MAGGIE STIEFVATER

GREYWAREN

📖 SCHOLASTIC

Published in the UK by Scholastic, 2022
1 London Bridge, London, SE1 9BA
Scholastic Ireland, 89E Lagan Road, Dublin Industrial Estate,
Glasnevin, Dublin, D11 HP5F

SCHOLASTIC and associated logos are trademarks and/or
registered trademarks of Scholastic Inc.

First published in the US by Scholastic Inc, 2022

ISBN 978 0702 32373 7

A CIP catalogue record for this book is available from the British Library.

Printed by CPI Group (UK) Ltd, Croydon, CR0 4YY
Paper made from wood grown in sustainable forests and other controlled sources.

1 3 5 7 9 10 8 6 4 2

www.scholastic.co.uk

Cover design by Christopher Stengel

to every reader who ever woke with flowers or feathers

Yet if you take the time to look closely at your subject, to analyze the shapes of shadows and their edges, and to record them in terms of value, you will achieve a convincing likeness.

—William L. Maughan, *The Artist's Complete Guide to Drawing the Head*

It takes a long time for a man to look like his portrait.

—James McNeill Whistler

If the dream is a translation of waking life, waking life is also a translation of the dream.

—René Magritte

PROLOGUE

At the beginning of this story, years and years ago, two dreamers arrived at paradise.

Niall Lynch and Mór Ó Corra had just bought a beautiful, secret piece of Virginia countryside. Sloping, open fields. Oak-covered foothills. And in the distance, the ghostly Blue Ridge Mountains acting as sentry. It felt like a magic trick to Niall and Mór, the acquisition of this verdant stronghold. Yes, the farmhouse at its heart was full of the towering stash of the hoarder who'd died before they arrived. And the multitude of outbuildings that gave the parcel its name—the Barns—were in even sorrier shape, every one of them knock-kneed and sloughing paint.

But to Niall and Mór it was a new kingdom.

"Sure, it'll come round," Niall said, full of his usual optimism.

Niall was a charming young buck, handsome, persuasive, fast-talking. If the rubbish inside the house and the barns could be convinced to move itself, he was the man to do it.

Mór (not yet called Mór then) said, "We'll have to take care the baby doesn't get lost in all these weeds."

Mór was a tough young hero, unsentimental, unflinching. A year before, she'd chopped her golden hair to chin length so it wouldn't get in her way, and a month before, she'd done the same to her past.

Niall smiled that big, sudden grin of his, tucked his long hair behind his ear, made himself pretty for her to stare at. "Do you like it?"

Shifting young Declan in her arms, she turned her flinty-eyed gaze over the property. It was everything Niall had said it would be. It was lovely. It was enormous. It was miles from the closest neighbor and oceans away from the closest family.

But that wasn't the most important thing to her.

She said, "I won't know 'til I've slept, will I?"

Both Niall and Mór were dreamers—literally. They would fall asleep and, sometime later, wake with their dreams made real. Magic! Rare magic, too—they'd never met anyone else who could do it . . . or at least, no one else who would admit to it, and was that really a surprise? Easy to see how someone with bad intentions might try to exploit a dreamer for profit.

In truth, exploitation was easier said than done. Dreaming was a slippery business. Niall and Mór often lost their way while hiking through their own subconscious. They would intend to dream of, say, money, and instead wake up with, say, handfuls of sticky notes with the words *pound* and *dollar* printed on them.

The most useful dreams were focused dreams.

The most focused dreams were dreams of the forest.

The Forest.

On the surface, the Forest seemed much like an ordinary deciduous forest, but when Mór stood inside it, she could tell its roots went far deeper. Past dirt. Past rock. Past anything humans had ever seen, looking not for water but for something else. When she visited it in her dreams, Mór could tell that something sentient lived within the Forest, but she never saw what it was. She only heard it. Or felt it.

Whatever it was, it was very interested in her.

She was very interested in it.

"Sure, don't worry," Niall told Mór, reaching out a hand for hers. "You'll find the Forest here."

Because he, too, dreamt of the Forest. It was interested in him, too.

(Niall was interested in the Forest, but he was mainly interested in Mór.)

He'd done his best to find a place where the dreaming was good and clear, where it was easy to choose to visit the Forest each night. Part of him had hoped she might also fall in love with the beauty of the place, with the promise of what their life together would look like, but he knew what she really wanted.

So that first night, Mór dreamt, and Niall waited. Finally, as the sun rose, Mór joined her young partner on the farmhouse's rickety porch. Niall held out his arms for Declan and hugged him as they looked out over the misty fields.

He didn't ask Mór if she'd dreamt of the Forest that night. He knew. They dreamt of the Forest; the Forest dreamt of them.

"I heard a word in the Forest last night, love," he said. "It wasn't English and it wasn't Irish, either."

"I saw a word last night, too," Mór replied. "Written on a rock."

She wrote it in the pollen on the railing just as he said it aloud:

Greywaren.

I

Art crime used to be funny.

Not ha-ha funny, but strange funny. A lot of crime goes in and out of fashion, but art crime is always in. One would think that art lovers would be the least likely to tolerate theft or forgery, but in fact, they're often the ones who find it the most intriguing. It's art appreciation on steroids. Art appreciation as a board game, a team sport. A lot of people will never steal a statue or forge a painting, but a lot of people find it interesting when someone else does. Unlike when seeing someone stealing a handbag or a baby, a reasonable number of onlookers might secretly root for the thief.

The stakes never seemed that high. Art was valuable, but it was never a matter of life or death.

But the world had changed.

Now, if someone owned a piece of art, it meant that someone else didn't.

And that *was* a matter of life or death.

No one so much as glanced at Bryde as he headed into the Museum of Fine Arts. He was just a tawny-haired man in a gray jacket too light for Boston's winter weather, dwarfed by the scale of the column-fronted museum as he jogged lightly up the stairs, hands in pockets, shoulders shrugged against the cold. He did not look like someone who had destroyed valuable things in the recent past or like someone who intended to steal valuable things in the near future, although he was both.

Desperate times, etc.

It had only been thirty-six hours since tens of thousands of people and animals had fallen asleep all over the world. They fell all at once, all together. It hadn't mattered if they were jogging down the sidewalk or tossing their child in the air or stepping onto an escalator: They fell asleep. Planes dropped from the sky. Trucks rummaged off bridges. Seabirds rained into the ocean. It did not matter if the sleepers were in a cockpit or behind the wheel of a bus; it did not matter if the other passengers were screaming; the sleepers kept on sleeping. Why? No one knew.

Well, some knew.

Bryde walked in his quick, neat way to the ticket counter. He blew on his cold fingers and shivered a little. His bright eyes looked here, there, back again, just long enough to note the guard lingering by the toilets and the docent leading a group into another room.

The young woman behind the ticket counter didn't look up from her screen. She asked, "General admission ticket?"

On the news, a rotating cast of experts had used phrases like *metabolic disturbances* or *zoonotic disease* or *toxic gas inversions* to explain all the comatose people and animals, but these morphed as the experts struggled to come up with an explanation that also included the hundreds of windmills, cars, and appliances that had also failed. Did it have something to do, one expert postulated, with the billions of dollars of industrial sabotage that had been happening on the Eastern Seaboard? Perhaps it was all an attack on industry! Perhaps the government would reveal more data in the morning!

But in the morning, no new information came.

No one claimed responsibility. The sleepers kept sleeping.

"I need a ticket for the Vienna exhibit," Bryde said.

"They're sold out until March," the counter attendant replied, in the tone of someone who had repeated this many times already. "I can put your email on a waiting list."

The once-in-a-lifetime traveling exhibition of Vienna Secession artists had sold out the day it was announced. It was bound to. At its center was Gustav Klimt's *The Kiss*, a painting that never left its home country. *The Kiss* is a knockout of a painting that most people have seen even if they don't think they have. It features two lovers completely consumed by both a gilded blanket and each other. The man kisses the woman on the cheek. He wears ivy in his hair; his hands touch the woman prayerfully. The woman kneels serenely on flowers; her expression is certain she's adored. How adored? Hard to say. Previous Klimts, less famous, had sold for one hundred and fifty million dollars.

"I need to get in today," Bryde said.

"Sir—" The counter attendant lifted her gaze to Bryde, looking at him for the first time. She hesitated. She stared too long. At his eyes, his face.

"Bryde," she whispered.

It was not only the sleepers whose lives had changed the day planes fell from the sky. The dreamers—far less numerous than the sleepers—had lost their ability to take things from their dreams, too. Many didn't know it yet, because they dreamt so rarely. And many had already been failing (at dreaming, at living) for a long time.

Bryde had visited some of them in their dreams.

"The Vienna exhibition," Bryde repeated quietly.

Now there was no hesitation. The counter attendant took her own badge from around her neck. "Put your, um, finger, over the photo."

As he walked away, looping the lanyard over his neck, she put her fingers to her mouth and stifled a little cry.

It can be a powerful thing, to know one isn't alone.

A few minutes later, Bryde calmly lifted *The Kiss* from the wall of the busy *Vienna Secession* exhibit. He took it with the quiet certainty of someone who was supposed to be taking a painting, which is perhaps why none of the other visitors realized anything was amiss at first.

Then the weight-sensitive alarm began to scream.

Thief, thief, thief, the piercing electronic tone warned.

Now the visitors stared.

Bryde staggered back with the painting, which was every bit as big as he was. What a piece of art *this* scene was: this light-haired man with a hawklike nose, something about his proportions neat and predictable, and this beautiful painting, with its own elegant balance.

The corner of the frame hit the floor. He began to drag it toward the exit.

Now it was obvious that the painting was being stolen. This was not how one carried priceless masterpieces.

And yet the onlookers did not stop Bryde; they watched. That was what one owed art, after all, wasn't it? They watched him stop long enough to rummage something that looked like a paper airplane from his jacket and hurl it at a docent hurrying into the exhibit. As soon as the plane struck the docent's chest, it melted into an oozy coating that glued him to the floor. Another docent got a faceful of glittering powder that shrieked and sparked when it touched her skin.

A third docent skidded to a halt as grass and brambles grew rapidly from the floor, released from an ordinary-looking tennis ball Bryde had tossed from his pocket.

Bryde struggled farther on.

At each turn, he faced more guards, and at each turn, he found yet more odd knickknacks in his pockets to distract them, like he was pulling from a gallery of works by disparate artists. The objects were beautiful, strange, frightening, mind-bending, loud, apologetic, shameful, enthusiastic—all gifts collected in the last thirty-six hours from those who'd thought they were alone before Bryde had reached out to them. In the past, he could have dreamt new weapons to keep the guards at bay, but not now. He had to make do with gifted dreams from *before*.

But he did not have enough of them to get him out of the museum.

There were more walkie-talkies crackling from deeper in the building and more alarms shouting and ever so many stairs left to go.

He was nowhere near escape.

One could not simply stroll into one of the largest museums in the world, select a Klimt from the wall, and drag it out.

It was bound to fail from the start.

"Don't you want them to wake up?" Bryde snarled to the bystanders.

These words landed more powerfully than any of the dreamt

gadgets had. They invoked those not there, the sleepers, who slept and slept and slept. In loved ones' spare rooms. In nurseries with doors left hopefully cracked, the baby monitors' batteries running dead. In geriatric wards devoted to sleepers no one had claimed as their own.

A handful of onlookers rushed forward to help Bryde carry the painting.

Now it was truly a work of art, Bryde and this group of museumgoers shouldering *The Kiss* past the displays describing Klimt's process, the arduous journey this painting had made already, the acts of rebellion Klimt performed again and again in his artistic life.

Out they strove, five, six, seven people carrying the painting as far as the museum's front entrance, other museumgoers pitching in to blockade the guards.

On the grand stairs of the MFA, the police were waiting, guns raised.

Now that he had run out of gifted dreams, Bryde was just a man with a famous painting held tight in his grip. It took only a few officers to relieve him of it. Really, it was not surprising that the theft had failed. It was surprising that it had taken so long to fail. But that was art for you: hard to predict what would stick and what wouldn't.

As they escorted Bryde in cuffs toward a parked cruiser, he stumbled.

"Easy there," said one of the officers, in a not unkindly tone.

"No need for anyone to get hurt," said the other officer.

Behind them, *The Kiss* was whisked back into the museum. The farther it got from Bryde, the slower his steps became.

"What were you thinking?" the first officer asked. "You can't just walk in there and take a painting, man."

Bryde said, "It was the only thing I could think of."

He no longer looked like the person who'd walked into the museum earlier. All the intensity was gone from his eyes. He sagged to the ground, a man in a jacket empty of dreams.

"One day," he told the officers, "you'll sleep, too."

Asleep.

2

Everyone wants to be powerful.. Ads tell every consumer: We are important and seen.. Teachers tell every student: I believe in you.. Embrace your power.. Be your best self.. You can have it all.. These are lies.. Power is like gasoline and salt.. It seems plentiful but there is only so much to go around.. Sharp blades want power to gain room to cut.. Dull blades want power so sharp blades will not cut them.. Sharp blades want power to do what they are meant to do.. Dull blades want power to just take up room in the drawer.. We live in a disgusting world.. The drawer is full of ugly blades made for nothing..

—NATHAN FAROOQ-LANE,
The Open Edge of the Blade, page 8

3

Ho hey, the working day.

Declan Lynch woke early. He didn't eat breakfast, because breakfast was the meal most likely to upset his stomach. He did drink coffee, even though it *did* upset his stomach, because without the urgent mewling of the coffee maker in the morning he wouldn't have a compelling reason to get out of bed on time. In any case, Matthew had once said that morning smelled like coffee, so now it had to continue smelling like coffee.

After coffee was started, he called Jordan Hennessy—her workday would be ending now, just as his was starting. As the phone rang in his ear, he carefully wiped coffee grounds off the counter and fingerprints from the light switch. He liked most things about his Boston apartment, especially the Fenway location, barely a mile away from Jordan, but the older building would never be as pathologically clean as the soulless place he'd left behind in DC. Declan liked things neat. He rarely got his way.

"Pozzi," Jordan said warmly.

"You still awake?"

This was a bigger question than it had been just a few days ago.

"Shockingly," she replied. "Stunningly. The crowd watches with anticipation; even the coaches have no idea what to expect."

Awake, awake—why was she awake when so many others were sleeping? What would he do if tomorrow she wasn't?

"I want to see you tonight," he said.

"I know," she replied, then rang off.

Ho hey, the working day. Declan's dress shirt was a little wrinkled, so he hung it in the bathroom and started the shower. In the mirror, young Declan Lynch eyed him. It was not the same Declan Lynch who had looked out just a few months before. That Declan had been forgettably assembled from mass-produced parts: perfect white smile, tamed dark curls, discreet grizzle, a confident but unthreatening stance. This Declan, on the other hand, razored into memory. Behind those blue eyes was now something coiled and barely restrained.

He had not thought before that he looked very much like his brother Ronan, but now—

(Do not think about Ronan)

Once he was dressed, caffeinated, and nursing an acidic coffee burn in his stomach, Declan tackled a little bit of work. Since coming to Boston to be near Jordan, this had become his job: high-end concierge babysitting. Clients left him their phones for the weekend, for the month, while they were out of town, out of the country, in prison. Some clients gave their phones to him permanently. In their high-stakes worlds, it wasn't always easy for them to address their clients with a cool head or without unwittingly promising something either emotional or physical. So they had Declan do their talking for them.

Declan had been training for this his entire life: making exciting things as boring as possible.

His clients wanted a discreet business associate fluent in the unspoken language of sweetmetals, the rare art pieces with the power to wake sleepers. That was Declan. He knew to call those vulnerable to becoming a sleeper *dependents*. He knew to be tactful when asking about a dependent's origin, to never reference dreams or magic: Most of his clients had acquired their dependents through marriage, but some had inherited them through a last will and testament, and still others had purchased a dependent child or spouse on the black market. These clients generally didn't know anything of how dependents came to be so dangerously at risk of sleep. They didn't want to know. They just wanted to know how to keep their family awake.

Declan understood that perfectly.

He checked his watch and called Adam Parrish. "You got something for me?"

Adam's voice cut in and out; he was walking. "The ley line's still gone. Everywhere. No change."

"Any word from . . ."

Adam didn't answer. That meant no. Not a good sign. Adam Parrish was the person Ronan cared about more than anyone else in the world. If Ronan wasn't calling him, he wasn't calling anybody.

"You know where to find me," Declan told Adam, and hung up.

(was Ronan dead?)

Ho hey, the working day. Early-morning Boston groaned awake as Declan stepped outside: garbage trucks clanged, buses hissed, birds fretted. His breath was visible as he unlocked his car just long enough to retrieve the air freshener diffuser hanging from the rearview mirror.

He was casual about it.

Just an air freshener. Not my life savings. Nothing to see here.

"Good morning!" one of his neighbors called. She was a

medical resident. He'd run a background check on her, along with the rest of the people on the street. Good fences make good neighbors. "Hey, is . . . your brother okay? Marcelo said he fainted or something?"

She could be a dream or a dreamer; there were some things background checks couldn't uncover. It was unlikely, but not impossible. When this all began, he'd thought he was the only one living with dreams. Now he knew from the news that there were others. Not many. But more than he had imagined.

More than there were sweetmetals, for sure.

"Low blood pressure," Declan lied smoothly. "Congenital. Mother's side. Do you do any work with that sort of thing?"

"Oh! Ha, oh, no, I do the, I do the guts and grime," she replied, gesturing to her midsection. "I'm glad he's okay."

"I'm glad you asked," he lied again.

Inside, standing well away from the windows, he pulled open the diffuser, revealing the necklace pendant hidden inside. The pendant was a delicate thing, wonderfully made, a silver swan twisted around the number seven. Who knew what the symbol originally meant; something important to someone, he supposed, or the pendant wouldn't still have value to him now. He seemed to remember a story Aurora used to tell about seven swans, but the details escaped him. His fine trap of a memory seemed to have only worked to contain his father's stories.

The pendant sweetmetal had cost so much.

He already missed the art he'd sold to get it.

"Time for school!" he called as he climbed the stairs to Matthew's room. In the doorway, his feet got tangled in a pair of enormous, ugly sneakers. He tried to extricate himself, but the quilted, bright footwear was out for blood. Declan went flying.

He caught himself on the edge of the mattress with a grunt; Matthew's golden curls didn't move against the pillow.

"Matthew," Declan said. His nervous stomach burned.

The boy in the bed looked seventeen, looked seven. This was the magic of Matthew's cherubic features. He kept sleeping. Declan pressed the swan pendant directly against Matthew's neck. His brother's skin was warm and vital beneath his fingers.

"Mmmf." Matthew sleepily pawed up to clasp the necklace's chain. Tightly. Like it was a security blanket, and wasn't it? "I'm getting up."

Declan let out his breath.

The sweetmetal was not yet spent.

"Hurry up," he said. "You've got twenty minutes."

Matthew whinged, "You could've woken me sooner."

But Declan couldn't have. The most powerful sweetmetals tended to be inconveniently well-known paintings: John Singer Sargent's *Madame X*, Klimt's *The Kiss*, Georgia O'Keeffe's *Black Iris III*. These and other Mona Lisa smiles hung in museums, owned and loaned by corporations and the super rich. Slightly less powerful sweetmetals lived in the hands of dreamt CEOs and heiresses, or undreamt CEOs and heiresses who had acquired or found dreamt children or spouses. That left the less desirable sweetmetals to circulate on the black market. These pieces were less potent, short-lived, uglier, clumsier . . . and still very expensive. Now that every dream needed a sweetmetal to stay awake, the price of even the worst had shot up in just days.

Currently, Matthew received the swan pendant in time for breakfast and relinquished it directly after school. He hadn't seen a sunset for days; he wouldn't see a weekend for months. The pendant had to last until the end of the school year. Declan couldn't afford another sweetmetal. He'd barely been able to afford this one.

(He lived in guilt, he wallowed in guilt, he was nothing but guilt.)

"I have a hypothermic question," Matthew said, a few minutes later. "Hypothetical, I mean."

He had appeared in the doorway of the kitchen, mostly assembled for school. He'd even washed his face and was holding his malevolently ugly sneakers in one hand so Declan's floors would stay clean.

He was sucking up.

"No," Declan said, swiping up the car keys. "The answer is no."

"Can I join the D&D club at school?"

Declan struggled to remember what D&D was. He had half a mind it involved whips and leather, but that didn't sound like Matthew, even in his new rebellious phase. He said, "Wizards?"

"You pretend to have battles with trolls and shit, yeah," Matthew said.

Declan did not have to *pretend* to find battles with trolls and shit. He would have liked to pretend he didn't. Less D&D. More B&B. "Are you asking because this involves evenings or weekends?"

If only Matthew could stay awake without a sweetmetal, just as Jordan did, but who knew how that was happening—

"Just Wednesdays. Do Wednesdays even count as days, really?"

"Let me think about it."

(He would rather not think about anything.)(Was Ronan dead?)

Ho hey, the working day. Declan drove Matthew to his new school; he had to account for his movements at all times. The day the dreams had fallen asleep, it had taken hours for Declan to find where Matthew had fallen. He couldn't bear another day like that. The not knowing.

"Have you thought about DnD?" Matthew wheedled.

"It's been twelve minutes." Declan pulled into the school drop-off line, where every other car was driven by someone in their forties or fifties, by a parent who hadn't been beaten to death with a tire iron in their own driveway before their kids reached the age of majority.

Declan *felt* forty or fifty.

(WasRonanDeadWasRonanDeadWasRonanDeadWas—)

"Have you?" Matthew repeated.

"Matthew, get out," Declan said. His phone had begun to ring. His phone, his real phone, not a client phone. "Don't drink soda at lunch. Don't hang on my car door. It's not a piece of gym equipment." His phone was ringing, ringing. He answered it. "Declan Lynch."

"This is Carmen Farooq-Lane."

His mouth went dry. When he'd last spoken to her, just a few days before, it had been to give her Ronan's location so she could capture Bryde and free Ronan from his influence. What a cluster.

Guilt scissored his guts.

(Ronan, Ronan, Ronan)

Matthew was still hanging on the car door. Declan waved a hand at him to make him go inside the building, but Matthew stayed, eavesdropping.

"It was kept pretty quiet," Farooq-Lane said, "but maybe you heard Bryde was arrested at the MFA a few days ago."

Declan's stomach soured. Already, his mind had perfectly conjured a scene of a lengthy shoot-out, Ronan sprawled in a pool of blood with some damning dream in his hand.

Please no, no, no, no, no, no, no

"Ronan—?"

"We need to meet," Farooq-Lane said.

He felt faint with relief. She had not said *Your brother is dead.* "Where?"

She told him.

Declan stared at his dusty steering wheel, the leather clean only where his fingerprints had touched it. The dust exhausted him. How quickly everything returned to grime and disarray when Declan wasn't attending to it. All he needed, he thought, was just a day or two where things didn't run to ruin without him. An hour or two. A minute or two.

(Ronan, Ronan, Ronan)

"Deklo," whined Matthew, "what's happening?"

Ho hey, the working day.

"Get back in the car," Declan said. "You're not going to school today."

4

The apocalypse had been averted, but it still felt like the end of the world.

Who are you now?

Someone who stopped the apocalypse.

Carmen Farooq-Lane kept telling herself that, but the answer that kept coming to her instead was different.

Farooq-Lane and Liliana sat in a car in the parking lot of the Medford Assistance Center, waiting for Declan Lynch. In the passenger seat, white-haired Liliana knitted something out of teal yarn that matched her cloth headband, humming to herself. She was good at whiling away the hours. In the driver's seat, dark-eyed Farooq-Lane had dug her fingernails into ten places around the steering wheel, and she kneaded it, white knuckled. She was not good at whiling away the hours.

Who are you now?

Someone who killed their brother.

Declan Lynch had tried so hard to protect the life of his brother, a deadly Zed, and she'd done everything in her power to end the life of hers.

Farooq-Lane knew their situations weren't exactly the same. Nathan had already used dreamt weapons to kill a string of victims, marking every crime scene with an open pair of scissors; Ronan, on the other hand, was on the chopping block for the crimes he *might* commit, apocalypses he *might* start. But both brothers had one thing in common: far too much power for any one person to have. It made sense to take them out of the apocalyptic equation. To take all the powerful Zeds out of the equation.

So the Moderators and Farooq-Lane kept killing and killing and killing and—

Do you know who is the easiest to control? Nathan had asked her once. *People who are still running away from their last controlling relationship.*

Farooq-Lane surveyed their surroundings. After a very cold start, the day had gotten suddenly warm, too warm for this time of year in Massachusetts. Now the hazy sky looked wrong behind the bare tree branches, out of step with the season. In the distance, a pedestrian's rapid progress reminded her of how Nathan used to look as he walked, so fast and intentional, leaning forward like the figurehead on a ship's prow.

Stop thinking about the past, she chastised herself. *Worry about the present.*

It was all over: Plug, pulled. Dreams, stopped. Possibility of fire, extinguished. World, saved.

Right?

Right.

She'd lost her entire family to this mess. Her entire career. Her entire soul. And in the end, what had brought this killing season to a close? A brief dream over a cup of hot chocolate had extinguished the source of the Zeds' power. In with a bang, out with a whimper.

"It all feels too easy," Farooq-Lane confessed. "Anticlimactic."

"Nothing about what we did was easy," Liliana assured her in her unusual accent, knitting one, purling one. The rhythmic clinking of her needles was like the ticking of a clock's second hand. "I, for one, am glad this is behind us so that we can just live."

Liliana: once the Visionary girlfriend, maybe now simply the girlfriend. Before the ley line was shut down, she'd periodically had dangerous visions, always of the upcoming apocalypse, that rotated her through three ages within her own timeline, but since the ley line vanished, she hadn't had a single one. The premonitions, like the dreams, seemed to need ley power.

It was nice to not have to worry about exploding from a deadly wave of sound during the visions. But it was decidedly discomfiting to have started a relationship with Liliana in her middle age and now continue it with a suddenly much older Liliana. Before, Farooq-Lane hadn't thought very much about the oddness of Liliana occasionally turning ancient, because she just as often cycled back to her middle age. But now the ley line was gone, and so were the visions, so it seemed like this age was here to stay. The shift had left Liliana still poised, still elegant, but nonetheless obviously decades older than Farooq-Lane.

Plus, without the visions, they were now blind to what the future held.

"I don't know what *just living* means anymore, though," Farooq-Lane said. "Can you believe I used to make my living planning people's futures?"

Liliana said, "I think futures will show up on their own."

Liliana put down her knitting in order to take Farooq-Lane's hand, squeezing their palms together. As always, her touch was immediately soothing. Mysteriously soothing. Farooq-Lane knew there was a bit of magic to Liliana above and beyond her visions, a magic that made people feel like a better version of themselves. She remembered something Liliana had said when they first met, about how humans were so fragile, something like that. One didn't make a comment like that unless one was making a joke or one didn't consider themselves exactly human.

And Liliana wasn't funny.

"Do you remember what comes next?" Farooq-Lane asked. It was difficult to completely wrap her head around the Visionary's shape-shifting through their own timeline, but she at least understood that there was one version of Liliana that was the *true* version, the one who was experiencing time correctly. The other ages were either looking back on events that had already happened or looking forward to a future that they had yet to catch up to.

Before this, Liliana, in her oldest age, had often had a little tidbit of a memory to offer. But now, she just said, "Let's think about what we'll do for dinner; Hennessy said something about curry and I think that sounds scrumptious."

"I hope it wasn't a mistake to leave her by herself," Farooq-Lane muttered. "I don't really believe she wanted to sleep more. All she does is sleep."

"Poor thing has a life of sleep to catch up on."

Liliana's voice was full of pity, and it was true that Hennessy's life *was* pitiful. Years of dreaming the same relentless nightmare; years of knowing she had the ability to make that nightmare real. *Pity her*, Farooq-Lane told herself. *Pity her!* But it had taken just days for Farooq-Lane to decide Hennessy was the most aggravating person Farooq-Lane had ever met.

Supporting evidence: Hennessy was loud. She seemed to feel that if a monologue was worth delivering, it was worth delivering at top volume, from atop furniture or cars or roofs, an ocean of relentless, throbbing words.

Hennessy was unpredictable. The first night after she'd shut down the ley line, she'd vanished for hours. No warning. No explanation. Just as Farooq-Lane and Liliana tried to decide if they needed to track her down, she returned with a car, something unbadged with a roaring, clattering exhaust that—like her—shouted and talked constantly unless it was locked away in the vacation cottage's garage. It seemed as if it might have been either very cheap or very expensive. Farooq-Lane was afraid to ask where it had come from.

More evidence: Hennessy was destructive. She needed constant supervision or, like a feral fox, she began to dismantle her surroundings. The few days she'd been with them, she'd managed to get water pouring from bathtubs, fire dancing from stoves, windows broken, and neighbors staring as Hennessy painted an enormous copy of *The Scream* on the garage door while music screamed from her (possibly stolen) car. Farooq-Lane was never going to get her damage deposit back.

Even more evidence: Hennessy was also always trying to die. Or at least, she was not taking enough care to keep living. She jumped off heights that weren't necessarily survivable. She submerged herself in water with slightly too little air in her lungs. She drank things that in high concentrations were not safe to humans. She ate things and then threw them back up and then ate other things. She ran with scissors, and when they sometimes sliced her open as she fell, just peered inside her broken skin with curiosity instead of horror. She laughed so hard sometimes that Liliana would start to cry in sympathy.

These last few days had felt like years.

But Farooq-Lane couldn't just turn the infamous Zed out. Because under the lure of saving the world, she and Liliana had taken the unicorn's horn and given it nothing in return.

Who was Hennessy now, without the dreaming?

Who was Farooq-Lane?

Someone who stopped the apocalypse.

"There he is," Liliana said pleasantly.

A gray Volvo pulled up, parking several spots away. Declan Lynch was in the driver's seat. His golden-haired younger brother Matthew was in the passenger seat. Two-thirds of the Lynch brothers.

"Let it all go," Liliana advised her. "This is the first step."

You stopped the apocalypse.

Taking two greeting cards from the door pocket, Farooq-Lane made her way to Declan. They each stood on one side of a painted line. It seemed a little like it was a handshaking situation, but neither of them stuck out their hand, and after a strained silence, it became too awkward for either to attempt it, so instead, Farooq-Lane just sighed in a meeting-opening way.

"Is he dead?" Declan asked, without preamble.

Instead of answering, she handed him the first of the two greeting cards.

He tipped it open. In printed cursive it read, *Happy Valentine's Day to a very special son and daughter-in-law!*

Beneath that, in her handwriting, she'd added:

I have not heard from the other Moderators since the rose garden. I am no longer associated with their directives, but they might still be watching me. In case my phone, person, or belongings are tapped or I am being followed and surveilled, I have written down what you need to know instead.

The Moderators' silence had been eerie, not comforting. It wasn't only her they'd ghosted, either. When the Feds notified her about Bryde's capture, they said they'd unsuccessfully tried several other Moderator contacts first before reaching out to her. Where were they? The Moderators were like junk mail or fungal infections; they didn't usually go away on their own.

She gave Declan the second greeting card.

This one had a printed message inside, too (*Turns out I like you a lot more than I originally planned! Happy Anniversary, Sweetheart!*), but it was nearly impossible to read, because she'd covered every centimeter inside with a handwritten explanation of everything she knew of the situation.

Declan read it. His expression betrayed nothing.

He glanced over his shoulder at the Medford Assistance Center, and then back at his golden-haired younger brother, who watched them with the intensity of a dog left in the car.

She pitied him. The feeling came so much more easily for Declan Lynch, who crushed all outward appearance of suffering, than for Hennessy, who detonated unhappiness in every room she entered. She couldn't understand Hennessy, but she knew what it was to be the sibling keeping it together.

Finally, Declan murmured, in a very passionless tone, "You didn't have to contact me."

"I made you a promise before. I'd collect Bryde; you'd get your brother back. I didn't keep that promise. This is all I can do."

He studied her for a long moment, then clucked his tongue. It was a peculiar and particular gesture. A decision-making cluck. He rummaged a business card out of his jacket and jotted two numbers and an address on it. "I don't want to feel like I owe you anything."

She took the card. "Should I say thank you?"

"I think you'll find some answers there."

She couldn't imagine what answers he might possibly think she wanted, but she said, "All right, then, thank you."

He shook his head a little. "Fair's fair. Now we're even again."

"Spies on a bridge," murmured Farooq-Lane.

"The only adults in the room," Declan corrected her. He still appeared brisk and professional, but now there was none-theless something restless about him; he was thinking over what she'd written in the greeting card. This agitation temporarily lifted the illusion of age, and for a fraction of a second, he looked very much like his brother Ronan.

Well, like Ronan the last time she'd seen him. Not now.

Farooq-Lane freed him from the meeting with a handshake. "Good luck, Mr. Lynch."

"That," Declan said bitterly, "is the only kind I never have."

5

R onan Lynch was dreaming of the Lace.
He was moving in it. Through it.
Branches crisscrossed over him.

Shadows connected beneath him.

Intricate patterns: light dappling an ocean, veins complicating a surface, everything tangled and snarled together.

He thought: *Oh, I* know *you.*

The Lace said, *I know you, too.*

And then the dream was gone, and instead, he found he was in a sea of emptiness. A world with nothing in it, or nothing that his senses had been made to see.

After some time, a moving, bright shape punctuated the dark sea. It was hard to tell if he moved toward it or it moved toward him, but once the shape was close, he discovered it was a grove of shining currents, undulating like the fronds of underwater plants.

They were beautiful.

He wanted to be closer, and eventually, he was, drifting right into the closest tangle of shining currents. The moment he made contact, immersive images overtook him. He found himself in disparate places: high-ceilinged mansions; deeply green graveyards; a shipwreck drowned in the ocean; dim bunkrooms with many cots; dark, close vaults; bright, open lakes; museums at night; bedrooms by day.

He lingered in each place as long as he could, taking it all in, but he was always eventually tugged back out into the empty sea.

In time, he understood: These places were real.

Not real for *him*. But real for those who lived in them. The people. The humans.

He found them beautiful, too.

These people seemed to be attracted to him, too. They peered at him intently. They leaned in close enough for him to see the tears caught in their eyelashes or hear the intake of their breath. He was held in the palm of this hand. He was kissed chastely by those lips. This cheek leaned against him appreciatively. That heart beat against him. He was watched, he was embraced, he was carried, he was bartered, he was strung around necks and wrists, he was worn, he was put in drawers, he was hidden in boxes, he was dropped in growing pools of warm blood, he was gifted, he was stolen, he was wanted, he was wanted, he was wanted.

Eventually, he understood that people weren't seeing him. They were seeing the objects he was looking *out* of: sweetmetals.

To them, he was the painting in a marble hall, the locket against a breastbone, the hound sculpture hugged by generations of children, the broken clock displayed on the mantel. He was the ring on the finger and he was the handkerchief in the pocket, he was the carving and he was the tool that carved it, but more than that, he was what was inside the sweetmetal, too; he was the love, he was the hate, he was the life, he was the death, he was everything that made a sweetmetal a sweetmetal.

Sweetmetals, sweetmetals, that word: *sweetmetals*. Had he known they existed before he came to this place? Some part of him must have. They were the secret heartbeat of the world. They were so knitted into society, into everything people believed and wanted.

Like the humans on the other side of them, he could not get enough of the sweetmetals. He spent as much time inhabiting the sweetmetals as he could. It wasn't just the sights and sounds of the human world he was attracted to; it was the emotions. Everyone looking at the sweetmetals came with their own enormous feelings. Anger, love, hate, excitement, disappointment, grief, anticipation, hope, fear.

He found these emotions beautiful, too.

There was nothing like them in the empty sea he drifted in. How wonderful and terrible these emotions seemed. How all-consuming, how complicating. He wondered what it would be like, having such big feelings. He seemed to remember some were nicer than others.

Now he was confused. He *remembered* that?

But he had no time to mull this puzzle over, because suddenly, as he entered another bright sweetmetal, he realized he was looking at a face he *knew*: Hennessy. He had forgotten that he could know people. And how he knew her! Her face, her name, what her tears felt like pressed into a shoulder.

She was in a studio surrounded by finished and unfinished portraits—it was their collective sweetmetal energy that had drawn him. Moreover, a slight charge surrounded Hennessy herself. As she slathered varnish on the canvas before her, he could actually feel energy crackling. It seemed possible the act of making the sweetmetal was itself a kind of sweetmetal, an ouroboros of creator and creation.

Slowly, he realized that he wasn't actually watching Hennessy, but rather, Jordan. This young woman wasn't hectic enough to be Hennessy. He realized, too, that he recognized the person in the portrait on her easel. The portrait featured a seated young man, suit jacket tossed across his leg, fingers loosely laced, face turned away in a mostly hidden smile. It was—

Declan.

Fast on the heels of that name came another one: Matthew. Why did they go together? Declan. Matthew. *Brothers.* Yes, they were brothers.

They were—

They were *his* brothers. He remembered that now. He remembered—

With a jolt, Ronan Lynch remembered *himself.*

He had not always been here in this void. He had been a person. He had had a body. A name.

Ronan Lynch. Ronan Lynch. Ronan Lynch.

Jordan's studio was disintegrating before him; the lurch of emotion had jerked him toward the empty sea. He tried desperately to stay.

Jordan! he shouted.

But his voice was not one with sound, and the sweetmetals were not a window that opened.

Ronan Lynch. Ronan Lynch.

What if he forgot himself again? Was he already in the process of forgetting it? Had he done this before? Oh God, how long had he been here, doing this, forgetting and remembering, forgetting and remembering?

He found himself back in the dark, empty sea.

Now he fretted. Memories were coming to him, of a valley full of sheds and barns, of paddocks full of forever-sleeping cattle. He'd been trying to find sweetmetals there. No. He'd been trying to *make* them. If only he'd had one for Matthew. For his mother. It would have changed everything. His fractured family, the Lynch family.

How had he forgotten all this? What else did he still have to recall?

Ronan Lynch was a hallway he illuminated inch by inch.

He turned his attention to the sweetmetals threading brightly through the dark. Before, he'd been curious. Aimless.

Now he knew what he was looking for.

Declan, Matthew, Ronan. The brothers Lynch.

A parking lot, crusted with dirty ice. Cars scummy with salt residue. Decorative trees, naked of leaves. A low, flat building surrounded by dismal shrubs. Late winter or early spring.

Ronan wasn't sure how much time he'd spent looking through sweetmetals; time didn't register the same way in the endless sea. At first, it had been agonizingly slow to sort through the sweetmetals, but he'd gotten better as he went. And now he could reap the fruits of his labor: As his consciousness slowly poured into the air of the parking lot, he glimpsed two familiar figures heading through the building's sliding doors.

One of them had a sweetmetal, a swan-shaped pendant, worn around a neck. Not the most powerful sweetmetal Ronan had inhabited so far, but strong enough. Strong enough, anyway, to allow him to feel quite present in the bright New England day, to haunt it like a ghost. He couldn't tell how hot or cold the air was, but he could pick up other information that his current form was built to collect. He felt the hum of the power lines a few yards away. He sensed an ocean seething a few miles away. He recognized a strange deadness in the atmosphere; not a *thing* but rather the space where a thing normally was. The absent energy of the ley line.

He floated after Declan and Matthew as they entered the low building. He was shocked by them. Matthew looked older than he remembered, much older, like a tall high school senior, his surly expression tempered only by the golden curls softly bobbing on his head. And Declan was younger than he remembered, just a guy in his very early twenties, looking older because of his expensive clothing and restrained mannerisms.

Declan had done something terrible to Ronan, hadn't he?

The name of the act came to Ronan even if the details didn't. *Betrayal.*

Was Ronan angry about this? It seemed far away. Perhaps he would feel anger later.

Inside, Declan and Matthew passed empty wheelchairs and empty armchairs to check in with a woman behind a plexiglass window, then headed through a heavy, wide door. On the other side, the hall was lined with stretchers and other unspecific medical supplies. Ronan could feel the fluorescent lights jittering unpleasantly against him. It all had the look of a vet clinic or hospital, the sort of place that got mopped more often than other buildings, but didn't seem to be either. He couldn't yet tell why the brothers were there.

Matthew seemed equally confused. "What are we doing here? It smells like old juice box."

Declan's stride didn't waver as he continued to the elevator at the end of the hall.

"You'd tell Jordan," complained Matthew.

"Matthew, please, not now," said Declan.

An elevator journey took them to an equally empty second

floor. At Room 204, Declan—mysteriously—consulted a greeting card before punching #4314 into the keypad.

The latch unlocked with a *clunk.*

Declan had been so casual about the entire experience that it was only when he hissed "hurry up" to Matthew that Ronan realized the brothers were doing something furtive.

The door clunked again as it locked behind them.

Inside, Room 204 was dim, the only light pooling from beneath some clinical-looking cabinets. A curtain divided the room. On the closest side was a neatly made nursing-care bed. Although whatever lay beyond the curtain was hidden from view, Ronan could *feel* it. Something in the room tugged at Matthew's sweetmetal with a sucking hunger.

Matthew fidgeted uneasily.

Declan found the light switch. The fluorescents buzzed to life as Declan pulled back the curtain, revealing—

"Is that . . ." whispered Matthew, *"Bryde?"*

The memories came in fast. It was as if the more Ronan recalled, the stronger the gravity of that old life grew. They pummeled him.

Bryde, Ronan's mentor, the one who'd found Ronan and Hennessy, who had led them on a destructive campaign to improve the ley line's power, who had introduced them to other dreamers in need of hope. A dreamer dreamt to have a plan.

In the clinic bed, Bryde looked small. Dusty. Someone had secured his ankles and wrists to the bed's handrails. Some official-looking paperwork in clear plastic had been fastened to the bed, too, keeping it all in a single package, like he was a product waiting for sale, or a corpse waiting for autopsy. But he wasn't dead. He was asleep.

Matthew peered at him. "Why's he tied to the bed and stuff?"

"He's being detained. He tried to steal a painting."

Regret washed over Ronan. As before, the strong emotion threatened to eject him into the empty sea, but, with effort, he clung to the scene before him. He'd rather be here, feeling this hideous feeling, than out in the darkness, feeling nothing.

"Uh, Deklo!" Matthew barked, alarmed.

Bryde's eyes had opened.

Declan said, "Good."

Bryde did not look at either of the brothers. Instead, he gazed up at the pebbled ceiling of the room. His throat moved as he swallowed. He seemed absolutely defeated.

Declan's voice was neutral, but his expression was electric as he leaned over Bryde. "I'll keep this short, because I don't want to spend any more of his sweetmetal than I need to keep you awake, you piece of shit. Where's Hennessy?"

Bryde simply shook his head a little.

"That's not good enough," Declan said.

"It will have to be. She left us at the rose garden."

Ronan remembered that she had physically left them at the rose garden, but their real goodbye had happened later, in a dream. She'd tricked both Ronan and Bryde in order to dream an orb that shut down the ley line. She'd known the orb would send Jordan to sleep and might kill Ronan, but she'd done it anyway.

Did he feel anger yet?

No. It still all felt very far away.

Declan demanded, "Next question: What's wrong with Ronan?"

"It's obvious you don't know anything about him," Bryde said.

"You can play games with Ronan, but you can't play games with me," Declan said tightly. "You had him for a few months. I had him my entire life. I spent my childhood keeping him from danger, and what did you do with him? Ruin his life. Throw away everything he'd built."

Bryde said, "Tell me, older brother: Did you want to keep him from danger or to keep him from being dangerous?"

Matthew glanced from Bryde to Declan and back again.

"You don't know anything about Ronan except what he put in your head," Declan said.

Bryde bared his teeth in a tiny snarl. "Then tell me what this means: *Greywaren*."

The word hung there in the room.

Greywaren. Ronan was closer to understanding it than he had been before. Something about this vast space, something about looking out at this world through sweetmetals—

"This game still has squares to jump to, spiraling like the shell of a snail. Jump, jump, jump, to the center. This game is . . ." Bryde trailed off. There was something very unhappy about his mouth. Turning his face away, he whispered, "Even the lights here make noise."

Matthew blinked fast. His eyes were very shiny.

"Declan," whimpered Matthew. It was hard to tell if he was unhappy about Bryde draining his sweetmetal or simply because Bryde looked drained. He had just as much in common with Bryde, after all, as he did with Declan.

"Tell me, Bryde," Declan demanded. "No riddles. What's wrong with him?"

"It's simple: He's a more complicated machine than I am. What was I meant to do? Make it all worth it to him. What was he meant to do? More." Bryde looked at Matthew. "What do you feel?"

Matthew whispered to Declan, "I want to go home."

I'm sorry, Ronan told the dreamer tied to the bed, but he still had no audible voice.

Bryde said, "I feel nothing."

The lights went out. Declan had turned away without any further conversation. As the lock clunked behind the brothers again, Bryde swallowed and stared up at the dark ceiling.

Ronan didn't want to leave Bryde here alone. He was beginning to realize that he'd birthed Bryde into hell, a world he was designed to hate. Ronan had not dreamt any optimism into him, any simple joy, so happiness was a skill Bryde would've had to learn for himself once he was in the waking world.

It seemed unlikely he was going to learn anything now, trapped in this room, zip-tied to a bed.

Ronan was pulled from the room just as Bryde fell asleep.

Matthew's sweetmetal dragged him to another hallway in the center, where Declan was again consulting a greeting card, but this time, only to confirm a room number, not to get a passcode. Already Ronan could feel a vast, starving pull from the other side of this door, which bore a temporary label beside the number: JOHN DOE. The nickname for an unknown patient or victim.

Matthew hugged his arms around himself. "Can I go wait in the car?"

"Please don't fuss," Declan told Matthew, turning the handle.

But Matthew did fuss, and so did Ronan. He didn't want to

go in this room, either. Part of him already knew what was on the other side of the door. He simply didn't want it to be true.

Declan pressed the door open to reveal the interior of this room. The occupant of this bed was sleeping, too.

It was Ronan Lynch.

6

Ho hey, the working day.

"So you're a thief," Sarah Machkowsky said. "That's how it is? I didn't hold on to my face, so you took it?"

In the Newbury Street art gallery Machkowsky & Libby, just a few miles away from Declan and the Medford Assistance Center, all eyes were on Jordan Hennessy. The other two women in the gallery wore sleek suits; Jordan Hennessy had dressed as the talent, in a long tapestry coat over a white vest. The flowers of the coat mirrored the roses tattooed on her neck and fingers, and the pale vest glowed against her dark skin. She'd pulled her natural hair back into a bun that was behaving, but only just. She had a face like a poem and a smile like a punch line.

Hennessy answered breezily, "Don't worry. You still have the original."

Machkowsky & Libby was one of Boston's oldest and most prestigious galleries, and it looked it. It had a winning combination of cutting-edge lighting and the odor of centuries-old mold. The many-paned windows faced a busy, tourist-filled sidewalk. Inside, the historic building had been carved into small rooms with high ceilings, each sparsely hung with paintings that shared not a style but a swagger. They bore name tags, but no prices. The first and second floors of this gallery embodied a career most aspiring fine artists could only dream of. But Hennessy wasn't here for that. She was here for what she heard they kept in the attic.

"What did you use for this?" Machkowsky asked. She was browsing Hennessy's portfolio, a combination of actual art and reproductions in a binder.

"Egg tempera," Hennessy replied. "Just like Mama used to make."

Egg tempera was a bit of a flex. Did an artist need to know how to use such a historical technique these days? Absolutely not. Did a forger? Possibly.

"Unusual," Machkowsky said. "Many unusual decisions."

Her brow furrowed to match the piece she was looking at: a portrait Hennessy had hastily painted of her. She'd spent an entire night looking up the gallery owner online, studying the photos and videos in an effort to see not only what the stranger's face looked like but also how she inhabited that face. At the time, the portrait had felt like the tempera, like a cunning and funny way to capture Machkowsky's attention. Now, though, watching Machkowsky touch her still-sticky portrait and rub her finger and thumb together, unsmiling, the gesture felt squirmy and childish. This was a real gallery in the real world, not a party or a Fairy Market. The living artists displayed here were winners of a war where the weapons were art-school credentials and networking chops. In a room upstairs, a Renoir was for sale, a real Renoir, and Hennessy had come here with parlor tricks.

But you're selling *parlor tricks*, Hennessy reminded herself. She wasn't here to audition for the real gallery. She was here as Jordan Hennessy, the combination human that was Hennessy plus Jordan, to make a devil's bargain for a sweetmetal. The contract was unspoken, but she knew the terms: In exchange for the use of a sweetmetal (not even ownership of one!), she would have to work for Boudicca, an all-woman syndicate that, depending on who you asked, protected the interests of their talented clients . . . or exploited them for their own purposes.

Boudicca had been trying to recruit Jordan Hennessy for ages, unknowingly approaching both Jordan and Hennessy with various deals. Jordan hadn't wanted any part of it. She didn't like being trapped. Hennessy hadn't been tempted, either. Boudicca hadn't had anything she wanted.

Now they had something she wanted.

Machkowsky turned to the rest of the portfolio. Hennessy had included copies and forgeries in all sorts of styles, on paper, on canvas. She had examples of the document seals she'd forged, the signatures she'd copied, the provenances she'd devised for past forgeries.

Machkowsky paused on a neat copy of da Vinci's *Vitruvian Man*, identical to the fifteenth-century original except that the naked man now dangled a cigarette between two of his fingers. She said, "Bernie told me you were funny. Did your mother teach you anything before she . . . passed away?"

J. H. Hennessy. "Jay," as she was known. The mother. The ghost in the room.

Machkowsky & Libby had represented her works in Boston before she died, which made a reasonable question even more reasonable.

Just don't say anything at all, Hennessy told herself, but she'd never been good at listening to advice, even her own. "Dear old mum. What did she teach me? Mmm . . . Don't leave cigarettes burning on the piano, never mix pills on a school night, stay single, die young."

Machkowsky's mouth hardened; she didn't look up from the art. She said, "I always wondered what it must have been like to be her daughter. So she was no different at home, then?"

Hennessy hesitated.

"I had hoped her behavior was more of an act," Machkowsky said. "Performance art. I'm sorry. That must have been difficult."

It was unexpectedly jarring to be seen. Hennessy had not come here to be known. She had not come here for sympathy from a stranger, especially not for a childhood she'd thought only looked appalling from the inside. Did it matter, to know that someone had thought about her in her youthful suffering?

She would have liked the answer to be no. It was simpler. But the way her breath felt all tangled up in her throat told her that the answer was yes. It mattered.

Machkowsky asked, "Do you think you're at all like her?"

Hennessy blinked her burning eyes before flashing a huge, empty smile. "Do you see a similarity?"

"Your technique is more old-fashioned," Machkowsky said. "You use color like an old man. If I put your mother's work beside yours and didn't know any better, I would have thought you were the older woman and she the younger. But your gesture is very good. Much truer."

This compliment threw Hennessy off just as surely as the sympathy had. She was a forger, a copier, in a gallery of originals. She made her voice light again. "Now who's the funny one? I'll give your compliments to Sargent. It's his talent you're ogling."

"I can see your handwriting in the sketches," Machkowsky said. "In the line weight. Your mother never cared much about learning technique. Or observing other people. I can see you have taken your time."

Grief seared the back of Hennessy's throat, sudden and unexpected. Once upon a time, Hennessy would have taken all these words back to the hive, to the other girls who wore her own face. She would have repeated them as accurately as possible so the girls could not only luxuriate in the compliment they'd all earned, but also so that later, if they found themselves in conversation with Machkowsky, they'd all be able to be the Hennessy Machkowsky had already met.

But the girls were dead. There would be no rambunctious celebration, no wild laughter, no drowsy commiseration. Just silence. There were only two Jordan Hennessys left, and those two weren't on speaking terms.

Yet.

A sweetmetal would make the surviving Jordan Hennessys equals, and then everything would be okay.

"Jo!" Stacking the forged sketches neatly, Machkowsky tipped her head back to better project her voice into the other room. "Jo! Kai, is Jo Fisher back there?"

A voice called back, "She just got in."

"Send her out here," Machkowsky said. To Jordan, she asked, "How long are you in the city?"

"I live here now," Hennessy lied, adding, in a slightly thinner voice, "Near the Gardner."

"Love the Gardner," Machkowsky murmured. "Jo, come meet this young woman."

Jo Fisher turned out to be a young woman who looked as if her entire person had been flat ironed. She held her phone at the ready, as if she might need to type a critical missive into it at any time. When she saw Hennessy, her eyes flashed recognition. "Jordan Hennessy."

Uh-oh.

Hennessy had never met this woman. That meant Jo Fisher and Jordan had some sort of history Hennessy would have to navigate on the fly. This was the familiar but difficult territory of forging two Jordan Hennessys into one.

Hennessy said, "Jo. We meet again; we ride at dawn, etc."

Machkowsky observed this exchange with satisfaction. She said, "So you know each other. Perhaps you already know, then, that Jo works with developing up-and-coming artists' profiles. Artists who might not otherwise have the platform or experience to show in our gallery or in other spaces we represent. Jo helps bring them up to speed, streamlines the process. Now, I've got another appointment, but, Jo, take a look and let me know your thoughts."

Hennessy and Jo Fisher were left alone with only the art between them.

"For someone who doesn't want to work with us, you sure do keep walking into our offices," Jo Fisher noted. "You want to be a star?"

"I thought you wanted a forger," Hennessy replied.

Jo gestured vaguely at the walls around them. "And I thought you wanted this."

"What every child dreams of: a rigged career in the arts."

"A child's guide to the economy, by Jordan Hennessy," recited Jo Fisher.

"Ow."

"What is it you think Boudicca does?" Jo Fisher asked. "Do you actually know, or is it some comic book imagining of what we do? We collect talented, powerful people so other talented, powerful people can find them more easily. And we take a small percentage for our trouble. That's it. We're really just a bunch of businesspeople trying to make the world run a little more smoothly while paying our mortgages."

"Mortgage! You don't have a mortgage," Hennessy shot back. "You have a dead houseplant, a personal massager, and a two-year lease for a place you never sleep in."

Jo Fisher glared.

Hennessy smiled widely. She added, "A child's guide to adult relationships, by Jo Fisher."

"I think we've gotten off on the wrong foot," Jo Fisher said, although it clearly took some effort for her to make nice. "You want to be in this gallery, in this life. You want to travel all over the world for openings and paint famous people before they die. I don't see why you shouldn't. You're pretty and you sound clever and you're talented enough to do it and you're not too old to be boring. You will photograph well. But you didn't go to school, you don't know anyone who's anyone, you're a criminal, and you need a sweetmetal. You're not going to *get* that life or that sweetmetal without us. So are you going to sign on the dotted line or not?"

"What makes you think I want all . . ." Hennessy spun her finger around to indicate the gallery, the life, the promise. "Maybe my deepest aspiration is to be your friendly neighborhood forger."

Jo Fisher squinted at her. Then she tilted her head and squinted at her some more. "Oh. I get it now. You're the other one."

"What?"

"You're the other girl. The one I talked to before, she's your twin. Sister. Dependent. Whatever she is. She's the one with the big dreams. You're what—the talent? The user?"

They knew.

They knew.

All this time living as Jordan Hennessy, as one person, keeping anyone from knowing, and now the secret was out. She supposed it was inevitable. Boudicca had already guessed "Jordan Hennessy" was a dreamer by the time Jordan had gotten to Boston. And with Hennessy spending the end of last year destroying public property with Bryde and Ronan, and Jordan living it up in the art scene with Declan Lynch in Boston—

The secret was out because they had stopped keeping it.

"I'm crafting a denial in my head," said Hennessy. "It's very witty and convincing. Give me a just a second."

"You don't have to, you know. We've been keeping your secret just as well as you have. We have lots of secrets," Jo Fisher said. "I don't know or care why you pretend to be one person, but it is making this conversation really stupid. Do you want to keep pretending, or do you want to tell me what name *you* go by, so I can keep you straight?"

"Hennessy," said Hennessy, and it was a relief to not have to pretend to be the Jordan half of Jordan Hennessy anymore. "I'm Hennessy. Did Jordan really ask about showing original stuff here or is that some Boudicca BS?"

"Jordan, cute." Jo Fisher smirked. "So you both have half. Jordan and Hennessy. Jordan Hennessy. You really are nothing like her, you know. I should have guessed right away. Is it for you, the sweetmetal?"

The question wasn't meant to be an insult, but it was like the opposite of Machkowsky's compliment earlier. Of course, from Jo Fisher's point of view, Hennessy looked like the dependent. One half of Jordan Hennessy was living like an original, like someone with power. Blasting into Boston, tearing up the art scene, making connections, working on her own art, flirting with Boudicca over the possibility of a legacy, not just a career. And then there was the other girl. Slouching in here and pretending to be her in exchange for lame prizes.

The most overwhelming feeling Hennessy had wasn't failure, though, but rather yet more grief. She missed Jordan and her soaring optimism. In their final months together, Hennessy had just been trying to survive and have a good time while doing it. Jordan had been walking through galleries and imagining herself there.

"My ferret. It's for my ferret," Hennessy said. "I'm so damn attached to the thing. Have you ever looked at your socks and thought, *I wish they could love me back*? That's what she is to me, this ferret, she's—"

"Whatever," Jo Fisher said. "Let's move on."

Before the discussion could proceed to more productive places, Hennessy's eye was caught by a very familiar-looking face outside the window, standing out among the strangers on the sidewalk. And the figure saw her, too. It was staring right back at her.

It was Jordan. The real Jordan.

"How long's this offer good for?" Hennessy asked.

Jo Fisher looked as if she had gotten something small and scratchy in both her eye and her nose at the same time. She inhaled sharply. "Two minutes."

"Har de har," said Hennessy. "But, really, how long's it good for?"

"I'm not going to waste my breath trying to convince you. If you decide to pull the trigger, you can come to the Fairy Market next week in New York. The pickings will be slim by then, because sweetmetals are going like wildfire. And I won't make the offer again. But I think you're being stupid and deserve a week to realize it."

Jordan was making the universal sawing across her throat gesture that meant *stop fucking things up!*

"Hold that thought," Hennessy said. "I gotta check in with my other half."

7

Jordan remembered the first time Hennessy ran away from home.

At the time, home was a split-level in a tidy Pennsylvanian suburb, a home ruled over by Hennessy's father, Bill Dower, who'd retired from racing and now taught performance driving at Pocono, an hour away. It was a small house and a small suburb and a small life to hide four identical girls in: Hennessy, Jordan, June, and Madox.

It was a prison of Hennessy's making.

After Jay's death, Bill Dower had persisted in London for a space—or, rather, he'd let Hennessy stay in their London residence. As before her death, cars took him away for the better part of the year, and Hennessy was left in the hands of various housekeepers, all easily run off the moment he was gone. This came to an end after Hennessy's arrest record grew daunting. Once Bill Dower realized there was nothing for him in his dead wife's birth city but endless trouble, he relocated his troubled daughter to his childhood home in Pennsylvania (a feat that, for Hennessy and the girls, had involved multiple hotel rooms and a passport mailed across the Atlantic multiple times, Hennessy herself sent first and Jordan sent last, as she was the most trustworthy alone—their secret had always required a lot of paperwork in order to be kept).

Pennsylvania! Jordan and June were not as much like Hennessy as Madox was, but they were in universal agreement: They all hated Pennsylvania.

They made the best of it. They cut class. They took joyrides in Bill Dower's cars. They drove a few hours away to clubs and danced in twos and, very occasionally, in threes, but only if June was the third, because she'd straightened her hair, which made her into an entirely different person in the shuttered lights of a club. They made art. Jordan and Hennessy, in particular, made art. They made art and they made money and they made their collective name mean something to a certain kind of person.

Hennessy continued to dream. She dreamt Alba, who died in a car. She dreamt Farrah, who died just outside of one.

"That's one way to get out of finishing that Leighton sketch," Hennessy had said when Farrah killed herself. She was being extra mean about it because June wouldn't stop crying. June felt responsible, because she'd been the Hennessy who'd first met the married man who broke Farrah's heart.

"You cow," June told Hennessy, only she used a different *c* word. "Go dream yourself a fucking heart."

"Yeah, crumbs," Jordan said. "Show a little . . ."

"Finish the sentence," Hennessy shot back. "Where are *your* tears, Jordan? I haven't seen one. Alba just bit it and now we have to wear widow's weeds over Farrah, too? You want to do this *every time* someone dies? Better buy more black. I wish you were all fucking dead already, actually. I wish you were all dead so I didn't have to fucking look at my fucking face all the time. What a cock-up that nature let you all out of my head."

June stared. Finally, she said, "You don't deserve us."

Jordan didn't agree out loud, but she didn't disagree, so that was that.

That night, Hennessy ran away.

She neither answered her phone nor returned, but none of

them fell asleep, so they knew she wasn't dead. June and Madox fretted she might be gone for good, but Jordan knew better. She pinched a car for the night and drove to all the places she and Hennessy had ever hung out. The train caboose that had been rehabilitated into a motor home before falling back into disrepair. The iron bridge they liked to climb because it was obviously not meant to be climbed. The narrow alley formed where the high school met the gym; if one was athletic, one could shimmy up by bracing one's back and feet against the two walls and then smoke directly above teachers' heads without them realizing where the smell of smoke was coming from.

Eventually, she found Hennessy under the bridge where they'd been painting a mural and waging an intermittent war with taggers. This time, blackguards with spray cans had tagged over half of Hennessy's painstakingly re-created version of the *Last Supper* (it featured her face on each attendee), and instead of repairing the painting once more, Hennessy was spraying a lengthy response back.

"You want yellow or blue?" she asked when Jordan sauntered up, as if nothing had happened.

"Blue," Jordan replied, as if nothing had happened.

Later, the other girls had wanted to know how Jordan had been able to find Hennessy, but the truth was easy: because she'd wanted to be found.

Jordan had spent more time with Hennessy than any of the other girls by virtue of existing long before them, and so she'd seen it before, again and again. Hennessy had run away because she was jealous. She was jealous of Farrah for dying. She was jealous of Farrah for getting June to cry over her. She was jealous of Farrah for getting Jordan to speak up for her. So she'd said something mean and run away, but not too far, close enough that she knew the game would be winnable. The game of Hennessy getting Jordan to look right at her and nowhere else for as long as possible.

Not long after that incident, the girls had run away for real, all together, which was how Jordan knew it would stick. All the Hennessys were tethered together. The dreams couldn't leave the dreamer, because they needed to keep her alive so they could stay awake. And the dreamer couldn't leave the dreams, because without them to look at her, who would reassure her she existed?

So here they went again.

Jordan had seen Hennessy only once since moving to Boston, just long enough for Hennessy to say something awful and then run away. As always. She didn't mean any of it. She just needed to leave so she could come back. Pull the rubber band tight so it could zing faster in its flight.

But things had changed.

"You look fit," Hennessy said as the gallery door swung shut behind her.

"What are you doing here?"

"No hello? No kiss? No tongue? After all this time, and you don't even notice my hair looks fabulous?"

It didn't look fabulous. Hennessy looked strung out. Hard to say if it was on substances or on just being Hennessy. Her eyes looked hollowed and her mouth was even unhappier than usual, even though she was grinning at Jordan. Moreover, time had done something to Jordan's perception of her, even though it had only been a few days. She was now freshly shocked by the reality of Hennessy, her double. Jordan. Hennessy. Jordan Hennessy. *She has my face*, Jordan thought. *She has my body.*

Only after did she realize she used to think *I have* her *face. I have* her *body*.

Things really had changed.

"Thirty minutes ago, someone called me to say they'd seen me walk into Machkowsky & Libby and to let them know how it went," Jordan said. She had not even begun to craft a story in her head to explain her trip; how quickly she'd forgotten how this used to be everyday life. "What were you doing in there?"

"'Someone'?" Hennessy wagged her eyebrows.

Her jaunty demeanor made Jordan want to slap her. "Yeah, 'someone.' You wouldn't know who, would you? You haven't been here. You don't know anybody here."

Hennessy flashed an enormous smile at her. Gorgeous smile she had, gorgeous smile both girls had. "I do *now*. Jo Fisher's a perfectly lovely little bitch."

The idea of people interacting with Hennessy, thinking she was Jordan, made Jordan's cheeks go hot. Hennessy, prattling through a conversation with a gallery owner Jordan would see again at a cocktail party in a few weeks, with the girls behind the desk at the art supply store, with Declan.

With a glance around at the tourists on the street, Jordan took Hennessy's upper arm and threaded through the people on the sidewalk, her portfolio bag slapping against her side in time with their strides.

"Manhandle me!" Hennessy encouraged Jordan.

Jordan didn't answer. She didn't stop walking until they'd entered a narrow alley at the end of the block. It was cold in the shadows, and the garbage bin smelled like old fish, but it was more private. She threw Hennessy away from her. "You can't just go round in my life!"

"Says the girl who lived in mine for a decade," Hennessy said. "I was doing it for you, anyway, you know. Getting you a sweetmetal."

"For me?" echoed Jordan with a disbelieving laugh. "You went in there to promise away my life to Boudicca for a sweet-metal? What sacrifice! Where were you three days ago? I could've been asleep somewhere in a field. I could've died."

"You didn't, though," Hennessy said. "Look at you! The picture of health. Bright-eyed. Bushy-tailed. How could the beauties of spring ever compare to a woman in love? Is that why you're awake?"

There it was.

Ordinarily this was where Jordan and Hennessy would go round in circles in banter. She could already tell that Hennessy was longing to take Declan, or whatever she thought Declan was, and smush his relationship with Jordan into something grimy and disposable, loathsome and depraved.

"No," Jordan said.

"What's that?"

"No. I'm not doing this," Jordan said. "Why are you really here?"

"I'm here because you summoned me," Hennessy replied. "Do I or don't I have three voicemails asking where I am? Did you or did you not send queries out to ye olde forums to find out if I had been seen in the wilderness of Massachusetts? Have you or have you not been waiting for me to magically manifest in your life?"

None of it was untrue, but also, all of it was. How had Jordan put up with this for so long? Because she'd had to. No, that was unfair. Hennessy was her best friend, after all . . . her best friend who'd told Jordan she wished she was dead and then waited days to investigate Jordan's welfare after all the other dreams had fallen asleep.

Suddenly, Jordan said, "*You* did this, didn't you?"

"Did what now?"

Jordan wasn't sure how she knew, she just *knew*. It was the most horrible thing she could think of, so it had to be right. "The ley line, the dreams falling ill, it's you, somehow, isn't it? You did it. You killed it, the ley line, so you wouldn't dream anymore. Didn't you?"

She'd taken Hennessy by surprise. Normally she was nothing but words, but for a bit, she didn't have any. This was how Jordan knew for sure she was right. A denial would have been easy. An explanation or justification—that took a bit of time. Jordan could see the exact moment Hennessy finished processing the shock and began, instead, to craft a sassy response.

Jordan cut her off before she could say anything. "Tell me: Is the ley line permanently dead? Can what you did be undone?"

Hennessy said, "What a boring conversation this has suddenly become, in every way imaginable."

All those messages Jordan had left on Hennessy's voicemail over the last few days seemed different now. She thought she'd been ringing to make sure Hennessy was all right, to reassure her that Jordan was awake, but now she thought maybe that wasn't it at all. Maybe she'd just called to find out if Hennessy had finally killed herself, so that she could stop holding her breath and start to move on. Maybe those weren't really phone calls at all. Maybe they'd just been flowers at the grave of a friend she used to love a lot.

"For years you've been telling me you wish I could have a real life, that I deserved a real life, but every time I get close, you absolutely unravel," Jordan said. "*I* want this life. Do you understand that? We're not the same person anymore! I want a nice studio, swish galleries, fancy whips, a big future. I want Declan.

You don't have to want it. Because it's all mine, do you understand that? Can you be happy for me? Can you at least respect I'm happy?"

"I can't respect the titty paintings you share space with at that studio," Hennessy said. "Looking at them, I could feel my own tits melting."

All of a sudden, Jordan wasn't even mad anymore. She was only disappointed. "Can you undo what you did or not?"

Hennessy didn't answer. She was stacking all the remaining dried leaves that had fallen on one of the closed garbage bins.

"You think you spared me the memories of Jay because you hated her, but you know what I think? Deep down, you didn't give me your memories of Jay because you didn't want me to know that you were a lot like her."

Hennessy's eyes simmered.

Jordan could tell she was doing her best to formulate a comeback that would cut Jordan as deeply. She didn't give her the time. "I don't need you anymore, Hennessy, but I thought I might *want* you. I was wrong. You're ugly and you make everything you touch ugly. It's over."

"Sure it is."

"Do me a favor: Lose my number. Get out of my city."

"Very camera-ready, this convo," remarked Hennessy.

Jordan took a step back. "It's over."

Hennessy's eyes blazed. "You'll change your mind."

Just like her. Hennessy always changed her mind.

But Jordan wasn't really anything like Hennessy. Not anymore.

For what felt like the first time in her life, she was the one walking away.

8

Not far from where Jordan Hennessy had broken up with Jordan Hennessy, things were also going badly for Declan Lynch. It hadn't taken long for the day to go pear-shaped after he'd picked up Ronan from the assistance center. Declan's ten-minute detour to pick up a client's emergency parcel from the airport turned into a two-hour delay after a crash in the tunnel left them stranded beneath the Inner Harbor. Cars ahead, cars behind. Brake lights simmering red as far as the eye could see.

The three Lynch brothers were finally all together again. Declan, behind the wheel. Matthew, anxiously pivoting in the passenger seat. Ronan, silent and motionless in the back.

Of course it felt all wrong. It was always going to feel all wrong.

Ronan hadn't woken up when his brothers entered the room at the assistance center.

Ronan hadn't woken up when Matthew ran to him and hugged his head.

Ronan hadn't woken up when Matthew helped Declan get his limp body out to the car and then adjusted his hands this way and that way next to his motionless legs, trying to make him appear more Ronan-like in the backseat. But there was no way to capture the ferocious potential that Ronan, awake, normally implied. Matthew's arrangements had done nothing but make him look like a Victorian corpse portrait.

But he wasn't a corpse. He was more expensive than a corpse.

Declan was unhappily reminded of arranging the not-dead, not-living body of Aurora Lynch in a chair back at the Barns. What a hellish hamster wheel he'd been born on.

"Do not say anything until we get home," Declan had told Matthew when they left the center. "Please just let me think."

That had lasted until the brake lights in the tunnel. They crawled to a stop. Five minutes of sitting, and Matthew had begun to fidget. Ten minutes, and he'd begun turning around to look at Ronan. Fifteen minutes, and—

"Why is he sleeping?" Matthew asked.

"I don't know," Declan replied.

"Is he a dream?"

"I don't know."

"Why isn't he waking up with my swan thingy?"

"I don't know."

"Has he *always* been a dream?"

"Matthew, I *don't know*." Declan's phones were buzzing against him. The cars in front of him were not moving. The cars behind him were not moving. He needed to make a plan for this, but he couldn't wrap his head around it. *He's a more complicated machine.*

"Why is he draining my swan if he's not waking up?" Matthew whinged.

Draining? Declan hid his alarm. He'd hoped Ronan's failure to wake meant he wasn't affecting the sweetmetal. Instead he was trapped in a tunnel with two hungry dreams and one sweetmetal. "I don't know."

"What *do* you know?"

Declan wondered why it was Ronan who got to sleep forever instead of him. "I know that this sweetmetal cost everything I had to spend at the moment, which means I have to make this one last if you want to make it to the end of the school year."

Matthew's face turned suddenly horrified. "Are you going to make me sleep through summer?"

"Let's not get ahead of ourselves," Declan said, realizing too late he'd made a terrible mistake. His phones were still buzzing against him. The jackass behind him honked. No one was going anywhere, Boston. Ho hey, the working day, the working day. "Come on. I'm sick of listening to that idiot's exhaust in front of us. Turn on the radio."

But Matthew had the bit between his teeth. "Wait a sec. Wait, like, a solid-gold sec. What are you going to do with him when we get home, anyway? Are you going to *store* him somewhere, like a piece of furniture? Is it going to be like M—"

"Matthew," Declan interrupted, "are you going to be quiet?"

Instantly, the car fell silent. Long ago, Niall Lynch had always begun his stories with this question, asking it the same way each time, holding the *going* like a sung word, pattering out fast *to be quiet*. Together the boys would crowd onto Matthew's bed to listen, Aurora gathered in the nearby chair. Declan wondered how such a short-lived animal—the Lynch family—could have left such an impression on him. The day would come upon him soon when he'd lived longer without it than with it, and yet the memories still owned him thoroughly.

In the passenger seat, Matthew was small, tucking his hands into his lap, pulling his neck down into his shoulders.

"It used to be, before you were born, before I was born, before my father's father was born and so on, that Ireland was a place of many kings," Declan recited. He could hear the cadence of his father's voice in the beginning, but he could not bring himself to erase it. Storytelling was one of Niall's only fatherly attributes.

"No," Matthew protested. "Not an old story."

"They're all old stories."

"They weren't all old, I remember."

Niall had rarely peppered his older stories with newer ones, all in the same genre: Matthew, the plucky young hero, getting into accidental trouble, and Niall, the incorrigible comic relief, arriving just in the nick of time to get him out of it. Sometimes Declan and Ronan featured. Declan, a fussy lawman; Ronan, an agent of chaos.

Declan knew why Matthew wanted it, but he had neither the mirth nor flexibility to conjure such a fantasy on the spot. But he knew what Matthew wanted. He wanted a tale of that brief-lived animal. He wanted a tale of when things used to turn out all right.

With a sigh, Declan cast his eyes over the unbudging traffic and began, "Dad gave me a dream, once."

Matthew's eyes widened.

"I brought it to Aglionby," Declan continued. "It was in the town house, too. I brought it here. I got rid of all the others. Sold them, traded them. I don't know why I kept this one. I suppose I kept it because it was beautiful. Monet—do you know Monet? You must, he did the water lilies, everyone's seen the water lilies. Monet once said, 'Every day I discover more and more beautiful things. It's enough to drive me mad.' Or maybe 'drive one mad.' Either way. I think probably it was that. The dream was just so beautiful, I was obsessed with it. I was driven mad."

Still driven mad, because he still had it, even after all this time. He had just the two dreams he would never sell: this one, from his father, and the ORBMASTER, a golden little handful of light Ronan had given him months and months ago.

"What was it?" whispered Matthew.

"A moth. Enormous. The size of Dad's hand. White, or green, or both. The color of a moonlit garden, that's what color it is." The moth was a dream. It could be whatever color Niall wanted, even if the color didn't exist in the waking world. "It had such eyes. Big as this—" Declan held up his fingers to indicate the size, big as a marble. "Black and shiny, and clever as a pig's."

"Ew!"

"No, no. The moth had eyelashes like yours," he added, and Matthew touched his own lightly. "Big, feathery antennae. It wasn't disgusting, it was an animal, that's all. It was . . . it is just beautiful."

"Moths are bugs," Matthew murmured.

"They have wings like tapestry cloth. Next time you see one, look up close, as close as you can get. But don't touch," Declan said. "I wanted to touch it, but Dad always told me no. If you touch a moth's wings, he told me, it'll knock off the fur, and then they can't fly. But to see the moth is to want to touch it, Matthew. You want to *feel* that green-white color."

"Mmmm," Matthew said, soothed by the story. His eyes were half-lidded as if he, too, were imagining the moth. Ahead, brake lights flashed, but only to demonstrate their irritation, not to indicate a change in traffic status.

Can we make a home for it? Declan had asked Niall. *A box? To keep it safe?*

It'll flap around in there, Niall had replied. *Moths want to fly. It's not meant to live long. It's just meant to get out there and do its mothy thing and get eaten or fly into the sun, that's what moths do. I don't think this one'll even eat, has it even got a mouth?*

Tears had gathered in Declan's eyes, against his will, either because of the futility of the moth's brief existence or just because of how beautiful it was, and Niall had said quickly, *If it's got glass on the front of the box, sure, it'll be able to see out and nothing can get in. If that's what you really want.*

"Dad made the moth a little box. With his hands, not his dreams," Declan said. That had seemed important at the time, that Niall had sworn and sanded and pounded out in the work shed instead of slipping into a dream. Now, for some reason, Declan's insistence that it be a *real* box instead of a dreamt one made his eyes burn again, years later. He wished he could take that part back. "So I could carry it with me when I wanted, so I could have it and look at it."

How the moth had beaten against the walls for those first few days, until it learned it could not escape. And then, when Niall had died, it had of course fallen asleep, and it didn't know whether it was in a box or free anyway.

"Do you still have it?" Matthew asked.

"I used it to test your pendant. I could show it to you when we get home, if you want," Declan said, although he didn't want to make the offer. A third dream tugging on the sweetmetal. How many could he carry? It. How many could it carry?

"Oh no! Declan!" Matthew exclaimed.

He'd twisted to look in the backseat. In the dim light, Ronan was positioned just as before, but one thing had changed: a thin trail of black had begun to trickle from one of his eyes.

Nightwash.

So many days Ronan had come to visit Declan and Matthew at the DC town house, only to be driven from the city—which wasn't close to a ley line—by an onslaught of nightwash. The rules of nightwash were myriad and ever more severe. Ronan had to manifest dreams, or the nightwash began. He had to return to a ley line often, or the nightwash began. He had to manifest more and more dreams, or the nightwash began. He had to *stay* on a ley line, or the nightwash began.

Now Ronan was breaking both of these rules. He could not bring a dream back if he could not wake up. And there was no ley line to return to, just Matthew's ever-weakening sweetmetal.

"No," repeated Matthew.

In the backseat, a second string of nightwash trickled to match the first. Ronan didn't stir. The traffic didn't stir. His self-destruction was the only moving piece.

This, Declan realized, was why Bryde had been stealing that Klimt.

A world-famous sweetmetal, because an ordinary one wouldn't do the trick. The bottomless abyss needed more, more, more.

No more, Declan thought. *No more.*

Matthew was trembling. His knuckles were white. His fingers pressed into his temples hard enough that Declan could see his nails digging red moons into his skin. A little sound was escaping him. His eyes were glassy. Once, not long after Ronan had given Declan the ORBMASTER, Ronan's nightwash had gotten so bad that even his dreams had started to ooze black. Including Matthew. He wasn't oozing nightwash now, but it was clear he remembered it.

"Matthew, calm down," Declan said. "We'll manage it."

"No," said Matthew. The sound reverberated inside the car. "No. No. No. No. No. No. No. No."

Everyone has their max capacity, a man had once told Declan. The man was not Declan's father but rather one of a variety of men Declan had combined into a parental scarecrow in the final years of his teenhood. These men were teachers, counselors, employers, acquaintances, small appliance technicians, pediatricians, dentists, librarians. They loved giving advice. They took him aside at parties to deliver it. Frowned and doled it out over the coffee machine in the break room. Emailed it to him with subject lines like "thinking more about our convo." Declan was always meeting people more excited about giving him practical skills than Niall Lynch.

When people hit their max capacity, this man had told Declan, considering the pens in his drawer and selecting the most worthy specimen as his weapon, *they get pegged there. Yeah, you don't want to mistake almost max for actual max. People can get close and still pull themselves back together. Someone who's truly at max capacity, though—it doesn't matter if the pressure comes off, even a little bit. The accelerator's already mashed on their breakdown. They might look fine, but they aren't. Very next thing that happens, no matter how little: Snap! That's when you make your move.*

Declan couldn't remember if this guy had been talking about business or politics or dating. He just remembered the phrase. *Max capacity.*

"No. No. No. No." Matthew kept saying it the same way over and over again, the timing and inflection identical each time, the volume the only thing changing. "No. No. No. NO. NO. NO. NO. NO! NO! NO!"

Matthew had hit max capacity. No longer sounding at all human. Just sounding like a thing, like a ceaseless, mindless alarm, triggered by disaster.

Declan didn't think—he just ripped the swan pendant right from Matthew's neck.

It was as if his hand knew exactly where to grab it to make sure his fingers would snag the cord, and then jerk it so that the clasp snapped.

Matthew didn't have time to react before Declan threw open the car door and scrambled into the noisy tunnel. He backed one, two, three steps, up to the wall before he paused to see if he was far enough. His heart was pounding. Everything stank of toxic exhaust and dead fish.

"Declan?" Matthew said.

Through the open car door, Declan saw his brother peering at him. He hadn't moved an inch to counteract the theft; no part of him had suspected Declan might take the pendant from him.

The bewilderment on his face was complete as his eyes dimmed. His head nodded. He had lost the fight against this particular foe so often that he knew better than to struggle. Instead, he leaned against the shoulder of his seat, his gaze still on Declan. With a shuddering sigh, he closed his eyes—and fell asleep.

Declan stood against the humid edge of the tunnel, feeling the rumbling of all the waiting vehicles through his feet. He told himself that if he didn't preserve the sweetmetal, he'd be the only Lynch brother left. He told himself Matthew wouldn't have handed it over willingly. He told himself he was doing what had to be done.

But it felt like now he'd betrayed both his brothers.

No more, he thought.

But there was always more.

Aware of the eyes of other drivers on him, he turned to the wall and pretended to throw up. Then he wiped his mouth, went to the trunk, and tucked the sweetmetal in the very furthest corner from the passenger seat. He made a big show of retrieving a bottle of water, as if that had been the reason for opening the trunk in the first place.

Then he returned to the silent car.

His two brothers slept.

His phones had stopped ringing. He wished they hadn't. He would have loved to snatch one up just then, to solve some other problem that *was* solvable, to cross *something* off a list. But he knew better. Problems solved in the heat of the moment were rarely actually solved—that was why he had a job.

So instead he breathed through his mouth a dozen or so times, leaned across Matthew's quiet form to get an antacid out of the glove box, and took several with his bottle of water. He wiped down the top of his steering column, which had gathered dust. He scrolled through vandalized photos Jordan had texted him of *The Kiss* with her face subbed in for the woman's. Only then, after his stomach had stopped hurting, did he navigate through his contacts so that he could start once more to make a plan, to execute it, to handle it.

The car was so, so quiet.

Declan stared out the window at the stagnant traffic. He wasn't going anywhere. No point fighting it. He placed a call.

As soon as he heard it pick up, he said, "I need your help."

9

"How did you know this place existed?"

"Lucky guess."

"You must have a lot of luck."

"I do a lot of guessing."

Ronan had been drawn into the waking world again.

It was impossible to tell if he was indoors or out. The only light came from a phone's flashlight function; it illuminated Ronan's slack body and not much else. As before, his consciousness floated above his physical form, and he found, now, that he was quite sentimental about his human body. Look at that poor asshole lying on that packed dirt, look how lovingly tattooed his skin was, each mark a small confirmation that even though it felt like he hated his life and his body, deep down, he wanted to keep it, to redecorate the place to his own liking.

Black trails oozed from his body's eyes, nose, ears.

From this vantage point, Ronan understood the nightwash in a way he hadn't before. It wasn't caused by an absence of ley line energy, but rather by an excess of the human world's energy. The two energies existed in balance, one pushing against the other. That body down there had been built for a world with a different atmosphere, one pressurized with magic. Without it, this world would slowly kill him. It was neither good nor bad. It was simply a side effect of being him here.

The flashlight swung around to illuminate the space,

revealing a claustrophobic windowless corridor. One wall was brick with a skeleton of naked framing. The other close wall was cinder block, painted heavily with colors nearly bright enough to pierce the dark. Directly behind Ronan were colorful scales, claws, a twisting tail, but the bigger picture remained hidden.

Ronan recognized that this was the sweetmetal that had brought him here. A mural. The entire wall behind his prone body felt alive with its energy. For the moment, it held the night-wash at bay.

"Why is it bricked up like this?" the first voice asked. Declan. Ronan recognized him now.

"What's that?"

"What's what?"

"Sorry, I'm deaf in this ear. What did you say?"

The flashlight swung to point at the second speaker. His features were gaunt and exaggerated, like a drawing of a young man rather than an actual young man. His long, knobby fingers touched one of his ears, an unconscious gesture. He was dressed very stylishly for a dusty cubby hole, in pressed cotton and smooth wool, but his dusty hair was cut jaggedly.

Elation overtook Ronan.

Even before he put a name to the face, he was overwhelmed with a single thought: *It is going to be okay.*

The second voice belonged to Adam Parrish.

Declan asked, "Why is there this double-wall situation?"

"I reckon . . ." Adam stopped, then restarted with less of a Virginian accent. "I suppose they did it when they were building that addition upstairs. Needed a bigger footprint to support it. So this was an exterior wall, but now *that's* the new exterior wall. The painting—mural—would have originally faced the street."

Memories were surfacing of a slightly different version of Adam, a younger one, a less polished one. Images, bright as sweetmetals, came to him. Aglionby Academy, an unloved trailer, a bare apartment, an abandoned Virginia warehouse, the slanting, long fields of the Barns. Midnight drives, anxious journeys into pitch-black caves, charged glances over school desks, knuckles pressed against mouths, tight hugs goodbye.

Ronan's elation was giving way to something more complex. He was beginning to remember that things had ended poorly between them. Part of him wanted to blame Adam—he remembered feeling misunderstood, ill-used—but most of him understood that the unpleasantness had been all Ronan's doing. Whatever future that spiky, vibrant past had been building to was no longer an option.

"Do you have any idea why he's sleeping?" Adam asked. He glanced at the body and then away. Ronan saw now that he was as far from it as he could possibly get, his own body turned as if he were already leaving.

Unlike Adam, Declan didn't flinch from the reality of Ronan's failing body, although his expression was grim. He leaned forward quickly to wipe the nightwash from Ronan's face with the bent-over cuff of his jacket. "I was hoping you would know. My father can't have dreamt him. He would have needed a sweetmetal all this time."

Adam worried a finger at the sewn edge of his pants pocket; there was not a hole there, but it was a place holes liked to appear. Ronan noticed Adam's watch then. For the first time, he was able to pull up a memory as easily as he had when he was wearing his physical body. He'd dreamt that watch for Adam when he left for Harvard. It was the closest he could come to a love letter;

the language of affection had never felt right to Ronan. Clumsy. Overblown. False. Ronan speaking the language of another country, vocabulary learned from watching films on YouTube. But the watch—the watch told the time for whatever time zone Ronan was in, and it said exactly what Ronan meant to say.

Think of where I am, it said. *Think of me.*

Currently, the watch's hands were motionless.

Adam still wasn't really looking at Ronan. "Where is Chainsaw, by the way?"

"Farooq-Lane didn't mention a bird," Declan replied.

"Ronan will be pissed if something happened to her."

Declan retorted something about how Ronan wasn't in a position to make further demands on his time, but Ronan tuned it out and instead let himself repopulate his memories around Chainsaw. Wings, talons. Trees. Cabeswater. Lindenmere. Opal. The words and images attached to the dreamt raven came in quickly. Soon, he thought, he'd have them all. He'd be Ronan Lynch again.

He just needed to wake up.

Somehow.

"I'm going to give you the key to this place," Adam said to Declan. "Just come when no one is in the shop and you'll be fine."

"How often do you have work here?"

Adam shook his head. "Oh, no. I can't do that. I'm not going to . . . I showed you this place, but I can't be the, like, I can't come here and . . ."

Declan's tone turned cool and businesslike. "He was going to *move* here for you."

The two of them faced each other, a clear divide between

them. On one side was the land of adulthood, where Declan lived, his expression weighted with disappointment and judgment. On the other was the nebulous country that contained everything *before* adulthood, and that was where Adam remained, his eyebrows drawn together uncertainly, once again glancing toward Ronan and away.

"Look," said Adam, "Ronan chose his side. It wasn't me."

This struck Ronan as profoundly unfair. The world had chosen for him. The black smudge all over Declan's sleeve was proof of it. Left to his own devices, Ronan had chosen Adam, he was sure he'd chosen Adam. Hadn't he come to Cambridge, even though he hated cities, even though he loved the Barns? Hadn't he played cards with Adam's new Harvard friends, even though he hated them? Hadn't he had a list of apartments he was going to look at, hadn't he tried?

"Ronan wasn't himself," Declan said. "He was under the influence of Bryde."

Adam's tone was the dry, rueful one Ronan knew well. "He gets into trouble in school, you ask Gansey to fix it. Gets into trouble here, you blame Bryde. If anything, Bryde's *his* victim. He was doing what he was made to do."

Declan made a face. "Dreams are their own people. They can make their own choices."

"Too bad Ronan's not awake to hear you say that," Adam said. "There was a time it would've meant a lot to hear you say it."

What bitter fights Ronan and Declan had had over their mother Aurora's sleeping form. How much bad blood underneath that bridge. How many frenzied night drives Ronan had taken, trying to outrun his brother's factually presented arguments: Aurora was nothing without Niall, which meant that she'd been nothing with him, too. How many days with her had Ronan lost by Declan using everything he had to minimize her as a person instead of digging deep enough into the world of dreams to discover the existence of sweetmetals. What if, what if, what if?

Declan had the good grace to appear pained. He said, "At least I'm showing up now."

"Yeah, I guess," Adam admitted. He glanced again at Ronan, visibly warring with himself, and finally, crossed the corridor to him. Crouching, he undid the band of his dreamt watch. Ronan understood at once what was happening.

No.

He laid the useless watch on top of Ronan's wrist.

No.

He fastened the band, checking to make sure it wasn't too tight on Ronan's wrist.

No.

Gently, out of the view of Declan, Adam subtly traced his fingers over Ronan's scarred wrist, the back of his hand. He swallowed. This was goodbye.

Ronan felt a new emotion: misery.

Adam, no.

Adam suddenly leaned in very close to Ronan's slumped body. His lips were right on Ronan's ear. In this close space, even a whisper was audible to Declan, but his words were just for Ronan.

"*Post tenebras lux,*" he whispered.

Light follows darkness.

Adam added, "*Tamquam . . .*"

Alter idem, Ronan thought. But he had no voice. The body lying slumped in this corridor was the one who had a voice, and it couldn't wake up to say anything.

So Adam drew back uncontested. He gave Declan the key.

For some reason, a clear memory, unattached to anything else, returned to Ronan. A plain wooden mask, with round eye holes and gaping mouth. It was not a horrific mask, but it felt horrific to look at nonetheless.

"Thanks for the temporary solution," Declan said, not bothering to hide the contempt in his voice. His hand closed over the key in a fist.

"If you need more help," Adam said from the doorway, "don't call me."

10

Hennessy was dreaming of the Lace.

The Lace dream was different than it used to be. Before, it always began in the dark. She was meaningless in this version of the dream. Not a cog in the machine, not a blade of grass in a field. Possibly a speck of dust in the baleful eye of a loping beast, blinked away. But nothing more.

Slowly, the dream illuminated, and the light revealed a thing that had been there all along. A thing? An entity. A situation. Its edges were jagged and geometric, intricate and ragged, a snowflake beneath a microscope. Brilliant light shone from behind the Lace, blinding in its intensity. It was enormous. Enormous not like a storm or a plant, but enormous like grief or shame.

The Lace was not really a thing one only saw. It was a thing one felt.

Then—and this was the worst part of the dream—the Lace noticed she was there. How awful to be seen. How awful to have not realized how wonderful a life was before being seen by the Lace, because now there was only *after*. The Lace stretched toward her, growing like crystals, thin as paper, sharp as razors. Its hatred of her was thorough. It hated what she was. It hated who she was. And most of all, it hated that she had something it wanted.

Hennessy could be a doorway for the Lace. All she had to

do was give in, and the Lace could manifest in the waking world, where it would destroy everyone.

For years, she had defied it, and for years, the Lace had punished her for this defiance. The jagged edges pierced her like hair-fine needles, and she woke with a million tiny holes in her skin, each beading blood. She became see-through. Like the Lace.

But since Hennessy had shut down the ley line, things were different. It wasn't just that Hennessy couldn't manifest the Lace, even if she wanted to.

The Lace itself was different.

Now when she fell asleep, its jagged form still grew to fill the darkness. It was still sharp and deadly. It still delivered the usual threats. But it didn't really matter. The dread was missing. She felt she was having a dream of the memory of the Lace dream, rather than experiencing the real Lace. Without the creeping dread and the fear of destroying the entire world through a moment of weakness, the Lace's dialogue came off more like a recorded message of all the terrible thoughts Hennessy already had.

The Lace hissed at her: *You ruined things with Jordan. You know she's going to have a wonderful life without you, don't you? You're going to miss her forever and she's not going to think of you for even a second once you're too far to see in the rearview mirror. You'll have plenty of time to decide what's worse: dying alone, or living alone.*

"You're singing a song I already know the words to," Hennessy said.

The Lace lashed out. She let the pain jolt through her.

It was just pain. Hennessy could handle pain.

Just pain.

No fear.

Hennessy woke with a start.

"Oh, she's right there," she said.

Just inches away were Carmen Farooq-Lane's enormous and luminous brown eyes. As always, they were full of beauty and judgment, like a smiting angel. When the smiting angel eyes saw that Hennessy was awake, they narrowed.

"You can't sleep all day and all night," Farooq-Lane said.

Classic Carmen Farooq-Lane. Hennessy had only known her for a few days, but it hadn't taken very long to get her number. Carmen Farooq-Lane liked rules. Carmen Farooq-Lane liked rules other people had come up with. Carmen Farooq-Lane liked rules other people from long ago or in a different branch of government had made so that she didn't have to think too hard about whether the people who made the rules were actually clever or not.

Some examples of rules Farooq-Lane had attempted to impose already: Meals were to be eaten at regular intervals, at the same time each day, and not in portions left half-eaten around the house. Sleep was to happen at regular intervals, at the same time each day, and not in portions left half-eaten around the house. Clothing was to be appropriate to the temperature outside. Crop tops were not cold-weather apparel. Fur coats were not indoor apparel. Furniture was to be used in the way the maker had intended. Sofas were to be sat on, counters were not. Stools were to be stood on, tables were not. Beds were to sleep in, bathtubs were not.

Zeds were for killing, except when they weren't.

Farooq-Lane hadn't found that rule very funny, when Hennessy asked her about it.

"Eight hours of sleep is a fallacy invented by the working man," Hennessy informed her now. "Eight hours of sleep and no more, leaving the remaining sixteen—is that the math, is it sixteen? Eight plus six is . . . okay, yes, that's right—for you to work for the Man. The forty-hour workweek and the eight-hour sleep cycle are a couple, do you understand? They were married by corporations who gave a dowry of suffering; mankind is meant to be like a leopard, lying in a tree all day except for the—"

From the kitchen, Liliana called in her crackling, sweet voice, "I've made some broth for us to take with us, Carmen! I think you will enjoy it, Hennessy."

This was their dysfunctional family, for the moment. Mother Farooq-Lane, laying down the law. Other Mother Liliana, gently softening the blow. Child Hennessy, the dutiful adopted adult daughter brought on because the guilty Mothers had stolen Hennessy's teeth from her, and wanted to make it up to her by spoon-feeding her structure and love.

Hennessy hadn't been born yesterday. She knew baggage when she saw it.

For the past few days, the three of them shared a shingle-sided house in a revoltingly domestic corner of the greater Boston area. It was clear Liliana had chosen the rental, as she was the one who liked it best. She was a demure, ancient goddess of a woman, with skin so pale it was greenish in some lights, offset by the turquoise hairband she nearly always wore to keep her snowy hair back. Hennessy could already tell that Liliana had never met a domestic task she didn't like. She liked to simmer bones for hours. She knitted scarves, sweaters, and bags for scarves and sweaters. She liked hot beverages and things called *mulling spices*. Houseplants unfurled at her touch. Children melted under her gaze. Altogether, Liliana had a soothing, loving vibe that had initially comforted Hennessy and now made Hennessy feel like she had a pillow over her head, and her legs were just about to stop kicking. Liliana and Farooq-Lane also seemed to have this December–May relationship thing going on, and Hennessy wasn't one to judge—she just had questions.

"We have an errand to run. Do you want to come with?" Farooq-Lane asked.

"I have moved into a post-want stage of my life," Hennessy said. "This is what I believe Buddha meant when he said *desire is the root of all evil.*"

Liliana came around the kitchen to offer Hennessy a steaming travel mug. She looked like the most perfect grandmother one could possibly imagine, her deep-sunk eyes wise and caring. "Do you want to talk about how you feel? Your face looks different, sweetheart, did something happen while we were gone?"

She was so nice that Hennessy immediately felt like being awful to her. She fought the impulse as hard as possible. "Is this a mug of soup? Am I meant to swallow this? That doesn't seem at all like a thing I would want to do."

"It's nourishing," Liliana said, at the same time that Farooq-Lane said, "This from the person who's eaten nothing but beer for three days. Cheap beer."

Hennessy waved both of these statements off and asked, "What's this errand you're talking about? Is it a real errand, like, work, or is *errand* just a funny figure of speech, a code word for something more interesting, like going clubbing or stealing a horse?"

"Declan Lynch gave me an address to investigate."

Hennessy recoiled from his name. "I don't want anything to do with that."

Farooq-Lane's expression sharpened. "Does that mean you know what it is?"

"What? What what is? No, it means he's a boring man with a boring face and I don't want to get close to his awful life in case I get some of his boring microbes and shit into my aura. If you knew what was good for you, you'd take some, like, bug spray or something to make sure you kill any of the boring things that might fly out at you as you got close to his life."

"I don't know," Liliana said with a wry smile, "that sounds a lot like an adventure, Hennessy."

Farooq-Lane saved Hennessy the work of giving her a frown. "If you want to come, then get up. If you want to stay, stay. I'm not your mother."

Straightening, she drew her curtain of hair into an effortless knot, causing a wave of appealing floral scent to wash over Hennessy. It was truly amazing how much of the past few days Hennessy had spent either fantasizing about Farooq-Lane or having that fantasy ruined by the reality of her.

Liliana patted Hennessy's cheek, as if she were a small child. Each time she did, Hennessy felt a little burst of unwilling good feeling. Liliana said, "I got supplies for you today, all the ones I heard you talking about." Hennessy didn't remember talking about anything money could buy. "They're in the basement."

"Counterpoint: Can I have my sword instead? Have I been good, Mum, can I have it yet? I'll clean my room."

Farooq-Lane zipped up her boots. "I told you I'd give it to you when you were sober. That hasn't happened yet."

For all her Honorary Mothers' guilt about taking her dreaming to save the world, Hennessy wasn't here because she couldn't think of anywhere else to go. She was here because of her sword.

It was one of a set, or had been; she and Ronan had dreamt them at the same time. His, engraved with the words VEXED TO NIGHTMARE, bristled with shining daylight. Hers, engraved with the words FROM CHAOS, glowed with the power of the night sky. They cut through just about anything except each other. How hopeful and stupid Ronan and Hennessy had been. What could you do with a sword these days? Strike a cool pose. Look like you knew what you were doing. Cut flowers very fast.

Farooq-Lane had once saved Hennessy's life with that sword. Instead of letting a tiny bit of Lace kill her while she was paralyzed, she'd snatched the blade up and sliced the Lace to nothingness. And Farooq-Lane had kept the sword—she still had it, in fact. Why would a Moderator do that?

Hennessy didn't understand, and intended to stick around until she found out.

She raised her voice so that Farooq-Lane could still hear her as she fetched her coat from her bedroom. "Seriously, though, it's my sword and it's sort of fucked up that you're keeping it from me!"

Liliana handed Hennessy a box of shortbread cookies. Hennessy had no idea where she'd had it this whole time, but that was Liliana for you. Comfort in every pocket. "Put a little something in your stomach and you'll feel a lot better."

"Paint a portrait of Liliana and I'll give your sword to you," Farooq-Lane said, returning to the room. "Or get sober and I'll give it to you. Your choice."

Hennessy strained her neck so that she could shout over the back of the couch. "So really that means I could paint Liliana while completely smashed and still get the sword, right, just so we're clear? Because I think you used the wrong Boolean operator and I just want to be absolutely on the level before I bother drying out."

Farooq-Lane held the door open for Liliana. "Don't burn the house down."

Liliana joined her. "Have a good time, dear."

After they left, Hennessy closed her eyes again, but she was annoyed to find that Farooq-Lane had been right about one thing. She *couldn't* sleep all day and all night.

Slowly, she ate the entire box of shortbread cookies while wondering what tedious scavenger hunt Declan Lynch had sent them on, and then she drank the travel mug of broth while wondering just how old Liliana really was. She was the oldest-looking person Hennessy had ever seen outside of a black-and-white photograph. Then she went into the kitchen and got a soda to wash down the broth while thinking about what Machkowsky had said about being J. H. Hennessy's daughter.

Then she went to the basement to see what supplies Liliana had gotten for her.

When she pulled the cord attached to the single lightbulb over the stairs, it illuminated just enough of the basement to show her that Liliana had set up an easel, a canvas, and a tray of paints. A tiny little studio carved out just in front of the old washer and dryer. It was a very Liliana thing to do, very thoughtful and unobtrusive, even if Hennessy still couldn't remember ever mentioning supplies to her.

Maybe she would, she thought. Maybe she *would* paint. Imagine the look on Farooq-Lane's face when she returned to see Hennessy had actually picked up a brush.

Hennessy lingered there, fingers lightly touching the cord to the lightbulb, her foot balanced on the edge of the stair's rounded lip, and thought about what Jordan had said about suspecting that Hennessy was probably a lot like Jay.

Mum?

Jay said, *You won't miss me.*

Pulled the trigger.

Hennessy pulled the cord again, plunging the basement back into darkness.

She wanted to go get a beer. She pictured what she would look like going into the kitchen, getting a beer. She presented herself with a list of all the ways she'd feel better with a beer. She presented herself with all the reasons why she deserved the beer.

She didn't go for a beer.

She didn't want Jordan to be right.

She pulled the cord a third time, and then she went into the basement to paint.

11

"You should not let her ruffle you," Liliana said as the two of them navigated the narrow roads of Peabody, Massachusetts. Old houses and buildings cast crooked shadows across the asphalt as the sun fell behind the trees and rooftops. "It teaches her bad habits."

"Teaches her? She came preloaded with them!"

"Don't we all?" Liliana pointed to a parking spot on the crumbling curb. "I believe this is it."

The radio spontaneously began to play opera at top volume, a thing it had begun to do with increasing frequency. *Okay, Parsifal*, Farooq-Lane thought. She peered at the run-down warehouse, which was labeled ATLANTIC SELF STORAGE, and then consulted the business card Declan had given her. Now the numbers made sense. The first was a unit number. The second a passcode. Not dissimilar to the information she'd given him for Bryde. Information for information. Spies on a bridge.

The only adults in the room, Declan's voice came back to her.

As they stepped onto the overgrown sidewalk, Farooq-Lane shivered, not just because it had suddenly snapped cold again, but because the hair on the back of her neck felt prickly, like she was being watched. She asked, "What do we think is waiting for us? Do you know?"

Liliana shook her head.

Inside, the unmanned storage facility was a concrete-floored maze of blue metal doors the size of garage doors, each unit numbered. It was heated, but only barely. The unit Declan had directed them to was on the far side of it.

She was uneasy. Waiting for the other shoe to drop.

You stopped the apocalypse, she reminded herself.

"It's okay," Liliana said softly.

Embarrassed, Farooq-Lane replayed the last few seconds in her head, trying to tell if she'd actually said the words out loud. To her further embarrassment, she couldn't tell. She hesitated, then confessed, "I don't know what's wrong with me. I feel like I'm losing my mind."

Liliana folded Farooq-Lane in her arms for several long minutes in the barren hallway, and Farooq-Lane let herself absorb the otherworldly comfort. Liliana inhaled the scent of her hair, and then she murmured, "You are such an interesting person, Carmen. You try so hard, even if you don't know why you're trying."

Even if it is killing people.

Farooq-Lane said, her voice muffled by Liliana's shoulder, "Liliana, are you a dream?"

There was no pause between the question and the feeling of Liliana nodding against her. It wasn't a secret; Farooq-Lane had simply never asked.

"Who dreamt you?"

"She died long ago," Liliana said. "She looked a little like you."

Farooq-Lane found this notion disagreeable, and pulled back. To her surprise, she found Liliana looking a little mirthful.

Amused, Liliana shook her head. "I was dreamt by a man, and he looked like a vulture. I wasn't sorry he died. I just wanted to see if you could be made jealous or not. Ah, there she is, your beautiful smile." She touched Farooq-Lane's mouth.

Farooq-Lane kissed Liliana's thumb lightly. "I didn't know you could be funny." Then it occurred to her: "Your dreamer died? Shouldn't you be asleep?"

"Visionaries can stay awake without their dreamers," Liliana said. "That is what makes us Visionaries."

"Did Parsifal know this?" Farooq-Lane wondered. The previous Visionary had never mentioned anything like this. Moreover, he'd seemed so firmly and mulishly human that it was hard to imagine that anyone could have dreamt him.

"He must have," Liliana said. "We choose this life. We choose the visions to stay awake forever."

Farooq-Lane half expected opera music to haunt the storage facility at this answer—it seemed like the sort of conversation that should have prompted Parsifal's otherworldly attention—but none came. The roar and clatter of a truck outside brought her firmly back to the matter at hand, however.

"I want us to talk about this more over a cup of tea when we're home later," she told Liliana, and Liliana's smile spread, surprised and genuine. "But for now, stay back. I don't know what is on the other side of this."

She consulted the business card, then knelt on the frigid concrete floor to key the passcode into the unit's digital lock. With a soft beep, it allowed her to slide the door up like a garage door. The rattle echoed through the warehouse.

The unit was occupied.

Occupied by the Moderators.

Lock. Business consultant and program manager, brought on as figurehead and point of contact.

Nikolenko. Explosive ordnance disposal, recruited for weapons education.

Ramsay. International brand strategy and investment manager, brought on for program strategy and travel expertise.

Vasquez. Retired intelligence officer, recruited for tracking Zeds through personal information.

Bellos. Black-ops, transferred for muscle.

Hellerman. Psychiatric nurse, brought on for experience with Visionaries.

Farooq-Lane fell to her knees.

She didn't even have time to break her own fall; she hadn't known her knees were going to buckle until they did. They slammed to the concrete and she caught herself from falling farther with her hand.

She was already shaking. Her breath was as ragged as if she'd been running.

The ferocity of her reaction shocked her.

These were the people Farooq-Lane had worked with for the past several months. She was just yards away from Lock, who'd recruited her at the beginning, who'd appealed to her sense of duty again and again.

You know who else is easy to control? Nathan's voice said in her head. *People who think they're doing the right thing.*

The Moderators lay neatly arrayed in the storage unit, on their backs on the concrete, their hands arranged by their sides.

Sleeping.

This was even more mysterious than Ronan Lynch falling asleep, than Bryde falling asleep. The Moderators had been merciless in their eradication of Zeds; scathing in their assessment of dreams. But in the end, what were they? Asleep in a storage unit like all the other dreams.

Something wasn't right, her subconscious had shouted. Something wasn't right.

And here was something.

Finally, she climbed to her feet and dusted off her knees. She tried to sound as composed as possible as she told Liliana, "I'm sorry about that. I just . . . I just . . ."

". . . hate them," Liliana finished for her.

Yes.

It was freeing to think it. She hated them. She hated them. She hated them. It wasn't a very complicated conclusion, but it was undeniably true, and that felt important.

"What are you going to do now?" Liliana asked.

This answer, at least, was easy. Farooq-Lane said, "We find out what the Moderators really wanted."

12

Time passed strangely for Ronan.

There were neither sunrises nor sunsets to mark the days. No schedule to mark the weeks. Minutes ticked by in a quite ordinary fashion while he inhabited a sweetmetal, but once he was back in the dark sea, he had no idea how many minutes passed *between* the sweetmetals.

He did not travel between them much now that he had seen his brothers. Instead, he stayed close to the sweetmetal that was keeping his body alive. He spent countless minutes in the dark corridor, listening to the sound of mechanics working on the other side of the wall, longing for Declan to visit, longing for anything to permeate the darkness, longing to wake up. Sometimes he let himself drift back out to the dark sea, sought out another sweetmetal in order to see the sun, but he always came back.

Let me in, he told his body. *Wake up, wake up.*

He did not know how much time had passed before light entered the corridor.

It came from a small electric lantern, the handle repaired with scuffed electric tape. The shoes of the lantern-carrier were visible as they stepped in. They were not Declan's dramatically styled shoes, the ones that always made his feet seem as long as elf feet, but rather a pair of scuffed leather sneakers.

Please.

Ronan didn't dare hope.

Adam Parrish quietly closed the door behind him. With one hand, he extended the lantern before him as he walked to Ronan's still-slumped body. The other he held close to his chest as if he were either favoring it or holding something close. Gingerly, he leaned over Ronan, examining Ronan's nightwash status, and then he put the lantern down and sat crisscross applesauce, awkwardly, using only one hand to balance himself.

Ronan took in every detail. The colorless brows, the light lashes, the unusual cheekbones, the unhappy, pensive mouth. The hair cropped unevenly across his forehead, still scissored in a mirror despite the more stylish clothing. One couldn't acquire haircuts secondhand. Even the shape of his hands was comfortingly familiar. The backs were badly chapped. The palms of them had numbers jotted on them, half-smeared from washing or age.

Adam said, "Shh shh shh."

But he wasn't talking to Ronan. He was slowly peeling his jacket open to remove a ragged black bundle.

"You'll hurt yourself," Adam said, then swore. The bundle had bitten him.

It was Chainsaw.

"Easy," Adam warned, as the dreamt raven shook herself free of his grasp. She let out a coarse protest before flapping up into the darkness; Ronan's heart was soaring up along with her. Overhead came the sound of her wings huffing against the air and her talons scraping against the walls. "Look who else is here. Chainsaw. Look who else is here: Kerah."

At that word—*Kerah*—the bird returned in an instant, diving from the darkness.

Adam's voice was soft; he pointed. "Look."

Chainsaw's neck feathers ruffled into a cartoonish collar. With a rippling purr, she careened into Ronan's unmoving chest.

How he longed to hold her. He couldn't feel any physical sensations now, but he could remember them. The cool, dry texture of her feathers. The weight of her on his shoulder.

But he could not hold her, of course, and as soon as she realized this, she began to caterwaul. At first she simply clucked and rocked. Then she plucked at the seams of his shirt, and when that did not rouse him, she began to peck at his fingers.

When she began to properly bite them, Adam hastily leaned forward to capture her, shushing. Cupping his hands over her neck and wings, out of reach of her beak, he made her sit in his lap, facing Ronan. "Just look for a bit, okay? Give yourself time to take it in."

She struggled for almost a minute, but he held her there, patiently, every so often stroking the back of her neck with his thumb.

"Shhh," he whispered again. Ronan had never seen him be so close with Chainsaw, but the ease with which he did it, and the way that she tolerated it, told him it must have happened before. "He's just sleeping. Like you were right before this. If I let you go, will you behave? Don't make me regret this."

Slowly, he set her onto the packed dirt before him, not lifting his hands. She stood, fairly quiet, her beak just parted a little from the insult of being contained. Finally, he released her and she shook his touch off as if she had never been fussing. Now that her panic had gone, there was just joy at the reunification; Ronan could hear her making a complicated, vaguely disgusting gurgling as she played. She busied herself stalking back and forth in front of Ronan, plucking at his bootlaces, jumping on his chest, crabbing down his arm, and then pecking the dirt around him.

Adam watched her closely through all this, his worry giving way to a reluctant smile at her increasingly performative antics.

She perched on Ronan's boot and cocked her head at Adam.

"Atom," Chainsaw remarked in her deep, strange bird voice.

Adam laughed a little. "Hi."

Both of them seemed more settled after this. Adam repositioned himself more comfortably, leaning his back between the framing on the opposite wall. His legs mingled with Ronan's long legs, a chaos of young men. Then he sighed and leaned his head back against the wall, eyes closed.

Yes, thought Ronan. *Stay.*

"I guess I'm an idiot," Adam said, after a space, his voice startling Chainsaw. She released a punitive crap dangerously close to his hand. "Chainsaw! Come on!" He scooted over an inch, then lifted his eyes to Ronan. "I know I said I wouldn't come back. I did mean it. And it's not like you don't deserve it . . ."

He drifted off, and it was hard to say if it was because he hadn't wanted to finish the sentence or if he had forgotten he was talking out loud.

Then he began again, "But I kept thinking about Chainsaw, I guess. I knew she had to be near wherever they found you. If she wasn't dead. Thrown out, eaten, whatever. I was in section and I just couldn't stop thinking about it. I had to at least look. And then when I found her—I can't believe I did, she's lucky she just looks like trash—I just kept thinking about how she'd feel to see you. I couldn't put it down, that thought . . ."

He drifted off again, and now Ronan was suddenly and fiercely reminded of praying. Not praying in a church, with a congregation, out loud, or reciting a memorized prayer. But instead the kind of praying he'd done when he was alone. Exhausted. Confused. Those prayers often faded into ellipses as he wondered if there was anyone on the other side of the line.

Adam couldn't know whether or not Ronan could hear him.

I hear you.

Chainsaw flapped chaotically into Adam's lap then, and he spent several long minutes pulling threads out of the pocket of his jacket for her to snatch and throw over her shoulder, a game rapidly invented.

"Do you remember when I asked you what you'd do if you accidentally dreamt another me?" Adam asked abruptly. "I thought about it a lot after that. What I'd do to that other Adam. Would I let him live my life with me, like Hennessy? Would I kill him before he could kill me? But you know what I got to thinking? That copy exists. *I* made him. I *am* him. There's a real version of me that stayed with you, I guess, that went out to Lindenmere every day and just learned everything he could about the ley line, about the *something else.* Or maybe who went with Gansey and Blue. Or who went to school in DC and came home every weekend. But this Adam killed those Adams so this one could win, this one who came to Harvard to go to class and write papers and buy waffles with the Crying Club and pretend like nothing bad ever happened to him and like he has all the answers."

Adam stopped then and suddenly, viciously, picked at his left hand with his right until a nearly healed wound grudgingly provided a tiny edge of blood. Angrily he swiped this away, as if annoyed the scab had given in.

"I lie to all of them. I lie to Gansey. I lie to Blue. I lie to my professors. It's like I can't stop. It's like I, it's like . . . I don't want this version to have anything the other version had, good or bad. So any time I need a past, I just make something up. New parents, new house, new memories, new reasons for how I lost my hearing, new me. I don't know what I'm doing anymore. Shit. You were, like, the place I stored all the reality in. Then I had to start lying about you, too, and it just all, it just all . . ."

He stopped then for a long time, looking off into the darkness.

"I found this place because I was looking for somewhere to scry. Declan wanted to know why I came and that was it. You know how there was no ley energy in Cambridge. I came clear out here. A lot more than I let on," he said, in a slightly more reasoned voice. A slightly more accented voice. This was his old accent, his Virginia accent, as warming to Ronan as the sun. "I could scry here pretty good. I knew it was dangerous, I could get stuck out there, I knew there was that Lace out there, but I did it anyway. I wasn't even looking for anything. I just missed it so bad, I just missed—"

He knocked his shoe against Ronan's.

Me too.

Now Adam's hands were fretting in each other again, prominent knuckles white and red as he squeezed them fervently. "I don't know if I hate it here or if I hate that I don't love it. I was supposed to love it. But I want to go—I think about it every day, just getting on the bike and going, and going, but where?"

He wasn't crying, but he quickly rubbed the back of his hand against one eye. "Anyhow, so I can't blame you that you lied to yourself about dreaming Bryde. 'Cause I made this fake version of me, right, and I was wide awake when I did it. We're both liars.

I don't know what to do. I miss . . ." He closed his eyes. "I miss knowing where I was going."

Then he did close his eyes and he *did* cry for a little. Not much in the way of tears, just the terrible, jagged sound one's breath makes when crying. Eventually, he stopped, and he sat there for a few long minutes, worrying his fingers over his deaf ear again and again.

Ronan couldn't do anything. He couldn't do anything at all.

Wake up, Ronan thought, *wake up, wake up*. But his body didn't move a muscle.

Adam gathered up Chainsaw, much to her protests, and tucked her back inside his jacket. He gathered up the lantern.

Tamquam, Ronan thought, furious that Adam was upset, euphoric that he'd come back. It hadn't been that long before this that he'd been wanting to know what emotions felt like, and now he had all of them at once.

Just before the door closed behind him, Adam said to the dark, *"Alter idem."*

13

For a very long time, the Barns were a paradise to Mór and Niall.

It was splendid to have so much room to spread out. Overgrown fields! Overgrown sheds! Overgrown woods! Overgrown life! Plants grow to the size of their pot, and the old Mór and Niall had been pot-bound.

It was splendid to have four seasons. The first summer produced so many hours of both beaming sun and bellowing rain that it seemed to add up to more than twenty-four in a day. Everything was green as a fairy tale. Autumn was sharp and red, the sloping fields half-hidden in the morning by white fog. In the evenings, unseen bonfires scented the air as crickets shrilled their goodbyes to the heat. In the winter, it snowed with such thorough confidence that it seemed white Christmases must be the norm (they weren't). And just when Mór and Niall had grown bored of hiding from the cold in the farmhouse, spring ferns uncurled in the forest, crocuses peeped out from under the newly repaired porch, and a new year's sky washed clear and fresh-faced above.

It was splendid to watch Declan grow up in this land that would be his kingdom. He was an easy baby, an easy toddler, with a nearly instinctive understanding of all the things that could make babies go bonk. The farmhouse didn't have to be baby-proofed. Declan choked gently on the edge of a pacifier once, and after that required proof of concept that everything that was put in his mouth was food. He was an unfoolish child.

It was splendid to dream. Soon the Barns began to get cluttered with silly nonsense items. Niall got it into his head that he wanted a herd of cattle and spent months reading books on cows, talking about cows, watching programs on cows, drawing cows, trying to provoke his subconscious into dreams of cows, cows, cows. He was not very good at bringing them back when he woke. More often than not, he came back empty-handed, or with a cow-shaped potholder or other cow knickknack. But every so often he managed the trick, and Mór raged that there was another cow in the house, and the multicolored herd out front slowly grew.

It was splendid to not be hunted.

For a while.

One day Niall blustered into the house in a way he hadn't in a long time. Niall wasn't a purposeful creature. He was a meandering sort of person, a person who liked to talk a road into being on the same journey as him. Mór was napping on the tatty wool couch; he shook her awake.

"She's found us. I don't know how she does it," Niall said. "Actually, sure, I do. She's got a nose for it. She's got that magnet of greed inside her that points her toward due north at all times. Due north being us! You were right. What a grasping witch she is. Have you ever known a woman who lived so far from a gingerbread house to be so likely to devour children? Are you not up yet? Jesus Mary, blink if you're listening."

Mór was paralyzed, as both she and Niall were after any successful dream. During this paralysis, the dreamer always watched themselves from above, like their body no longer belonged to them. Niall, knowing this, looked up at the ceiling as if he might guess where Mór's attention was coming from. He fidgeted, waiting for her to move. He plucked the silvery-blue oak leaves from her hands.

They both dreamt of the Forest so often.

"How do you know she's found us, what are the signs that you saw?" Mór demanded, sputtering to life.

"At the Lotus Mart," Niall said, referring to the only gas pump in Singer's Falls, a tiny, unbranded station attached to a professional garage. They sold curried potato salad sandwiches that both Niall and Mór were addicted to. "Dinesh said a woman came in who talked like us. 'What's she look like?' I say. 'A lot like you,' he says. Referring to—" He tapped his own chest. "Of course, not yourself."

"That can mean all sorts of things," Mór said, rising from the couch. Acorns spilled from the cushions around her. "A black-haired woman with a funny voice."

Niall looked dispiritedly around the sitting room at all the scattered dreams cluttering the place. They had not bothered with secrecy within the farmhouse. He asked suddenly, "Where's himself, where's Declan?"

"Napping," Mór told him. "I tried to get him to share the couch with me a little while, but you know how he is with his rules. 'Sleeping only happens in beds,' he says. I asked him what he thought he was doing in the car the other day, though, and he didn't laugh a bit. Love, do you really think it's her?"

Love was what Mór called Niall. It always sounded a little like it was the first time she'd said the word. The *her* in question was Marie Lynch, Niall's mother. She was the sort of species that was only dangerous to a very few, and usually only those related by blood.

"It is," interrupted a new voice.

Niall's mother had his dark hair. His intense blue eyes. His height. But where his energy made him seem alive and charismatic, she seemed reanimated and possessive.

She held Declan's hand tightly. He did not struggle. He just looked at his parents with an expression heavy for a toddler, a sort of weary look that seemed to imply that he had known the world was perilous and *now look.*

Both Niall and Mór stared at their son.

"Thank you for the welcome," Marie said. As Dinesh at the Lotus Mart had observed, she did have the same accent as Niall and Mór. "There's nothing a mother likes more than to be left in the cold."

They had not seen Niall's mother since they'd left Ireland. She was not the only reason why they'd left, but she was one of the big three, particularly after Niall's father had died (vodka rinsing him away over time like the letters on a sign).

Did Niall love her?

Did Niall hate her?

He had hoped to never see her again, which wasn't as conclusive an answer to those questions as one would think. She was one of those intimate villains, one of those species that was both poisonous and necessary to those susceptible. Too much of her would undoubtedly kill Niall Lynch, but too little might, too.

Mór cast a knowing look at her young husband, whose hands twitched at his sides. Niall's voice was chilly and unlike himself as he asked, "How did you find us?"

Mór said, "Declan, little hawk, come over here."

Declan tested his hand against the grip of Marie Lynch. She continued to cling to him tightly, even though she obviously wasn't paying any attention to him anymore. Her gaze was only on the young couple of dreamers before her. She pressed her other hand to her chest and said to Niall, "Did you think you could send things to that woman's eejit sisters and us not know about it? And why is it you're sending things to her family, after what happened, and not to your own, Niall? I came here to see if there was any chance that you might remember us, boy, or if you were still well caught in her wicked spells."

Mór didn't flinch away from the accusation.

"Ah, don't pretend, Ma," Niall said. It would have taken far more hours to get him round to this level of directness back in Kerry, but they weren't in Kerry anymore, were they? The pot had tipped over and their roots had spread out.

"What's that?" Marie Lynch's voice turned a little sharper still. "What's that you said?"

"Don't pretend you're not here for something of your own," Niall said. "I know how you are."

"It doesn't bring me any joy to see you like this," Marie said. "It doesn't bring me any joy at all to see you here, living in sin with *that* woman, already being against God in your own way, but you know I tolerate it, because you're my son, and who else will? Yes, I tolerate it, even if I don't understand it, but how about murder? Do I have to tolerate murder?"

It wasn't only the dreaming that had driven Niall and Mór across an ocean.

The Lynch family and the Curry family—that was Mór's maiden name—were all tangled up, on account of shared property lines and shared ugly business. First of all, the ugly business Niall's father and Mór's father were all netted up in back in Belfast, and second of all, the ugly business of Mór's uncle, the one she hated for reasons everyone knew but no one would say. The uncle who'd died that one night Niall came back after working in Manchester for months; the night he'd reunited with Mór again to catch up, see where you're at after all this time between us, would you like to go dancing; the night where everyone had seen Niall leave the house party furious, shouting about how there were snakes left in Kerry after all because he couldn't believe the number of forked tongues he'd just laid eyes on! And Mór left crying there as Niall stormed off, and if you knew Mór, you knew she never cried.

Yes, they all knew what had happened to Michael Curry, because what were the odds he'd be careless with his blades on a night when Niall Lynch was seen speeding in his little hatchback to Michael's cabinet shop?

"You tolerated plenty before he came to a bad end, didn't you?" Niall said in a low voice.

Marie let this pass without comment. "It would be nice for some affection, some gratitude, some family. Some acknowledgment I'm here, even with your old father in the grave, trying to see how you are."

"Acknowledgment," Mór echoed. "Just say 'money.'"

Turning dreams into money was easier said than done. Neither Niall nor Mór could manage enough specificity in their dreams to be sure their dreamt riches would hold up under a microscope, so dollar bills were right out, and so was gold or gems. Dreams always *felt* right, but that didn't mean they *were* right. Pressing on them too hard often revealed them as false, and that was exactly what Niall and Mór didn't want, to be revealed.

And yet somehow Marie Lynch had found them.

"Is that true?" Niall asked, subdued. "Is it money again?"

"I wanted to see my son," Marie said. "I wanted to see my grandson. Do you think I care you're not married? Do you think I care about all the things you said and did that night, in comparison to all the years that came before it? This isn't about money. Stop letting *her* tell you it's about the money."

Both Mór and Marie knew Niall well enough to see the turmoil in his expression. Love was one of this species' weapons. It had so many hooks: the knowledge it was conditional, the desire to believe it was real.

"I suppose you'll be wanting your plane ticket covered for a start," Mór said.

Marie just stared at her with glittering eyes.

"I can't believe we're doing this again," Niall said, which meant Marie would get her way.

If only she'd wanted oak leaves and acorns. In the end, Niall drove ten of his cattle halfway across the state to sell them at auction, tears in his eyes because he didn't want them eaten, and his fingers crossed because he hoped they would age and behave like normal cattle. Then he gave that money to his mother and drove her to the airport, and hoped that he'd never see her again, and knew deep down that he would.

The thing in the Forest whispered that it was a shame, it was a shame.

The stark fields looked robbed.

Paradise, paradise, why would they ever leave?

14

Farooq-Lane had been very excited to get her first job. Not her job at Alpine Financial, her adult job, but the gig she scored in high school. While her peers were getting jobs stuffing burritos and selling cute tops, Farooq-Lane got hired as a temporary assistant for an area accounting firm. They hadn't meant to hire a high schooler, but she looked so poised at her interview they'd thought her age was a typo.

She'd flourished at the firm. The tasks were repetitive, clinical, unforgiving, time-sensitive. In comparison, her parents' well-meaning rules now seemed changeable and short-sighted. Her brother Nathan's philosophical societal debates now felt like anarchy.

The firm was like a church for her. Things there were right and wrong, black and white.

Three weeks after starting, Farooq-Lane discovered during her filing that the senior accountant had defrauded the firm of fifty-thousand dollars. When she revealed this during the next morning's situation update, the firm had loudly fired the senior accountant on the spot.

They'd fired Farooq-Lane quietly a few days after.

It hadn't made her lose her taste for justice. It just taught her that some people mouthed the rules, but didn't really believe in them.

Like the Moderators.

In the days after discovering them sleeping in a storage facility, Farooq-Lane had thrown herself into finding out everything she could about them. She'd started with the records the DEA had on all of them, including herself, and moved outward from there, researching them with the same diligence she'd used to research the Zeds. She wanted to know if the Moderators had anything in common with each other.

If they were dreams, she wanted to know if they'd all been dreamt by the same person.

But as far as she could see, they had come from all walks of life. They all seemed to have long histories of existing in society for decades, with phone bills and school records and military enrollments to prove their existence. It didn't seem as if they, at least, had been *created* by someone with a grand scheme.

"I'm being played," Farooq-Lane told Liliana. "I have to be getting played."

Liliana glanced up from the armchair in the corner of the living room. She was either making or soothing something fuzzy; she kept brushing the wad of pastel blue fur with two slicker brushes. "I don't think that is a certainty, surely."

"Yes," Farooq-Lane said, "it must be. I'm the straight man in the joke. Everyone else was recruited because they were useful to the project in some way, above and beyond having experience with a Zed in their life. Why was I there? I was a mascot."

"But you were very good at finding the Zeds."

"They couldn't know that, though. I was unproven. And— Does she *have* to play the music so loud?" Farooq-Lane pressed her fingers lightly over her ear holes, but she could still hear the music from the basement, some bitter young woman spitting about war as a turbulent beat raged beneath her voice.

"At least she's doing something."

"Besides drugs." Farooq-Lane opened the spreadsheet she'd made with all the Moderators' victims, as far as she knew. She had included all the Zeds she had helped them track, as well as the few that the first Visionary she'd worked with had mentioned. It was a longer list than she'd thought, and she didn't like looking at it, but she didn't shy back. She'd been part of this.

"She asked me how old I was the other day," Liliana said. "And if I thought you were looking for a 'hot young sidepiece.'"

Farooq-Lane was trying to find out when the Moderators had decided to kill their first Zed. The federal contacts had been less useful than she'd expected; apparently the Moderators had been handed off to the Drug Enforcement Administration by way of Homeland Security, by way of the CIA. No one wanted to claim them officially, but no one wanted to disband them, either.

Farooq-Lane blinked up from the screen. "Was she referring to herself?"

Liliana gave her an amused smile.

"I should wake them up," Farooq-Lane said suddenly. "With a, what do you call it. Sweetmetal."

This made Liliana pause in her fur-brushing. She looked a little worried. "I think I prefer life without them, don't you?"

"I can't just ignore this. People *died* because of them. I helped them find victims. I have to know what they were doing." Farooq-Lane paused. It was unlike Liliana to throw on the brakes like this. "Right? Am I missing something?"

Liliana looked a little sad. "No, you're right. I think I have just grown used to choosing the option that keeps me alive. You choose the option you think is morally right. I would rather we try to live like you."

Putting her computer down, Farooq-Lane went to Liliana and kissed her temple. "I'm committed to choices that keep you alive, too, don't worry. If we—*that music*."

As Farooq-Lane marched across the room and down the basement stairs, she invoked the image she always used to keep herself calm. A feather floating on the surface of a perfectly still lake. *I am that feather. I am that feather.*

At the bottom of the basement stairs, she was greeted by the sight of Hennessy crouching on top of a stool like a gargoyle, dabbing paint on a canvas, surrounded by an attentive audience of crushed soda and beer cans. She was smoking. There was a dead mouse laid out so perfectly in the center of the worktable that it must have been put there intentionally.

And of course music blared from an old radio.

Farooq-Lane tugged out the cord for the radio. "I'm trying to work."

"Can I have my sword?" Hennessy asked, not looking up from the canvas.

"Conditions were supposed to be met. And you don't look sober."

Hennessy continued scrubbing paint onto the canvas. "Conditions were met, mon amie!"

"So I can see that portrait?"

With an enormous grin, Hennessy scooted her chair back to allow Farooq-Lane access. She was so pleased about this development that Farooq-Lane was certain there was something unpleasant waiting for her. Was she really going to give a deadly weapon to someone as unhinged as Hennessy just because she'd painted a portrait? She had said that she would. So she had to at least look now.

The painting was awful.

The painting was also awesome.

It was not done. Some parts were worked nearly to completion and some were still just barely scrubbed in shapes. There were preliminary sketches lying on every horizontal surface around. The woman on the canvas was unsmiling. She stood with one foot propped up on the rung of a chair, her elbow leaning on the back of the chair. She wore a business suit; the jacket had fallen open enough to reveal a somehow suggestive flutter of blouse, no skin showing, just that silk, but still too much.

It was not a portrait of Liliana. It was a portrait of Farooq-Lane. It seemed absolutely impossible that Hennessy had so thoroughly managed to capture a pose Farooq-Lane had unconsciously adopted many times over. The suit was not one she owned, but it was one she might have owned. The hands were hers, the throat was hers, the straight line of the full mouth was hers.

The portrait was intolerable.

Not because it was bad, and not because it was her instead of Liliana, and not because of the energy of that touchable silk over her breastbone.

It was intolerable because Hennessy had painted the bright reflection of fire in her eyes.

The unmistakable glow of things alight glimmered in Portrait Farooq-Lane's pupils as she looked on, unsmiling. Did this woman not care the world was burning? Or had she been the one to set it alight?

"You're——" Farooq-Lane started. But she didn't know how to finish the sentence in a way that wouldn't give Hennessy exactly what she wanted. Because the young woman was still sitting there, keeled back on her chair in a very typical Hennessy pose, looking as happy as she ever did with her situation, lapping up Farooq-Lane's reaction.

"I don't understand why you're this way," Farooq-Lane said finally. "I don't know what you want from me." She felt her cheeks get hot when she said that. "All you had to do was paint Liliana. Instead you painted that, like . . ."

"You're a very promising young woman," Hennessy told her, making her vowels round and American to sound like Farooq-Lane. "I don't understand why you throw it away like this."

"You're——" Farooq-Lane started. She finished, "the worst."

"I wondered how long guilt was good for."

Immediately, Farooq-Lane regretted giving her this much, giving her feelings this much. She said, "I misspoke."

"Oh, no, you didn't, and I enjoyed every second of that searing honesty. What'd you want, by the way? Why'd you come down to my lair?"

Farooq-Lane struggled to remember. The radio. The spreadsheet. "I was coming down for my laundry."

"I don't like it when you call me your laundry," Hennessy replied. "I'll make you a deal, by the way. I'll get you something to wake up the Moderators, if you let me shoot every single one of them in the face after you're done with them."

"What am I even supposed to reply to that?"

Hennessy shrugged.

"What do you actually want? Money? Oh—now that you've earned the sword, do you want the orb back, is this what that is aiming at?"

"The orb! You said it, not me. You're so crass," Hennessy said. She was still wearing all those teeth. Enjoying herself hugely, for the first time. "All you had to do was ask."

15

Ronan visited Jordan.

He was lonely.

He wanted to be with people he knew, but the people he knew didn't have sweetmetals. The company of strangers was barely better than the dark sea; the only advantage to that was that he worried less about forgetting himself again when he was inhabiting even a random sweetmetal.

But Jordan was not a stranger. There was a comfort to seeing her, even though he didn't know her like he knew Hennessy. Watching her paint reminded him of just how *good* Hennessy had been. She'd amazed him so often with her casual art. Anything could be a medium to Hennessy. A discarded pen, dust gathered on a dashboard, convenience store makeup, melted candy, leftover ketchup. Hennessy could be so mean and clever when she spoke; with her art, she was just clever.

Ronan hovered in the studio, just barely held by the charge in the air. He could tell the slightest disturbance would whisk him out to the dark sea. It took quite a bit of focus on his part to stay, but stay he did. He stayed even when the sun came up, and Jordan stopped working and went to sleep. He stayed even when the afternoon wore on, and she woke back up to go to work.

Jordan's art-making was less hectic and more studied than Hennessy's. Her job was keeping herself awake, and she worked hard at it. None of the portraits around her were sweetmetals, but it didn't seem to matter. The process of trying for sweet-metals was what kept her awake. Ronan was fascinated by this private skill. It reminded him a little of what Adam used to do with the ley lines back when they were in Henrietta. Adam had worked hard to learn how to focus the invisible ley energy, but it was more than that; he had a knack. Jordan was a hard worker, but she, too, had a knack.

Did Hennessy have the knack as well?

Just after Jordan's worknight began, Declan came over. He was in a suit. Not his old gray suit that he used to wear all the time, but a sharp dark one with a modern cut. He strode across the studio to stand next to Jordan's computer, which was put-tering and grooving its way through her music collection as she worked.

"I don't want you to work tonight," he said. "I want you to make yourself look nice and be ready to go in forty minutes. No, thirty-five."

Jordan, at the easel, moved one eyebrow and nothing else. "Do you now?"

"I want to be happy," Declan said, in a matter-of-fact tone. "I'm tired of feeling guilty. I want to take you to dinner, and then I want to go to Schnee's opening."

She made a face. "Schnee! What an asshole. I don't want to go to his opening. I'm not putting on fake eyelashes for that."

"And then," Declan continued, as if she had not interjected, "I want to make an enormous scene proposing very publicly to you at the afterparty, so it completely overshadows his opening."

Ronan was shocked enough to nearly hurtle back out into the black sea again. It was only by drawing close to the still-wet painting on the easel that he was able to stay. Declan! Getting engaged? He'd told Ronan when they were kids that he never wanted to get married, right before trying to knock Aurora's wedding ring into the sink drain. He'd been a joyless and relentless serial dater in high school and in DC, the invisible man with the invisible girlfriend. To marry someone, you had to be visible to at least one person, a choice Declan was unwilling to make.

Jordan's mouth quirked as she slid off the stool. To Ronan's surprise, she did not seem at all surprised, and it occurred to him they'd already talked about this future before.

"How about I just take you out of that suit now instead?"

They embraced, Jordan's fingers tightly entwined in Declan's hair, his fingers pressed tightly into her back. After a few seconds, they began to sway to the music. Then, spontaneously, they took a few proper dance steps together. Declan dipped her, and Jordan struck a pose.

Declan smiled, turning his face quickly away from her, hiding this from her, of all the things to hide. But Ronan could see his smile, and he could see it was one he'd never seen his brother wear before, not in all the years he'd known him. This smile wasn't *for* Jordan, it was *because* of Jordan.

Then, without any further discussion, Declan and Jordan broke apart. He removed his suit jacket, lay down on the orange couch, and took out his phone to answer emails, and she returned to her stool to resume painting, singing along with the track under her breath. They did not go out to dinner or to crash a gallery opening or even remove Declan's suit, but it didn't much matter.

Ronan knew his brother was happy.

Suddenly, he could see Declan's future in a way that he hadn't ever properly been able to see his own. Declan, ten years from now, twenty, in Boston, with Jordan, in his apartment, in her studio, then a row house, then a loft with white walls filled with the sharp, dark art that made Declan's eyes water to look at. Cocktail parties, gallery openings, transatlantic flights, auction houses, a curly-headed daughter, a phone full of contacts who knew Declan was the man for the job, a wife who looked better behind the wheel of their car than he did, an artist who made headlines and the suit who snipped them out for the box beneath the bed. It was not the life Declan had claimed to want all through his teen years, but that didn't really matter: Declan had been a liar back then.

Ronan lingered for a long time there, watching the boring but comforting scene of the two of them working into the night, until the sweetmetal was no longer strong enough to hold him there.

He thought of the life he had thought he wanted.

He wondered what he wanted now.

"One, two, three," Adam said. "Four, five, okay, six, seven . . ."

Ronan was back in his corridor, looking at his motionless body.

Adam had returned with his electric lantern. As Ronan drew closer, he saw that he was setting out odd objects on the dust in front of Ronan. Seven stones. A lump of bright copper. A twist of wire (a guitar string, possibly?). A dark blue soup bowl. Frowning, he bent over to use his middle and ring finger to draw patterns around them. Every so often, he paused and stared into space, thinking hard, and then added another line or dot to the pattern.

He filled the bowl to the brim with a bottle of water and then walked out of the light to place the bottle out of sight.

Returning, he sat in the middle of the pattern, careful not to disturb it.

Hovering his hands over the tops of the stones, he hesitated, and then moved them slightly.

Finally, he stretched over to place the bowl of water directly in front of him.

Ronan realized Adam was going to try to scry.

This was a terrible idea. Scrying was a risky business even when conditions were perfect. Adam had first begun doing it while he was in high school, throwing his mind out into the ether to get a better view of the world. Sometimes, all one needed to get a little perspective was to look at a situation from outside human space and time. He'd honed the skill further with his mentor, Persephone, a psychic who had eventually died scrying. Scrying was like dreaming, but while awake. The mind wandered away from the body during a dream, yes, but one could rely on the moment of waking to snatch it back. With scrying, there was no moment of waking. The scryer had banished the mind from the body while awake, and often it wouldn't return if it got too far away. The safest way to scry was with a spotter—someone to snap the scryer out of the trance before it got too deep. Before the body died.

But there was no one watching out for Adam in the corridor.

"It's too bad Chainsaw can't be trained to bite me on command," Adam said into the quiet, obviously thinking the same thing as Ronan. "Maybe she could, with enough time. Next project, I guess."

His eyebrows drew together. "I don't even know if you can scry with just a sweetmetal's energy. I did what I could to make it better." He fidgeted his hands over the stones again. "I've got to see if I can . . ."

Adam, don't.

Adam took a deep breath.

He leaned over the bowl of water, which looked black in the dim light. He swallowed.

Adam, don't.

Adam unfocused his eyes, looking both into the water and past it. Unhitching his mind from his body. His nostrils flared; his mouth worked. Ronan knew him well enough to know he was frustrated by the lack of energy.

But then he let out a long breath, moved the stones again, and tried once more.

Agitation rippled through Ronan. He didn't know where he should be. Here, waiting to see if Adam's expression went blank, signaling it had worked? Out in the sweetmetal sea, to see if Adam's plan worked, to make sure he didn't wander too far into the dark alone?

Back and forth Ronan dithered as the minutes went by and Adam patiently remained in place. Finally, entirely unsettled, Ronan threw himself out into the sweetmetal sea.

Most of him hoped Adam didn't make it out to him.

Some of him hoped that he did.

16

W e had a break-in a few days ago," Jo Fisher said. "We're moving things to a more secure location, but until then, we're shoring up our systems here."

It took Hennessy a minute to realize Jo Fisher was explaining why there were three cameras visibly watching her cross the threshold of the mansion. It didn't surprise Hennessy. It was that kind of mansion. Located in Chestnut Hill, a few miles outside Boston, the Boudicca-controlled property was an impressively constructed brick Tudor whose beautiful face was hidden away behind a gated iron mask.

"They didn't take anything, but they smashed up the foyer," Jo Fisher said. As before, she had a cell phone permanently fixed to her hand, and she addressed it more often than Hennessy. "So that's that. Cameras for everyone. Smile for them."

Hennessy did.

"All right, come inside, I just have to—" Jo Fisher hid the keypad from view as she let them into the house, never putting down her cell phone. Inside, the foyer was architecturally grand and furniturally empty. The paint between the exposed beams was spanking fresh. Some of the beams were new, too. Whatever smashing up had happened in here must have been significant.

Hennessy remarked, "I thought the sweetmetals were kept at the gallery."

"Everyone thinks that," Jo Fisher said in a pitying voice, as if she was sorry Hennessy was as stupid as everyone else. "It's part of the security."

"And yet here we are. Looking at the signs of a struggle."

"There's always going to be attempts," Jo Fisher said. She stamped the word *attempts* deeply into the sentence in a way that implied something terrible had happened to the *attempter*. "I'm going to cut you short before you do anything too embarrassing: You're Hennessy, right? Not Jordan. The one I talked to in the gallery. Don't bother lying, I have another appointment right after this one and do not have the time."

"I'm the most Hennessy possible," Hennessy said. "Absolut Hennessy."

"And where is Jordan?"

"Sandwiched right between Israel and Saudi Arabia, with Syria as a jaunty li'l hat."

Jo Fisher studied Hennessy, head cocked, and then said, "Oh, *I* get it. You're the asshole one. Right. Well, our offer *was* going to be a package deal. We assumed you were working together; the deal was for whatever the two of you do together."

"I am the whole package," Hennessy said. "Were you not listening? Absolut Hennessy. The deal for us should also be the deal for me."

"The deal for both of you," Jo Fisher said in a precise way, gesturing for Hennessy to follow her, "was for you to paint originals in public as a dazzling, promoted young voice, and, in private, forge occasional works for us, both for Boudicca's purposes and for clients we work with. Obviously, everyone you worked with through us would be aware you are a premier product, the best forger on the East Coast, the most promising new portraitist, etc."

"Do go on. No, I'm serious. Go on. Feel free to lay it on pretty thick."

Jo Fisher did not go on. She instead pointed to an unblinking man in a suit standing stiffly beside the elevator. "That man has a gun."

"Neat," said Hennessy.

Walking directly up to him, she put an arm around his neck and kissed him on the mouth.

A moment later she found herself on her back with the breath knocked out of her and Jo Fisher looking down at her with a cell phone in one hand and a Taser in the other. "Do I need to use this?"

"Depends on how stubborn satisfaction is for you," Hennessy gasped. Climbing to her feet, she limped after Jo Fisher into the elevator. "Just checking the threshold for humor."

"None," Jo Fisher said, pressing an elevator button.

Together they rode the elevator down a floor. The man with the gun rode down with them, too, frowning at Hennessy. It was the sort of frown that did not seem *for* her but rather *about* her. When the elevator door opened at their destination, Jo Fisher pointed to a spot on the floor just outside it and he went there and stood, like a trained dog.

"Stay," Hennessy told him. "Good boy. Who's a good boy?"

They were in what used to be a wine cellar. It still smelled like wine, but most of the space was occupied by easels and displays, all tastefully lit in shades of red and gold. Some contained jewelry, some clothing, some paintings, some pottery fragments, but many of the displays were empty.

Jo Fisher observed Hennessy taking it in. "So you really are the other one."

"Jordan saw this already?"

"Yeah. You two really are in splitsville, aren't you?"

"No one says *splitsville*, Jo Fisher," Hennessy murmured, stepping farther in.

But they were in splitsville. It was a strange feeling to imagine Jordan here without her, investigating these options for staying awake, weighing how much freedom she was willing to give up for a life without Hennessy. Hennessy found herself suddenly heated about it, actually. Jordan had been apoplectic when she found out Hennessy had pretended to be her, but who exactly did she think she'd been visiting these sweetmetals as? Hennessy had split her life right down the middle to make room for Jordan. If Jordan deserved to have her own life separate from Hennessy, then didn't that mean Hennessy deserved one separate from Jordan, too?

Hennessy had never thought of it this way before. She'd never wanted to.

"Everyone likes the sweetmetals." Jo Fisher handed her a tablet. She tapped the screen to bring it to life. "We are always bringing in new ones, but demand is higher than ever. We will travel with this collection to the Market in New York, too, of course, and you can expect that most of this will go then."

On the tablet, Hennessy swiped to the first listing, a photograph of *Self-Portrait* by Melissa C. Lang. It matched the first sweetmetal she could see in the exhibit, an antique mirror with half its frame ripped off in a troubled art student way. "And the deal was that if we worked for you, we got one of these babies?"

"Got the use of one of them," Jo Fisher corrected her. "Use of a sweetmetal with an equivalent value to the service you were providing. Obviously you would also be making a salary, bonuses, all of that. We don't provide an insurance plan at this point, but we can point you to agents who are familiar with our—"

"Got it," Hennessy said. She turned to face Jo Fisher directly. "Do *you* have the 'use' of one of these, or were you bought a different way?"

She liked how Jo Fisher didn't flinch back from this question, although her eyes glittered with irritation and surprise.

"Discretion," Jo Fisher said coolly, "is one of the traits that Boudicca appreciates, and it's impossible to imagine an associate without it."

"Something else, then. Something worse. Or something better. Interesting," said Hennessy. "And I'm not an associate yet, Jo Fisher. I hate to be discreet for free. Speaking of free, are you this evening, do you want to go someplace, do you want to do someone? I'm working the long game on someone, but it might be decades before it comes to fruition."

Jo Fisher exhaled slowly before ignoring Hennessy and gesturing to the exhibit. "You'll find the sweetmetals are in order of value. The ones closest to us are the most likely to be included in your deal. It would have to be a very unusual situation for us to include those beyond that, but not out of the realm of possibility. And the final two are not on the table."

Hennessy grinned at her. "I'll take a look-see."

As she walked slowly down the aisle, she thought about how Jordan would have probably been able to tell how strong these sweetmetals were as she walked past them, unlike Hennessy, who could just tell that all these art pieces were more appealing than they ought to be, based on merit alone. As Jo Fisher said—everyone liked the sweetmetals. She wondered how strong the sweetmetal would have to be to wake the Moderators, just for a little bit. She wondered how hard it would be to steal one. She wondered if the square on the wall upstairs used to hold a sweetmetal. She wondered if it had been successfully stolen that night of the break-in, or if it had been damaged or moved.

She wondered what it would be like to actually cut a deal with Boudicca.

If Hennessy gave herself over to a life of servitude in exchange for a sweetmetal for a good cause, would Jordan change her mind and forgive her? Maybe that was just how Jay would have thought when she was strategizing how to keep Bill Dower interested in her.

Hennessy stopped at the second-to-last sweetmetal, the first of the two that was too valuable to be considered for a deal. According to the digital tablet, it was a bottle of handmade ink. According to Hennessy's eyes, it was darkly pigmented fluid in a little glass bottle shaped like a woman. It was one of those art materials that was so gorgeous on its own that it would take a very gutsy artist to risk wasting it on something uglier than it was in its raw form.

Jo Fisher was right.

Hennessy liked it very much.

With great expectations, she turned to the most valuable sweetmetal Boudicca had in their collection.

For a very long time, Hennessy didn't move.

She couldn't really believe it.

She could *feel* the sweetmetal, of course, like the ink; she felt how she simply *liked* it. But that was so at odds with how she ought to feel about seeing it.

The silence stretched out.

It was awesome.

It was awful.

Finally, she began to laugh and laugh and laugh. She laughed until she was out of breath, and then she waited until she had it back and she laughed some more.

Boudicca's most valuable sweetmetal was a huge painting called *Jordan in White*, of an intense little dark-skinned girl posed in a white slip.

"What's so funny?" asked Jo Fisher.

"I don't need your deal," Hennessy said. "Because I painted that."

17

*C*reate your paintings for one specific person.

A fellow artist had given Jay that piece of advice while Hennessy was in earshot. At the time, Hennessy had thought it was garbage advice, because Jay already only ever did anything for Bill Dower. And then, after she began to make art herself, she still thought it was garbage advice, because why should an artist define themselves by other people's wants? Eventually, she'd realized it didn't mean either of those things—it was simply a call to specificity, to appeal strongly to the few instead of blandly to the many. And by then, Hennessy was decidedly a forger, not a true artist, so it didn't matter, anyway.

But after seeing Boudicca's collection of sweetmetals, she took it to heart. She created for one person.

Or rather, she created for one mouse.

She'd found the mouse in the corner of the basement. Its tail had caught her eye first, although she hadn't realized initially it was a tail. She'd just seen a glint out of the corner of her eye as she prepped the canvas Liliana had gotten her. When she slid off the stool to investigate, she'd found a dreamt mouse among the dust and spiderwebs. She knew it was a dream not only because it was sleeping, its furry little sides rising and falling, but also because its tail was plated with solid gold. *Vermin!* Hennessy had thought to herself, but she'd been somewhat charmed, even then. She wondered what kind of mind had dreamt a blingy mouse.

Taking it up by the gold tail, she'd laid it out on the worktable within view of her easel. A little mascot.

After her meeting with Jo Fisher, Hennessy was determined to wake it.

She wasn't sure what made *Jordan in White* a sweetmetal, but she had a few ideas. It was an original. It had been created under duress. It was a very accurate portrait. The portrait she'd begun of Farooq-Lane seemed like an excellent candidate to test these conditions again. It was also an original. It had also been started under duress. It was also a very accurate portrait. The delight Hennessy had derived from Farooq-Lane's reaction to it had been immense. That woman was always on fire, and always denying it.

Hennessy painted all night.

She painted to the point of exhaustion, and then past it, until she was wound bright and high.

Just like *Jordan in White*.

But as the hours passed and the portrait grew even more finished, there was still a difference between *Jordan in White* and *Farooq-Lane, Burning*—according to the mouse, only one of them was a sweetmetal. The mouse continued to lay motionless on the worktable beside Hennessy's sword, which Farooq-Lane had left there while Hennessy was meeting with Jo Fisher.

Hennessy took a different tack, returning to the preliminary sketches. It was easy to lose the life of a piece in the finished brushstrokes. Maybe she needed to return to the raw power of the early line work.

The mouse continued to sleep.

She'd painted *Jordan in White* in a frenzy, improving the accuracy of her mother's work; maybe she needed to improve the likeness of *Farooq-Lane, Burning*. She redid the face. She improved the texture of the blouse. She reworked the background.

The mouse continued to sleep.

Hennessy was amused, first, at how it escaped her.

Then she was puzzled by how she couldn't figure it out.

Then she was frustrated as she exhausted all her ideas.

And finally, she was just angry.

Why was this something she could do as a kid, when she had almost no skill, and not now, when she knew so much more? Did the art not have enough pain in it? Was it actually her mother's brushstrokes beneath Hennessy's work that had made *Jordan in White* a sweetmetal?

Hennessy began to throw things. First a tube of paint. Then a brush. Then her palette, then papers, then stools.

The tantrum didn't feel good exactly, but it felt not bad, so she kept at it, until she looked up and realized she was no longer alone in the basement.

Farooq-Lane stood, her arms crossed, managing to look somehow business-meeting-ready in her silk pajamas. Liliana looked disheveled and comforting with a blanket around her shoulders like a robe.

In a hollow voice, Farooq-Lane said, her voice froggy with sleep, "Hennessy, it's four thirty a.m."

Was that all? It was longer to dawn than Hennessy had imagined. She said, "Darkness is the time when the innovative work, while the wretched, mundane world is sleeping—"

Farooq-Lane flipped a hand at her to shut up. She stepped over the clutter to rescue a tube that was leaking a small worm of green paint onto the concrete floor. "No. No, you're not doing a monologue. Shut up."

In a sweet, sleepy voice, Liliana asked Hennessy, "What's wrong, dear?"

Farooq-Lane held her hand up again. "No. Do not answer her. Don't say anything. Do not do anything. Do not move."

She turned on her heel to climb back upstairs, leaving Liliana and Hennessy together. Liliana sank to the bottom stair, still wrapped in her blanket cape, waiting patiently until Farooq-Lane marched back downstairs with an unopened package of index cards in one hand and a permanent marker in the other. She took her time peeling the plastic off the cards and locating a trash can to throw it away in, an act of rebellion among the trashed basement. Finally, she slapped both cards and marker on the worktable next to Hennessy.

She said, "This is a process I used to do with some of my clients. You're not allowed to speak. I am going to ask a question and you're going to *write* or *draw* an answer to it on a card. You can think about the answer as long as you like, but you only have ten seconds to write it down."

Hennessy wasn't in the mood for a craft project. "Why shou—"

"No," Farooq-Lane said. "Don't say anything. Don't break the rules. This is unacceptable, and you know it. Sit down and shut up, or it's over, this whole experiment. I'll turn you in for industrial vandalism and you can deal with the real world's law. We are trying to establish whether or not *the entire world is going to end*, and I do not have the patience for any more of this."

Hennessy sat down. She shut up.

Righting a toppled, grimy lawn chair, Farooq-Lane leaned on the back of it. She would not have liked to hear it, but her pose was identical to her portrait. She asked, "First question: Who are you?"

Hennessy signed her name on a card and then displayed it like an infomercial. Big, goofy smile. Big, goofy body movements.

Liliana laughed gently, encouragingly.

Farooq-Lane did not. "Second question: What is it you're trying to accomplish down here?"

This puzzle was harder. The concept of painting a sweet-metal to wake up the Moderators in the storage facility was too long to write in ten seconds, so instead, she hastily drew two versions of the dreamt mouse, one asleep, one alert. She couldn't bear to not show off, so she hurriedly dabbed her finger in her wet paint palette and swiped a broad, thin swath of paint across the card for the mouse's body before hurriedly suggesting the finer details with the marker.

"Very pretty," Liliana murmured.

Farooq-Lane just frowned. "And why do you think you can manage that?"

Because she seemed to have managed it before, when she was a kid. Before she'd spent a decade learning how to paint like any old master in any museum, becoming the greatest forger on the East Coast. Because it felt like if she couldn't do it now, she truly had given *that* girl's promising adulthood to Jordan and kept only her shitty past for herself.

She wasn't going to tell Farooq-Lane that. She wrote: *I did it before.*

Farooq-Lane went on, relentlessly. "Do you care about this mouse? Is that why you threw all this stuff, because the mouse itself is important to you?"

Hennessy longed to deliver a flippant response to this, but she just glanced at the little mouse's sleeping body and shook her head.

"And do you actually care about waking up the Moderators?" Farooq-Lane asked. "Be genuine."

She was startled to realize she didn't care why they'd killed her girls. It wouldn't bring them back. And it wasn't like they could do anything else to her, trapped in a storage facility, sleeping. Grief extinguished any curiosity.

Hennessy shook her head.

"So why are you actually upset about this?"

Hennessy shook her head again.

"That wasn't a yes or no question," Farooq-Lane said. Her mouth was a sharp, unforgiving line.

Now Hennessy longed to bury her in a monologue. This was exactly a place words were called for. A treatise on binaries, perhaps, a prattling, unwinding lecture on the beauty of ambiguities. A drowning pool of meaningful words so tightly packed they became meaningless.

Because she could not deliver a monologue, she had to think about the answer.

Why had she trashed the basement? She had a beautiful painting of a beautiful woman on the easel, so it wasn't about the quality of her work. It wasn't about waking Jordan up, because Jordan seemed to have managed that all by herself. It wasn't about waking up the mouse, it wasn't about waking up the Moderators. It wasn't about a hypothetical end of the world.

Her world had already ended.

Jordan had left her. And Jordan had been right. She was like her mother. Just as Jay's actions were outsized cartoons to keep Bill Dower's attention, Hennessy had visited caper after caper on Jordan to try to make sure she never, ever left. When pain and anguish were lifted from Jordan's shoulders, she made a new life.

When pain and anguish were lifted from Hennessy's, there was nothing of her left. She was nothing but the shit other people stepped in.

Jordan was the real Jordan Hennessy.

Jordan was always trying to make herself better, and Hennessy was always trying to keep from being unhappy. Jordan was succeeding at her task and Hennessy was drowning. She'd lost her childhood ability to make art that kept people awake. She'd probably killed Ronan Lynch by shutting down the ley line.

Jordan had escaped her, and Hennessy was glad for her.

"Hennessy," prompted Farooq-Lane.

As her eyes burned, Hennessy swiped a thin, bleeding splash of red on one of the index cards, and then, with the marker, suggested the lines needed to show that it was an anatomical heart, bleeding paint. Beneath it, she just had time to jot angrily: OF FUCKING COURSE.

Her heart was broken, that was why she was really upset, her heart was broken, broken, broken because Hennessy wanted so badly to be as good at living as Jordan was and she never even got close. She flicked the index card across the table at Farooq-Lane.

The mouse woke up.

18

Matthew woke up.

He was mad.

He never dreamt, so the space between when he fell asleep in the tunnel and opened his eyes again was blank. Absolutely blank. Just a pause. Time, eaten. Maybe some people might have had a dream, a nice dream, that would have changed their mood. But Matthew just woke up in his bedroom with the still-fresh truth: Declan had stolen the sweetmetal right off his neck.

"Good morning," Declan said, already leaving the bedroom.

Like nothing had happened! Like it was an ordinary day! Like there was nothing to be ashamed of!

Matthew crashed out of bed to discover an even worse truth: He was still fully dressed. His teeth were furry with unbrushing. Declan had just hauled him up here like a sack of flour and thrown him in bed. Why had he even bothered with that? Matthew wouldn't know any different if his brother had just left him crumpled in the car. Instead, they were meant to play pretend that Matthew had somehow had a good night's sleep like a normal person. Ronan had always told Matthew that Declan was a liar, and Matthew had never really listened. What was a fib here and there?

But now he understood. Declan's lies were big, elaborate, three-dimensional stage plays, featuring Matthew debuting with a bit part.

Good morning! As a form of rebellion, Matthew didn't bother to change his clothes, only added a heavily patterned bomber jacket he knew Declan didn't like, and then thumped through Old Man Eyebrows (Matthew's name for the building) to the living room (Bashful Sloth)(he'd also named the rooms) to see how Ronan was doing, post-tunnel. The couch was empty. Matthew couldn't think of where else he might be—Old Man Eyebrows only had two bedrooms.

His heart squirreled faster with something that was either gladness (Ronan had woken up! Things would be okay!) or distress (Ronan had woken up and left during the night! Things would never be okay!). He poked his head into Doc Greed, the office, but there was no sign of him there, either.

In Happy Gluttony, he found Declan pouring himself coffee with one hand while rapidly scrolling through an email on his phone with the other. On his laptop, two separate windows displayed two separate inboxes.

"Where's Ronan?" Matthew asked.

"I took him to a place closer to what he needs," Declan replied, not looking up.

"What does that mean? Where? You could have brought me."

Already Matthew was preparing various volleys to whatever excuse Declan might give to this, but Declan wasn't even paying attention to the conversation. Instead, he had put down the coffee mug and swept up the phone to furiously tap away a response. Then he placed a call and put it to his ear.

"We talked about this," Matthew said. "You were going to treat me differently! Like—"

"Declan Lynch here. I wanted to follow up immediately on our email chain so we're on the same page about the priority of the situation. That container should not have my client's name anywhere on the paperwork. Everything that is associated with that container needs to go through C. Longwood Holdings. I'm sure you understand how you'd feel if your personal home address and children's names were printed on all of your manifests. It would be unsettling in the least to have perfect strangers know that you have a"—Declan glanced at his laptop where a chat window had popped up—"sister that you haven't claimed in an assistance center." He paused. Listened. "I'm glad we could resolve this misunderstanding so quickly. Can I have a tracking number with the new information sent to me so I can update the file? Thank you."

He hung up, sucked down some coffee, and immediately swiveled to the laptop, all in one smooth motion. He seemed to have completely forgotten Matthew's interjection. He said, "Get something to eat, get your laptop, and I'll show you what you're going to be doing for school."

Matthew didn't get breakfast or get his laptop. He squinted out the window, trying to discern what time it was. "Aren't we late?"

Declan mouthed some words to himself as he typed them into his laptop, and then he said, "I worked out a better solution. I managed to get you enrolled in an online school, which, I know what you're thinking, it's accredited, and I got the paperwork in to make sure you can get a diploma from the state."

This was not what Matthew had been thinking.

"I don't know why I didn't think of it before," Declan said, "but of course it's ideal. You can get the work done in convenient chunks, right here at the apartment, in far fewer hours a week than in-person school. Less drain on your sweetmetal, and you still graduate on time like you wanted."

Slowly, Matthew was working out what Declan meant. Being awake for just enough time to do the week's schoolwork, then sleeping through the rest of it.

Even more slowly, he was working out that this must have taken longer than a day to line up. He asked, "How . . . long has it been since I've been awake?"

He felt sick.

Declan's phone buzzed a text; he tapped a reply with thumb and forefinger.

"Declan," Matthew repeated. "How long has it been?"

Only then did his brother seem to hear something amiss in his tone, because he blinked up at him. "What? Don't look at me like that. It's not forever. I'm working my absolute hardest on negotiating another sweetmetal. Have you eaten anything? I need to get you up to speed on the school interface so we can maximize your time awake today."

That was when Matthew punched him.

It amazed him, the punch. Not the shape of the blow. Niall had taught all the boys to box when they were much younger, and although Matthew hadn't used this knowledge since then, it turned out his hands and arms and shoulders still remembered it in some deep, subconscious way.

No, what amazed Matthew about the punch was the fact that it appeared at all. The fact that his hand made a fist and the fist took a journey and the journey ended on Declan's face. The punch knocked Declan right off his stool and onto his back on the tile floor, fancy brogues pointing at the ceiling light. It knocked the breath right out of him (Matthew heard it) and it knocked the car keys right out of his pocket (Matthew saw it). A second later, his spilled coffee cup rolled off the counter and joined him on the floor with a clatter.

It amazed Matthew that his hand, right after punching Declan, snatched the car keys off the floor. It was like he was a whole different person. It was like he was Ronan.

"How do you like it?!" Matthew shouted daringly.

Sock feet sliding on the floor, he galloped to the door, stopping only long enough to shove his feet into the pair of rubber mud boots Declan kept there to protect his pant legs from dirtier jobs. He heard Declan say, "Matthew, I——"

And then Matthew was out in the biting cold of the morning.

The air was scraping his lungs. His heart was thumping so hard it hurt. He felt as if he were being chased by something far more fearsome than Declan.

What did he think he was going to do? Run away from home? The leash that tied him to Declan was only as long as his sweetmetal's strength. At the end of the day, Declan was right. Matthew couldn't do anything without——

Suddenly, Matthew knew where he was going.

With a last glance at the door to make sure Declan wasn't yet emerging, he got into the car, fumbled until he figured out how to start it (There was no keyhole! Oh, right, a button. That still wasn't working! Oh, right, foot on brake!). Then he lurched out of the parking lot and down the road.

His phone buzzed. At a stop sign, he risked a glance at it. There was a text from Declan: *Do not curb those wheels.*

Matthew didn't answer. Instead, he plugged an address into the map app on his phone and then tried to convince the directions to play over the car's speakers. He couldn't figure it out before the cars behind him started honking, so he just rested the phone in his lap and crept along, following its directions.

Another text from Declan: *I assume you're not going far since the car needs gas and you didn't take my wallet, too.*

Matthew didn't answer this one, either. He just kept winding through Boston traffic. It was easy to tell that the car was Declan's, because it was clearly still on his side. It kept trying to surprise Matthew so it could run back to its master. It lunged at green lights, hopped over curbs, shuddered to an uneasy, panting stop in difficult intersections. Matthew was quite certain it shifted round the gas and brake pedal at a few points. It certainly played hanky-panky with the gearshift, in his opinion, at one point coasting in neutral into the middle of an intersection and then screaming loudly at all the other vehicles that tried to approach it. It did not seem to like bicycles. It was always plunging at them with a barely heard growl, then rearing back when they gave it the finger.

Matthew was sweating a little.

All the honking was unpleasant, until Matthew realized that if he rolled his window down and smiled apologetically, the drivers would roll down their windows and smile back at him. The bicyclists even forgave him if he shouted, "I don't know what this car has against bicycles!" at them. As conflicted as Matthew felt about likability being dreamt into him, it came in handy.

Another text from Declan: *If you get pulled over without a license you'll never be able to get one.*

For the past several years, Matthew had always felt like the bridge between two buildings—one burning, one standing tall.

After their father had died (been murdered), Ronan had gone a little wild. Before, he used to get sad sometimes, but after Niall died, weirdly, that seemed to go away. Matthew never saw him sad anymore, only ferociously angry or ferociously smiling. Every word now sprang razors. Declan, who had previously seemed quiet, was now gratefully still, an unmoving body for Matthew to sob into, a calm voice to take calls from the school or funeral home or government. Matthew spent more and more time with Declan, especially after Ronan moved out of the Aglionby dorm and into his friend Gansey's warehouse. The whole time, Declan had quietly explained that Ronan wasn't a bad person, he was just messed up by Niall dying, so now he was doing his best to ruin his life and also theirs because he thought it would make him feel better. He told Matthew about how Niall had actually been the one to cause all this, with negligence, with lies, with careless behavior, with abandonment. Ronan, on the other hand, told Matthew how Declan was a huge liar and how wonderful Niall had been.

Now Matthew thought that maybe he'd mislabeled the brothers. Maybe it wasn't Ronan who'd been the burning building.

What else was Declan lying about? Wrong about?

Maybe everything.

Declan texted: *Find your own sweetmetal next time.*

Matthew caught sight of a donut shop and managed to yank the car's face in the direction of the drive-through. There was only a little scraping as he got it close enough to order some donuts, and then he used the cash Declan kept in the console for emergency tolls to pay for them.

He felt a little virtuous at managing it all, and felt even more virtuous a few minutes later when he actually managed to pull into the lot of the Medford Assistance Center. He curbed the wheels as he pulled into a spot right by the door, realized he was parked crooked, tried three times to fix it, and then finally pulled into a new spot, wedging the car on a partially melted slush pile.

Inside, the woman behind the glass at the reception signed him in and gave him one of her mints, and he gave her one of his donuts.

Then he walked back through the halls to Bryde's room. Victoriously, he punched the passcode in.

Matthew had woken up mad; Bryde woke up defeated. He just stared straight up at the ceiling, showing no curiosity as to who might have roused him this time.

"Hi, remember me?" Matthew replied. "Ronan's brother. Your brother, too, I guess, kind of. I didn't really think of it like that before now, but I guess we have the same hair, sort of. Yours is just a little mustier or something. Not in a bad way!"

Bryde looked pained. "What a strange world this is, that gods are being raised by children."

"Sure," Matthew agreed.

"Why are you here?"

Matthew touched the zipties holding Bryde's wrists to the bed, then squinted around the room for signs of scissors. "I want to talk about being a dream."

Bryde closed his eyes.

"And," Matthew said, "I brought you donuts."

19

Ronan was not alone.

The Lace was with him.

It moved slowly through the dark. Ronan was not sure at first how he had recognized it as the Lace, as it looked different now. Instead of checkered edges and jagged, split holes, it had become an entity more suited for moving around in the empty sea. Now its form was less like lace and more like lightning paused mid-flash, or like the splintering patterns in polished marble. It was the shape of energy. It was not, in fact, entirely unlike the sweetmetals, although they were bright veins in the empty sea, and the Lace was made of dark ones.

The Lace scissored slowly toward Ronan where he floated, and he could feel its curiosity, its suspicion, its judgment.

He sucked back, but it continued to spread toward him.

The Lace was communicating with him. Or rather, it was trying to. It was not using words. It was using some language suited to this sea, or perhaps some language suited to wherever it had just come from, because it seemed to Ronan that the Lace was a visitor to this sea just as he was. Whatever the language was, Ronan suspected that he might be able to speak it if he tried. He also suspected, however, that he would forget the *Ronan Lynch* of himself if he did. It was very difficult to hold both at once.

It felt like the Lace's language had no word for feelings.

And it felt like human language had no word for the Lace.

The dark, jagged veins of the entity created a thicket around Ronan as it tried to make itself understood. Ronan thought about how both Hennessy and Adam had seen the Lace before and been terrified, and he understood why. It was so vast, so strange, so inhuman.

Look, look at you. Was it worth it? Didn't we tell you?

With effort, Ronan made sense of the Lace's words. He asked, "Tell me what?"

The Lace did not fully understand. It twisted around him, trying to turn the words into its language.

Speak to us as you know how.

He didn't, though. He had suddenly caught a familiar scent. Or not a scent, exactly, but whatever the equivalent was here in the sweetmetal sea, a place without noses. It belonged to Adam Parrish. Ronan had no idea how long it had been since Adam had begun scrying back in the dark corridor.

Ronan said, "Get out of here. I'm waiting for someone."

So was the Lace. It seemed possible they were both waiting for the same person. He was struck then by the hideous idea of Adam appearing here now, with the Lace so present. He would be unprotected, nothing but his mind, no one to tear him back to awareness in the corridor.

It had taken everything Ronan had to pull his disparate memories back to himself when he first arrived in the sweetmetal sea, and he was a dreamer, more suited to this atmosphere than Adam, either through practice or through design. Adam, though—the Lace would pull out the things Adam liked about himself first, and then let everything he couldn't stand about himself dissolve him into screaming nothingness.

This was the plan, anyway. Ronan heard the Lace muttering

about it. How it hated Adam. Ronan could feel the hatred radiating, just as sure as he could sense that *scent* of Adam growing stronger.

"He's not for you," Ronan said.

The Lace replied, *He's not for you, either.*

Ronan ignored this. "Leave us alone."

This time, instead of shrinking back, he exploded. He hadn't known he could before then—there had been no reason to react to anything, not when it was just him and the sweetmetals. But now he saw energy crackle out from him, black lightning in the dark sea. The Lace retreated slightly, but Ronan didn't relent. Again he exploded, and again, and again, as that *scent* of Adam continued to grow.

He drove the Lace deep, deeper, deepest into the blackness.

"Stay away from him," he snarled, and then, because he was angry enough to risk trying the other language for it, he added, in the Lace's way of speaking: *Stay away from him!*

The Lace, as it retreated completely, was disbelieving. *He's not for you. None of it's for you, Greywaren.*

Then it was gone, just as Ronan realized Adam Parrish had arrived in the sweetmetal sea.

Introductory paragraph incorporating the thesis: After a challenging childhood marked by adversity, Adam Parrish has become a successful freshman at Harvard University. In the past, he had spent his time doubting himself, fearing he would become like his father, obsessing that others could see his trailer-park roots, and idealizing wealth, but now he has built a new future where no one has to know where he's come from. Before becoming a self-actualized young man at Harvard, Adam had been deeply fascinated by the concept of the ley lines and also supernaturally entangled with one of the uncanny forests located along one, but he has now focused on the real world, using only the ghost of magic to fleece other students with parlor trick tarot card readings. He hasn't felt like himself for months, but he is going to be just fine.

Followed by three paragraphs with information that supports the thesis. First: Adam understands that suffering is often transient, even when it feels permanent. This too shall pass, etc. Although college seems like a lifetime, it is only four years. Four years is only a lifetime if one is a guinea pig.

Second paragraph, building on the first point: Magic has not always been good for Adam. During high school, he frequently immersed himself in it as a form of avoidance. Deep down, he fears that he is prone to it as his father is prone to abuse, and that it will eventually make him unsuitable for society. By depriving himself of magic, he forces himself to become someone valuable to the unmagic world, i.e., the Crying Club.

Third paragraph, with the most persuasive point: Harvard is a place Ronan Lynch cannot be, because he cannot survive there, either physically or socially. Without such hard barriers, Adam will surely continue to return to Ronan Lynch again and again, and thus fall back in with bad habits. He will never achieve the life of financial security and recognition he planned.

Thesis restated, bringing together all the information to prove it: Although life is unbearable now, and Adam Parrish seems to have lost everything important to him in the present by pursuing the things important to him in the past, he will be fine.

Concluding paragraph describing what the reader just learned and why it is important for them to have learned it: He will be fine. He will be fine. He will be fine. He will be fine.

"Parrish," said Ronan.

Adam seemed very small in the darkness. Ronan had not understood the scale of the brilliant sweetmetals before now; Adam was a speck beside them. An odd speck, shaped unlike everything else here, clearly out of his world. He was a creature of round, intense feelings, a finite creature, a fragmenting creature. Without a body to contain them, his thoughts were drifting out in a million different directions. It was not hard to understand his alarmed expression.

Ronan hurried over, guiding some of these fragments back toward the center. It was not taking long for Adam to lose himself here; or perhaps Ronan didn't have a good sense how time worked for Adam.

"Parrish," he said again. "Adam."

The sound of his name made Adam's appearance resolve. The collection of thoughts now saw themselves again as the skinny young man they inhabited back in Massachusetts. He was no longer a fragile cloud of ideas, but rather a human floating in space. He was Adam Parrish.

Electric joy surged through Ronan, overpowering the worry.

Adam had come for him. All this way. He had not given up. He had risked everything.

Slowly, though, he was retreating from Ronan, not quite looking at him. His chin was ducked, eyes averted, as he drifted farther into the dark. For some reason, he was trying to inobtrusively sneak away. As uncounted time passed, however, he began to fragment again, his thoughts separating from the shape of Adam Parrish again.

"No!" Ronan snapped, circling round quickly to keep Adam's thoughts from spreading thin again. He pushed them together. "You idiot. Stay close!"

"Are you trying to help me?" Adam asked politely. He was looking everywhere but at Ronan.

"I'm trying to keep you from dying!"

"I appreciate that, but I think I'd better go," Adam said, trying to once again slip away, and all at once, Ronan realized what was happening and began to laugh.

"Don't you know who I am?"

Because of course Ronan realized now that he didn't look like that body down in the corridor, like the body named Ronan Lynch. He still looked like whatever form it was that could swim through this sea to the sweetmetals. Adam had seemed like a speck to him; he must seem enormous to Adam. Just as Adam was a disassembled collection of bright, human thoughts before he was intentionally gathered into a human form, Ronan was just some essential form of himself in this strange other place.

"Are you . . ." Adam hesitated and then said, very softly, ". . . the Lace?"

Ronan had not expected this answer.

Energy exploded from him, conveying his bewilderment and hurt.

Adam flinched.

He was afraid. He was afraid of Ronan. Calming himself, Ronan tried to see what Adam was seeing. He stretched, twisted, perceived.

Dark shapes stretched out from him. Like tree branches of liquid ink, they forked and split until they were nothing. They looked nothing like the drifting orbs of Adam's consciousness. When he moved quickly to once again gather Adam's drifting thoughts close, Ronan realized Adam was right: He *was* shaped like the entity he'd just driven away.

He did not understand.

"Ronan?" Adam said suddenly. "Are you Ronan?"

Relieved, Ronan replied, "Yes."

"Can you be smaller? Or tell me where to look? You're everywhere." But Adam began to laugh, a big, disbelieving laugh ragged with his newly extinguished fear, turning to look all around himself.

With some effort, Ronan twisted and compacted the branches of his form as small as he could. He was rewarded by Adam looking directly at him.

"Don't fuck off too far, though, because I'm not holding you together right now," Ronan said. "Is this better?"

"I can't believe it," Adam replied. "You look like—"

"I know, the Lace," Ronan said crossly.

"No, I was just, you were just— You *sound* like a jackass. But you *look* like energy. It's breaking my brain. Is it . . . is it really you?" His expression darkened. "Or is it just showing me what I want . . ."

Ronan could not blame Adam for his distrust. Only a little while before, Adam had shown up at the Barns to surprise Ronan for his birthday, and the first thing Ronan had wondered was: *Is it really Adam?* The difference was that, on that day, Adam could tell Ronan all the steps that had brought him to that point to convince him, and Ronan couldn't. He still didn't exactly understand how he had gotten here or why he was trapped outside his ever-sleeping body.

"Don't ask me to convince you," Ronan said. "If I were the Lace, I'd try to mindfuck you by telling you what I thought you wanted to hear. Use your own shit. Whatever you use when you scry other times. You've done this before without dying. Intuition. That's the word. Use your intuition. What do you feel?"

Ronan recognized Bryde's words coming out of his mouth, but before he had time to process how he felt about that, he realized that the bright orbs of Adam's memories and thoughts had already begun to dazzle out across the dark sea again.

Shit! Ronan dove, unfolding, unfurling, racing out to arc around Adam. He gathered them close and remained encircled around them, like a spiky fence, until Adam seemed to be more like himself. Then he retreated; he didn't want to see Adam afraid of him again.

"Wait," said Adam. He held out an arm. "Don't. Let me——"

He stretched his hand out, palm up. He swam slowly toward Ronan. He was obviously still intimidated, but he let himself drift close enough to drag fingers through the nearest darting strands of energy that made up Ronan's form here. His face held the same concentration as when he had placed the stones for scrying.

The effect of Adam's consciousness touching Ronan's. A startlingly clear memory jolted through Ronan, as fresh as the moment he'd lived it. It was the day Ronan had first come to Harvard to surprise Adam, back when he still thought he was moving to Cambridge. He'd been so full of anticipation for how the reveal would go and then, in the end, they'd walked right past each other on the sidewalk. They hadn't recognized each other.

At the time, Ronan had thought it was because Adam looked so different after his time away. He was dressed differently. He held himself differently. He'd even lost his accent. And he'd assumed it had felt the same to Adam; Ronan had gotten older, lonelier, sharper.

But now they were in this strange sea, and neither of them looked anything like the Adam Parrish and Ronan Lynch the other had known. Adam was a collection of thoughts barely masquerading as human form. Ronan Lynch was raw dark energy, alien and enormous.

And yet when Adam's consciousness touched his, Ronan *recognized* him. It was Adam's footstep on the stairs. His surprised whoop as he catapulted into the pond they'd dug. The irritation in his voice;

the impatience in his kiss; his ruthless, dry sense of humor; his brittle pride; his ferocious loyalty. It was all caught up in this essential form that had nothing to do with how his physical body looked.

The difference between this reunion and the one at Harvard was that there in Cambridge they had been false. They'd both been wearing masks upon masks, hiding the truth of themselves from everyone, including themselves. Here, there was no way to hide. They were only their thoughts. Only the truth.

Ronan. Ronan, it is you. *I did it. I found you. With just a sweetmetal. I found you.*

Ronan didn't know if Adam had thought it or said it, but it didn't matter. The joy was unmistakable.

Tamquam, said Ronan, and Adam said, *Alter idem.*

Cicero had written the phrase about Atticus, his dearest friend. *Qui est tamquam alter idem. Like a second self.*

Ronan and Adam could not hug, because they had no real arms, but it didn't matter. Their energy darted and mingled and circled, the brilliant bright of the sweetmetals and the absolute dark of the Lace. They didn't speak, but they didn't have to. Audible words were redundant when their thoughts were tangled together as one. Without any of the clumsiness of language, they shared their euphoria and their lurking fears. They rehashed what they had done to each other and apologized. They showed everything they had done and that had been done to them in the time since they'd last seen each other—the good and the bad, the horrid and the wonderful. Everything had felt so murky for so long, but when they were like this, all that was left was clarity. Again and again they spiraled around and through one another, not Ronan-and-Adam but rather one entity that held both of them. They were happy and sad, angry and forgiven, they were wanted, they were wanted, they were wanted.

20

All blades begin as raw metal.. Sharp blades and dull blades both start the same.. Before each blade is honed and put together it is impossible to tell which will cut and which will waste space.. Each must be tested.. Any blade can cut butter.. Some blades can cut wood.. Still fewer blades can cut another blade.. There is nothing to be gained by looking at the scissors in the drawer.. If you want to know their strength, you must use them..

—NATHAN FAROOQ-LANE,
The Open Edge of the Blade, page 10

21

Dawn had not even broken by the time Farooq-Lane and Hennessy headed to the Atlantic storage facility, the index card with the bleeding heart resting on the dash of the car; they'd gone as soon as they could, unsure how long Hennessy's new accidental sweetmetal would last. Liliana had reluctantly stayed behind. She said she was worried spending too much time in the presence of Hennessy's new sweetmetal might trigger a vision. Although Farooq-Lane felt they could use a hint of the future, she agreed that it wasn't worth risking draining the sweetmetal before they could wake the Moderators.

Peabody was dead quiet as they drove through it. The few cars they did pass on the streets seemed muted, as if it were too early for even the sound of commuters to be awake. The entire predawn had the charge of adventure, of fear, of anticipation, a holdover less from Farooq-Lane's days of hunting Zeds and more from her days of early-morning school field trips.

Hennessy was allowed to talk again after the exercise with the index cards, but she hadn't said a word. Being around her when she wasn't prattling was different. Her monologues, Farooq-Lane realized, weren't that different from Liliana's visions. Those were a wall of deadly sound, too, disguising what was really going on. The real Hennessy was hidden deep beneath that explosion.

How wild, Farooq-Lane thought suddenly, as opera began to spontaneously sing in a low voice from the car's radio, that she had spent all this time hunting the Zeds, and now she sat next to one of the most powerful of them on the way to see her sleeping bosses.

She glanced at Hennessy in the passenger seat, expecting to find her looking out the window, still disconsolate, but instead she found Hennessy was staring at the side of her head.

"What?" Farooq-Lane asked.

"Why didn't you shoot me in the face?" Hennessy asked. "At Rhiannon Martin's. When they shot *her* in the face. Why'd you go all hero on me?"

It was hard for Farooq-Lane to drag up the memory of that day. Not because it was painful, but because it was absent. A lot of her time with the Moderators was this way: checkered with gaps. All the violent bits had become one long death scene beginning and ending with Parsifal Bauer, the young Visionary who had always listened to the opera he was named after. Even though she'd spent months with the Moderators, mostly she remembered his body twisting into a deformed horror as he tried to control his vision long enough to connect Farooq-Lane to someone who woud be important to her in the future.

Liliana. He'd meant Liliana. That was where the vision had taken her.

"I didn't shoot people in the face," Farooq-Lane said. "That wasn't my job."

"Noble."

"I never said it was noble."

"Did you or didn't you think I was a threat to the world?"

Farooq-Lane put on her signal light silently and then took her time checking for traffic before turning down the next dim blue road.

"Should I get your index cards for you?" Hennessy asked.

Farooq-Lane struggled for an answer to the question. "You were very powerful."

Hennessy laughed hysterically, performatively, pounding the door.

"You can mock all you like, but I saved your life with a sword that can cut through nearly anything," Farooq-Lane said. "That you *dreamt*. That's power."

"So again: Why didn't you shoot me in the face, if you believed we were going to end the world?" Hennessy shot back.

"I think you should just be grateful I didn't. And speaking of shooting people in the face, I saw you put the sword in the trunk. Leave it. You are not chopping off any Moderator heads."

This turn of the conversation meant they were both pissy when Farooq-Lane parked the car outside the facility. Silently they made their way to the unit, and silently Hennessy stood with the single index card in her hand as Farooq-Lane punched in the code.

It was less shocking this time for Farooq-Lane to see the Moderators, because she knew to expect them. But it was still intensely off-putting to find them in exactly the same place as they had been before, waiting patiently for the door to open. They really were dreams.

She felt sort of sick to her stomach.

Hennessy took one-two-three strides forward to lay the index card inside the unit, and then just as quickly retreated. Her eyes were full of a terrible fury. There was a chaotic potential to the way her fingers were claws by her sides.

These people had killed everyone Hennessy had cared about but one.

Farooq-Lane was glad she had told her to leave the sword in the car. She didn't think she would have been able to stop

Hennessy from killing the Moderators. She wasn't sure she would have tried.

She didn't want to find out.

A scraping sound made Farooq-Lane startle.

Lock had woken.

His hand fumbled out from his prone body. The fingers walked and felt across the concrete floor until they found the index card.

He pressed it against his chest.

He did not open his eyes.

He did not sit.

But he was awake. The energy of the index card was sufficient for that.

"Carmen," he said in his deep voice, and she jerked. "Is that you? I can smell your perfume."

"You're a dream. After all this, you're a dream," she said accusingly. She tried to pull herself together. She didn't have time to be emotional over this. The sweetmetal was only strong enough to barely wake Lock. "Are all the Moderators? Everyone but me?"

"That's right," Lock said.

"You hypocrites!"

"Don't be hysterical, Carmen. It would be hypocritical to kill Zeds if we were *Zeds*. Since we're dreams, it's not hypocritical—it's complicated." The drowsy way he spoke was unsettling. His eyes were still closed, nothing moving except for the fingers gently touching the index card on his chest, as if looking for comfort. "Where am I? What happened?"

For once it was Lock who was in the dark. "I would rather ask the questions right now. How were you awake before?"

"I had a few sweetmetals. Bryde lifted one off me during one of their raids, but the others should still be working . . ."

Maybe in a world with a ley line, they would still be working. But without that underlying energy, the others must have drained very quickly. She asked, "Did the same dreamer dream all of you?"

"Oh, no," Lock said. "We're all orphans, like you. Your birth parents are dead; our dreamers are dead. Some of us haven't seen our dreamers for hundreds of years. Nikolenko has been bumming sweetmetals for nearly a thousand. We're related only by a common purpose. The ground is cold. Am I outside? Has it been long? Sometimes it is very long. Some of us are older than you might think, if you count the years we had to sleep."

Nearly a thousand years.

Magic kept finding a way to tug the rug from beneath her.

"Why kill Zeds if one made you?"

"You sound emotional, Carmen."

"You sound sleepy," Farooq-Lane said, and her voice was so cold when she said it that she thought of Hennessy's portrait and the fire in that woman's eyes.

He laughed drowsily. "Fair enough. Is this a deal that we're making now? Is that why you're tempting me? This is negotiation?"

"No," Hennessy broke in. Her voice was slightly raised so she could be heard from where she stood in the hall. She took one step forward, just so she could continue to be heard. Farooq-Lane had the sense that she was doing her absolute best to hold herself back, a restraint she wouldn't have imagined Hennessy had. "It's torture."

"Who is that now?"

Hennessy didn't answer the question. She continued, "You and the others are lying in the dark in a storage unit. No one but us knows where you are. Time's passing without you. There is no ley line anymore, so there's nowhere you could go to be awake without really fucking good sweetmetals. This is your life now. Or rather, your death."

"I never thought you were cruel, Carmen." Lock appealed to Farooq-Lane, as if she had spoken instead. "Surely you can see now why we would do it because of how easily you have imprisoned us. We have no power. There is not enough to go around. Zeds are always dreaming and dying, and when they die, what becomes of their dreams, of us? We are left to fight for the scraps of energy to stay awake without them. Overpopulation is a problem. Too many . . ." Lock's voice was getting slower; he was fighting sleep hard, but failing. "Too many wasteful Zeds. Too many hungry dreams. It is not . . . the dreams' fault. Dreams didn't ask to . . . they never asked . . . they had no power over coming into the world. The problem is with the Zeds, who will not stop. Cull them and there is more energy for all of us already here. Spay/neuter program, really."

Hennessy made a guttural sound.

Farooq-Lane had held a gun for these people. She'd followed them all over the world. Parsifal Bauer died for their genocide. Helplessly, she remembered him begging her to spare one of the Zeds. They'd both known this wasn't right. Why had they both gone along with it, then? "And the apocalypse—was that a lie?"

"Oh, we couldn't fake . . . the visions. There *is* a Zed who is going to . . . who will . . . there will be . . . fire," Lock said. Every pause was getting longer. "It was a good excuse. A righteous excuse. Look, we knew . . . we knew it was thin justification. We let ourselves believe him because we wanted to."

"Him?" echoed Farooq-Lane. She had been waiting for this with dread, she realized. She both wanted and did not want the answer. "If the Moderators weren't the originators of this plan, who was? Say his name."

Please say Bryde.

She knew he would not.

"A Zed," Lock said. "*Now* you can say hypocrite . . . we took orders from a Zed. A Zed with a plan. You . . . of all people . . . should know how appealing it is . . . for someone else to have a plan."

Hennessy snarled, "Whose plan? Don't be fucking coy."

Lock was quiet for a long time, before starting awake, fingers jerking around the index card. "You know . . . exactly who."

She wanted to say Bryde. She wanted to say Ronan Lynch.

But she knew neither of those were the real answer. She had known the real answer for a long time, if she was being honest. Or at least she'd been afraid it was the real answer for a long time. You can't be afraid of a thing you don't believe in at least a little bit.

Her voice sounded thin to her; it was getting all lost in her closing-up throat. "He's dead. I saw you shoot him."

"A copy. He knew it . . . was easier to . . . be hidden if . . . he was . . . dead . . . he . . ."

Nathan. Nathan. Nathan.

Her ears were throbbing with her own heartbeat.

"He's a *serial killer*," Farooq-Lane said finally. "That's not a person whose plan you follow!"

"There are no perfect heroes," Lock said, sounding very, very awake.

But when he closed his eyes this time, they stayed closed.

He was asleep again and the index card had become just an index card once more, stripped of whatever energy had originally made it more than that.

You of all people should know how appealing it is for someone else to have a plan.

The worst part of all of this was that Farooq-Lane knew Nathan was right. She was no better than the Moderators. She'd believed in their plan because she wanted someone else to have the answers, even though deep in her heart, she'd always known it wasn't right.

"What does that mean?" Hennessy asked.

Farooq-Lane said, "This is my brother's apocalypse."

Two minutes later, the first bomb went off.

22

It was an unusual bomb.

Nestled deep inside the building it had been hidden in, the weapon let out twenty-three ticks before exploding.

The explosion was not the unusual part.

The shock waves careened through the building, incinerating ceilings, floors, stairwells, and walls, leveling everything all the way out to, and including, the sign out front, which read: MEDFORD ASSISTANCE CENTER.

Physical damage stopped there, but the bomb wasn't done.

After the initial shock wave leveled the building and startled most of the Boston area, an additional wave continued to roll out from the site. This one was invisible and farther reaching. It touched every person for miles.

If they were awake, they began to have a vision.

If they were asleep, they began to dream.

They all saw the same things.

First, they saw the Medford Assistance Center explode. They saw it from the point of view of the bomb. They watched it unpeel the building and all the unclaimed dreams and night staff inside it.

Then the destructive scene melted away into the glow of a different afternoon. They were looking at an interstate packed slaughterhouse-full with cars. Everything shimmered with exhaust and smoke. Everyone who shared this scene moved along the shoulder, trying not to make eye contact with the people in the vehicles. They were fleeing the city that used to be at the end of the interstate.

It was on fire.

Everything that was not the interstate was on fire. A city, on fire. The world, on fire.

It would never go out, the fire whispered. It would eat everything.

Devour, devour

Everyone who experienced the vision had the crawling sensation of premonition. This did not feel like a nightmare. This felt like a promise.

And then, just like that, the bomb released them.

Those who were awake shook their heads, dazed.

Those who were asleep and could wake shot up, shivering with adrenaline.

Those who were asleep and couldn't wake fell back into darkness.

No one knew yet who had planted the bomb. But there was one person, at least, who knew who had *made* the bomb:

Carmen Farooq-Lane would recognize her brother Nathan's handiwork anywhere.

Slumped against a wall in a pitch-black corridor, Ronan Lynch didn't wake, but a single, ordinary tear ran down his unmoving cheek.

It had begun.

23

The Barns was enough, for a while.

Niall and Mór had plenty to keep them occupied. There was the dreaming, of course. They dreamt for the fun of it, to see what they could do, but they also dreamt things to sell to keep sending money back home. They didn't want a reappearance of Marie, after all.

They had settled into the kind of dreamers they were going to be. Niall dreamt more often but also more uselessly. He dreamt telephones that wouldn't stop ringing and watches with the same number printed twelve times around the face. He dreamt living dreams sometimes, which Mór never did. These sometimes looked like cows, but they sometimes looked like stuff one wouldn't imagine as alive, too, like small engines that needed to be petted and loved in order to run. These dreams seemed to cost more dream energy, though, and after he dreamt something that seemed alive, they often had to wait days or weeks before they could dream productively again.

Mór was a more precise dreamer, but also a slower one. She thought of the object she would like and then dreamt of it many, many times to try to hold all the possible facets of it in her thoughts in order to bring it into the waking world exactly as she meant. Every ridge on every bottle top would have been thoroughly imagined before she attempted to bring it back. Unlike Niall, who dashed out mistakes left and right, Mór's dreams usually appeared just as she intended them, because she took so long conceptualizing them. There was only one part of her dreams that she never intended that nonetheless always appeared: They always had pain in them. She would manifest a perfume bottle, a box of delicately patterned stationery, a set of useful clogs . . . and they all had pain baked right into them. The perfume bottle's lid bit into one's palm, whatever was written on the stationery prompted tears, the clogs gnawed blisters.

She had gotten so used to the pain, she didn't even notice it sometimes, but Niall avoided using Mór's dreams as much as he could. Not because he couldn't bear the pain, but because he couldn't bear thinking about how she'd managed to get used to it.

Together, they ran the farm. Niall, nostalgic for the successful farm he'd grown up on, was intent on making the Barns fill that hole in his heart and then some. Now the fields and barns brimmed with as many animals as Niall and Mór could take care of on their own. Niall was not a gifted businessman, but he did his best to try to turn this livestock into a livelihood, hoping they would no longer feel the need to make their living with dreams. He missed when it had been fun.

And they raised Declan, of course. He was an easy child, but still, he was a child. Mór never lost her temper, but she had a way about her when she was getting frustrated with having to watch him for a very long time instead of dreaming. Declan sensed it, and Niall sensed it even more, and so he got into the habit of towing Declan with him as often as he could.

Funny place for a child, he heard when he rolled up to the slaughterhouses with the cattle.

Sure, then I have company for my tears, Niall replied, to make the other farmers laugh, because he had a soft spot for his cows and didn't like to send them off, even if it spared the dreaming some of the weight of capitalism. *And he should know what he's eating anyway, I'm not raising a fool.*

It seemed like life might go on like this forever. But one day Niall brought back a virus without realizing it. The virus wasn't really a disease, it was a contact in a phone, it was a jotted word on the back of a farm receipt, it was a square business card with a woman's face on it, a cross painted over her.

"What do you think about being rich?" Mór asked Niall one afternoon. He was lazing on the couch after a morning of tending his animals with Declan. Declan never lazed, but he was quiet, anyway, sitting in the corner and organizing the record collection by color.

Niall laughed. "What would I be after with money? Don't I have everything I need here?"

Mór said, "I called one of the numbers on those little cards you brought home. It was interesting what she had to say. Powerful people in high places. Sounded like a spy movie."

"Put that record on, Declan," Niall said. "The one you've got in your hand right now. Do you know how to do it or do you need help?"

"Did you hear what I said?" Mór asked.

"I heard it," Niall said. "But what could we do for powerful people in high places?"

"Become them. The Forest says it could help. Did it tell you that, too?"

It had, but Niall hadn't been paying it any heed. The Forest had sounded a little too eager, which made him nervous. The look in Mór's eyes made him nervous, too, but he couldn't ignore her like he ignored the Forest. He didn't want her to grow bored of him or the Barns. So he nodded and asked her to tell him more.

This was what the thing in the Forest had been saying to them lately: *more*.

For a stretch the Forest had just lingered in the background of their dreams. A tree here or there on the horizon of a dream about something else. The smell of leaves in autumn. The sound of rain in a thicket. But lately it had been moving closer. In his dreams, Niall found himself pressing through branches to get to the clearings where cows were. Mór found herself deep in a hidden glade, the hanging vines touching her face.

The Forest sought them again and again. It held Niall when he was trying to wake. No, not held. Pressed against him, trying to slip out like a dog at a cracked door.

One night, Niall and Mór waited until Declan was asleep and then they made their best effort to dream together. They were in the Forest, and the thing was there. It was strange, Niall thought, how at first the Forest had looked like the forest near his parents' house where he was raised, and then it had looked like the Virginia forest that grew on either side of the driveway to the Barns, but now it looked like neither of those things, like a forest in a country he'd never been to. These were big, vast old trees. They seemed scaled for entities of a different size than he and Mór, a place or time when giants walked. Perhaps that was it, he thought. They seemed to come from an older time, a time long before humans were the dominant species, when everything could be bigger, when the air and ground were different.

He could feel the thing in the Forest agreeing with him, feeding this information in the way dreams do, where it feels like your idea but really you're just along for the ride.

As they dreamt together, Mór asked the Forest how to get more, to be more. The thing in the Forest listened eagerly. Niall could feel its longing and curiosity permeating every branch and every root. It answered her.

It wanted out.

Roots and branches, which way was up? Whose dream was this? Were they dreaming of the thing in the Forest, or was it dreaming of them?

"If we give it what it wants," Mór said, "it'll give us what we want."

"What do we want?" Niall asked.

Mór answered, "More."

24

It looked as if the apocalypse was still a go.

The area around the crime scene was a pleasant neighborhood, with large, neat older houses with ice-free sidewalks and very little dirty snow remaining. The residences farthest from the blast were missing some windowpanes; the ones closest were partially collapsed and skewered with debris. The Medford Assistance Center itself was completely gone. Where it had stood looked like a cross between a forest fire and a parking lot; it was now contained by a temporary metal fence as the search for survivors and bodies continued.

Hundreds. That's what they were saying. Hundreds of people had died here, everyone in the building presumed dead. Humans. Sleepers. Dreams. Whatever their differences were before, they all had something in common now.

Hundreds more people gathered around the temporary fence, craning their necks for a better view or taking videos as uniformed officers tried to shoo them away. There wasn't anything for them to see or record besides the wreckage, but Hennessy supposed she understood the impulse.

The mandatory vision had been a helluva waking dream.

The apocalypse.

Hennessy had forgotten that it was even possible for dreams to not be the Lace. Certainly not for her. Certainly not without Ronan or Bryde to manipulate her subconscious.

And yet, just as they got back to the car outside the storage facility, the vivid hallucination had hit, working through her thoughts as thoroughly as her Lace nightmares. She came to feeling as chemically scrubbed as she would have with any naturally formed nightmare. She had seen the apocalypse—an apocalypse *not* caused by the Lace.

She felt like everything was changing. The Lace dream was changing, how she felt about her paintings was changing, the world was changing.

Now Hennessy, Farooq-Lane, and Liliana were at the site of the explosion, and Farooq-Lane was on the other side of the caution tape, having gained access with DEA credentials. Hennessy found it darkly hilarious that the Moderators had managed to get the hunt for dreamers sorted into the Drug Enforcement Agency. All kinds of dreadful things could be done in the name of stopping the war on drugs; it was kind of brilliant. And weren't dreams sort of a psychoactive substance? Bryde's fancy little orbs had been.

And certainly this bomb had been, too.

"I'm not sure our friend Carmina Burana's doing so hot, old lady," Hennessy told Liliana as they stood on the civilian side of the police tape. The smell was weird and not good. It was the smell of things that were not meant to be broken open having been broken open.

Liliana peered at Farooq-Lane with a worried expression, the breeze whipping at her long white hair. Farooq-Lane was listening robotically to one of the recovery team members. Everything about her posture looked incorrect for her, as if someone had been asked to assemble a new Farooq-Lane from a written description alone. Liliana murmured, "Her brother killed her parents with a bomb like this."

"Shittola," remarked Hennessy. That explained her reaction after the vision. Farooq-Lane's eyes had gone completely dead. She hadn't answered anything Hennessy said to her as they drove away from the storage facility. It was as if she couldn't hear a thing.

"She is a good person," Liliana said. She frowned into the distance, where one could still hear the sounds of ordinary commuter traffic. As always, it seemed impossible that a normal day was proceeding just a few blocks away from a tragedy. "She is kinder than me."

Hennessy glanced over sharply, intrigued, but Liliana didn't go on.

Farooq-Lane finally rejoined them. She said, "Hennessy, there's no easy way to say this. Bryde was being held in custody in that building. The assistance center. They have found no survivors at this point."

Bryde wouldn't die. Not without delivering one last lecture to her. Not unless his death would somehow pit her and Ronan against each other for their own educational good.

"He's a wily fox," Hennessy said, forcing out a jocular tone. "You never know when he might have slid out, like a dolphin in margarine. So many metaphors! What a morning."

Liliana turned her pitying look on Hennessy, and when Farooq-Lane spoke, she sounded as tired as Lock had. "He was zip-tied to a bed."

The image came easily to Hennessy. It was a miserable one.

For some reason, even though it would have made her feel better to remember any of the times Bryde had made her feel like shit, she remembered, instead, when she had accidentally shown five little dreamer children the hideous Lace. Their mother had been furious with her; she thought Hennessy was a monster, and she hadn't held back telling her so. Bryde had sent Ronan and Hennessy to the car, but before they were out of earshot, Hennessy had heard him tell the children's mother, "You might remember that dreamer was a child once, too, not very long ago."

Hennessy. He'd meant Hennessy. It was the kindest thing he'd ever said about her, and it hadn't been to her. *Be soft to her,* he had meant. *Be soft because it would still matter.*

Liliana said, "I'm going to hug you now."

She did.

The strange comfort of Liliana's presence surrounded Hennessy. She stood there with her eyes open and Liliana draped on her, looking across the rubble.

"There was no sign of him," Farooq-Lane said, and something about the way she said *him* conveyed that it was not Bryde she was talking about, but Nathan. "But it was certainly one of his weapons. Everything we did was for nothing."

Liliana released Hennessy. "I don't believe that is true."

"Oh, it is," Farooq-Lane said. "Think about it. He must have them stockpiled. And if he has them stockpiled, any dreamer could have dreams stockpiled. That unending fire might already be burning in a jar in Topeka or a mine in West Virginia, and we just haven't seen it yet. The only thing we stopped was *new* dreams. Either way, I didn't stop the one person I thought I definitely had stopped. And now look."

They all did. For several minutes they simply stood there, staring at the wreckage with their own individual feelings about what they were seeing, and then Hennessy sucked in a sharp breath.

"Oh, shit," she said, her eyes fixed on an object on the other side of the rubble.

Liliana and Farooq-Lane followed her gaze to a car. Part of a car. It was enough of the car to be identifiable, although the windows were all busted in and debris had collapsed the roof and impaled the doors.

"What are you pointing at?" Liliana asked.

Hennessy replied, "That fucker Declan Lynch's car."

25

At first, Declan had hated Matthew.

After Ronan had dreamt Matthew into being as an infant, Aurora Lynch tried her absolute hardest to convince him to love his new little brother. She appealed first to his curiosity, then to his compassion, and then to his duty. *Don't you want to see how he'll turn out? Don't you see how he's smiling at you and waiting for you to smile back? Don't you think he deserves a smart older brother like you?*

No, Declan didn't.

Matthew was a mistake: a dream that managed to slip out of Ronan's head, despite Declan's best efforts to prevent it.

Matthew was also a usurper, a brother dreamt to be a better companion to Ronan than Declan.

No, Declan was not going to love him.

Even more frustrating was the knowledge that everyone else would.

Matthew, dreamt to be lovable and huggable, was always getting love and hugs from everyone. He was unflappably happy. Even when Declan refused to play with him or smile back at him or hug him, he just pluckily went on his way.

Nothing Aurora could say would persuade Declan to do more than tolerate him. Aurora was already a lie Declan was being asked to play along with. He would not play along with another.

Some years after Matthew had been with them, the Lynch

family took a trip up to New York (state, not city). This was a trip they often made, usually to see people the boys had been instructed to call Aunt and Uncle (Declan knew now they were neither). These trips usually coincided with other business Niall had, although in this case, the trip's purpose was to go to the yearly Fleadh, an Irish music competition and festival. All three of the boys had learned a musical instrument, with varying levels of devotion, and this was a chance for them all to get out of the house and show it off. It was also one of the only places they ever took long trips to as a family; Ronan had gotten sick on so many other trips away from home, forcing their early return. (Declan wondered now if this was the nightwash.)

At the Fleadh, the buildings were full of people and noise. Concertinas skipping along here. Fiddles shuffling there. Pipes barking here. Mandolins simpering there. Dancers with curls piled upon curls minced past; mothers holding extra wigs made of curls upon curls trailed after. Niall and Ronan had plowed right on ahead, Ronan bullying people out of his way with his pipe case, Niall making up for his son's violent path with cheery smiles and words. Declan and Aurora walked behind, Matthew between them. As the crowds grew thicker, Matthew reached up for Declan's hand.

It was just like that. There was Aurora on one side, Declan on the other, and Matthew could have chosen either, but he held up his hand for Declan instead. He did not question that Declan would want to keep him secure; he just assumed that he would.

Declan looked down at Matthew. Matthew smiled up.

At that moment Declan understood that Matthew was unlike any of the other Lynches. The rest of Declan's family members were knotted with secrets, memories, lives experienced behind masks. Matthew might have been a dream, but nothing about him was pretend. Matthew was the truth.

Declan took his hand and held it tightly.

"I understand that Matthew is dead," Declan said. "That seems to be the situation."

It was well into the orange-black night now, fully into Jordan's time. After a day of driving from place to place looking for definitive answers, of making and taking phone calls, he had finally asked to be dropped off at the police station to wait for news. She wanted to stay with him, but she needed to paint if she wanted to be awake for whatever he found out. Now he had finally returned to her at the studio. It was less comfortable than his apartment for talking, but she knew why he had. The apartment was supposed to have Matthew in it, and didn't.

Jordan said, "You can't know for sure. Your car was at the site. That's all."

With a sigh, Declan navigated to an email and handed the phone to her. While she read it, he took his coat off and hung it on one of the empty easels. He did it with quite a bit of care. Pressed out wrinkles even though the coat wasn't the sort to maintain them. Hung it very gently on the easel to keep from knocking it over, though it wasn't the sort to be knocked over.

"So a security cam an entire block over caught a photo of someone who looks like him going in," she said. "And even if it *was* him, that doesn't mean he was still there."

Declan opened his messenger bag and tugged out a bundle that continued expanding after it had been removed. "The recovery team found this in the rubble. The police said I could have it."

Jordan looked at Matthew's bright-patterned bomber jacket, now mostly gray with soot.

Declan's hand was steady as he held it, but nevertheless, the very ends of the sleeves jittered.

Jordan shook her head. "Surely not."

Declan could tell that, despite it all, belief still escaped her.

But it didn't escape Declan.

Part of Declan had always thought it would end this way. This was the fruit that grew from the seeds his father planted. Declan had tried so hard to make the crop something else, to make the outcome not simply *Declan Lynch, a man who used to have a family*, but it was always meant to be this. He was a hardier strain than the other Lynches, for better or worse, and so he went on as the rest of the orchard perished around him. He had been preparing to be the last man standing his entire life.

Edvard Munch—an artist who, like Declan, felt defined by his anxiety—had once written,

A bird of prey has perched in my mind
Whose claws have dug into my heart
Whose beak has drilled into my breast
Whose wingbeat has darkened
my understanding

Declan's understanding was dark with nightwash. Claws dug for his heart, only to find it gone.

"Declan—" Jordan said, but instead of continuing, she just put his phone back in his outstretched hand. Ferociously, she began a new painting, paint saying what words couldn't.

He started to make calls.

First he found out who among his clients was willing to vouch for him to attend the Fairy Market in New York the following night since he had not applied for an invitation.

Then he reached out to a few of the clients who had regular transfers they needed to make from Logan Airport to the New York area and let them know that if they provided the vehicle, he was willing to make the drive.

Once he knew he had a car, he called Jo Fisher of Boudicca. He put it on speakerphone, so Jordan could hear. He and Jo Fisher bantered in circles as he tried to find out how much she was willing to do for him with what he was willing to give ("Would you be willing to set up a meeting for us with your brother?" "Would you be interested in having access to all of Ronan's and my father's personal effects at our family property?"), discovered what he already knew, that the numbers did not do what he wanted them to do, not anymore, and that more bullshitting was required, more negotiation. He arranged for a meeting with Barbara Shutt at the Fairy Market, to make a case. Boudicca told him to come prepared to talk about the Barns. They told him to not come without Jordan Hennessy.

He called his attorney, whose husband had fallen fast asleep at the same time as Matthew, and he directed her to change Declan's will to leave his town house and his liquid assets to Jordan Hennessy. He told her he would be by in fifteen minutes to sign the papers.

Then he called the man who stored his weapons to say he would be by in forty minutes to pick up a gun and the metal flask he'd told the man not to open under pain of death.

Then he hung up his phone and slid it into his pocket.

He told Jordan, "I need you to take me to Ronan."

They went out to Waltham, to the garage where Adam Parrish worked part-time, or had, before he'd helped Declan hide Ronan's body in the walls of it. No one was there as they crossed the gravel in the cold light of the bulb over the main bay's door. Declan used the key Adam had given him to unlock the side door, turned on his cell phone's flashlight, and let himself into the dark corridor.

He went to Ronan's body. There was no new nightwash on his face. Just two very ordinary tears leaking from his closed eyes. Ronan had always worn his feelings on his sleeve.

Declan knelt in front of him. "Do you think he can hear me?"

Jordan didn't reply. She was watching the two of them, chewing one of her tattooed knuckles, brow furrowed.

He turned back to Ronan and said, voice quite calm, "You were right. I was wrong. I fucked up. I fucked it all up. Here is the situation. Bryde said I wasn't keeping you from danger, I was keeping you from being dangerous. I don't think— No. I was. That is true. What he said was true. I have been holding you back your entire life because I was afraid. I have been scared shitless every time you fell asleep since I was a kid, and I have been stopping you whenever I can. Not anymore. I am going to New York and I'm going to get a sweetmetal strong enough to wake you up."

Ronan did not move a millimeter, but one of the trails of salt water down his cheek glistened a little as one more tear was added to it.

"Find whoever killed him, Ronan," Declan told him. "Find whoever killed Matthew and make sure they are never happy ever again."

He and his brother never hugged, but Declan put his hand on Ronan's warm skull for a second.

Declan said, "Be dangerous."

Finally, having done all that, he turned to Jordan and let her fold her arms around his neck.

"You're not coming with me," he said. "They can have the Barns. They can have what they want of me. They can't have you."

She put her hands on either side of his face and just looked at him. Both of them had worn masks for so long, but there were no masks between them now.

"It was always going to be this way," he said blandly. "Jordan, it was always going to be this way. Our story was always a tragedy."

"Pozzi, it wasn't," she said.

"Not yours," Declan said. "The Lynch family's. The Lynch brothers'. It was written before I was born."

"Mine was, too. I rewrote it. I saw the angel in the marble—"

"—and carved until you set it free," Declan finished the Michelangelo quote for her. "Yes, you did, Jordan."

But he was still trapped in stone.

26

Ronan used to dream of being dead.

They weren't nightmares. They were good dreams, actually. He'd had them off and on for so long that he could not precisely remember the first time he'd had the being-dead dream, but he did remember a very early one. He was in Mass, and he'd been nestled up hidden in Niall's side, although he'd been a little too old for such a thing. The entire Lynch family would have been there. Ronan sitting beside Niall, Niall sitting beside Aurora, Matthew beside Aurora, Declan bookending one of his brothers. Even back then, Ronan had been quite fixated on Mass, so it was unusual for him to be lured to sleep during it, even during the endless homily, but on this particular occasion, he was exhausted. The night before, Declan had woken him right in the middle of a dream.

"I'll get rid of it," Declan had hissed to him, his eyes wild, but Ronan hadn't even known what he was talking about before his older brother left his bedroom. Ronan had already forgotten the dream he'd been having, and all he remembered was the sight of his older brother looming at the edge of his bed, his expression quite unlike himself, teeth bared in a violent, terrified snarl. He hadn't been able to sleep for hours after for fear of having a nightmare of Declan looking so scary.

In the church the following day, however, that fear seemed far away. Everything at St. Agnes was comforting to Ronan.

The presence of his wiry father, with his smell of lemon and boxwood. His mother entertaining Matthew by subtly casting shadow animals with her hands on the pew before them. Declan reading the bulletin with his eyebrows furrowed as if he very much disagreed with the way they were running things but needed to know anyway. God. Ronan always felt the presence of a god, capital G, when he was in church, but especially on rainy days like this, when the church was hushed and dim, all the stained-glass horrors in the windows dulled to dark gems, the interior lights shimmering and dreamy behind the incense and candle smoke.

Ronan was very comforted by a god, capital G. The world got more and more senseless as he grew, with rules seeming to contradict each other left and right, but the knowledge that there was someone out there who knew how it all fit together was relieving.

Why am I like this? Ronan prayed when he arrived at church, knees aching on the kneeler. *Show me a sign of what I'm supposed to do with myself.*

God had not yet answered, but Ronan respected the reticence. Fathers were not always there. They had other things to do.

In this Mass, he slept and he dreamt of being dead.

It was wonderful.

Not for the others, of course. Dead Ronan, in the dream, could see that the other Lynches were very unhappy that Ronan had died, but Ronan couldn't tell if this was because they missed him or because they had been left behind. He could understand the latter. Being dead had brought him to what he assumed was Heaven. Heaven looked a lot like the Barns, but clearer.

The light through the old farmhouse was bright. It cast all

the carved wood into sharp detail: the rugged floral pattern in the stair railing, the dog head on the end of the walking stick, the hawk and hare in the picture frame over the living room mantel. The light found all the stoneware plates and teacups from Ireland in the cabinets, the lace curtains in the kitchen window, the dried lavender in the antique washbasin in his parents' room.

When Ronan was alive, they rarely had guests over to the Barns, but now that he was dead, he could see out the window that a great host of guests was coming down the drive. It was a vast throng of them—hundreds, perhaps—all processing from the sheltered trees at the end of the drive and up the winding path to the house. How exceptional these guests were! They were dressed in all manners and they were all races and ages and genders and sizes. Some of them did not seem to be human. There were, for instance, some entities who seemed too long or too stretched beneath their flowing garments, and there were others who either wore crowns or had horns. Some, like Ronan's dream friend, the orphan girl, appeared to have hooves.

They were not frightening, though, because he saw that they were there for him. Some had already caught sight of him in the window and waved.

His heart burst with gladness. Gladness and relief. Thank goodness, he thought in the dream, that this was what the world was actually like. Some part of him had thought it must be. It could not be just mundanity and humans, because that felt wrong, like he had been made for something different, like he would always be seeking something more but never finding it. But this varied party, with their diverse shadows cast across these fields he loved, coming to celebrate with him—his heart thought, *of course, of course*. He just hadn't found all these pieces while he was alive, but in death, he had access to and knowledge of all the things that had been too far-flung or hidden for him to find before.

Thank you, thank you, thank you, Ronan thought. He could cry from it, such relief, such relief.

He rushed down the stairs to open the door of the Barns to them, and then he was surrounded by the visitors' strangeness. They rose above him with their inhuman enormity. Others swirled by with fragrances he'd never smelled before. Women wore flowers that didn't exist in Virginia. Men laughed and sang to each other in languages he'd never heard. The downstairs mudroom was filled not with shoes but with wild vines, ferns, and trees. A dapper, tawny-haired man with a distinctive hawkish profile stood at the door, continuing to welcome in ever more guests, making sure no one was turned away. Food had appeared, spread out on every flat surface in the Barns, all of it foreign and familiar at once. Everything was so bright, so clear, nothing hidden, everything just as it was before, but so visible, so seeable. He wasn't sure if this was his funeral or his baptism into this place, but whatever it was, it was joyful and thorough. He'd been confused and powerless in the capricious land of the living.

Here in the land of the dead, Ronan was a king.

Someone seized Ronan's hand, firmly lacing fingers with his, and he looked down at this gesture, this claim of possession. It was a boyish hand, all knuckles and veins, and it fit perfectly against his.

He heard a voice in his ear: *"Numquam solus."*

In the dream, he knew what it meant: *Never alone*.

How Ronan wanted to be dead.

Ronan was killing sweetmetals.

He didn't mean to be, but he was.

Somehow, in an instant, he had lost everything.

As the vision of the apocalypse rippled through everyone in Boston, it rippled through Adam and Ronan, too, somehow all tangled up in Declan's revelation that Matthew was dead, the two events compressed into the same event in the sweetmetal sea's odd sense of time.

Ronan spasmed with horror.

And in that one moment, that *one moment*, of vulnerability, the Lace attacked. He had not even had time to realize there was a gap in his protective fence around Adam.

There was a hoarse noise, complicated, high and low at once.

Then Adam was gone. He was just *gone*.

Ronan was absolutely alone in the dark sea, with nothing but the glimmer of the sweetmetals. There was no sign of the Lace. No sign of any of Adam's consciousness.

Horribly, Ronan was beginning to understand the sound he'd heard had been Adam's scream. The rasp in it grew worse every time he recalled it. And he *did* recall it. Over and over and over, as if punishing himself with the sound could erase his guilt.

Matthew, dead. Adam, lost.

He wanted to go back in time. He only needed to go back a second or two. He couldn't affect the bomb blast, but he could keep a grip on Adam. He could delete the sound of his scream from reality.

But for all the time strangeness in the sweetmetal sea, redoing time was not part of it.

What was done was done. He'd lost them both in quick succession.

Matthew, dead. Adam, lost.

That was when he began to kill sweetmetals.

He flung himself from sweetmetal to sweetmetal, trying

desperately to catch a glimpse of Declan, or Adam, or Matthew. He peered out of this painting, that sculpture, this tapestry, that wedding ring, searching every space he found himself in.

Ronan screamed in each room he was in.

At first he tried to shout his brothers' names, but then he felt himself shouting *Adam* as well, and then *God*, and then finally, just screaming. Static and noise. It wasn't a sound a human made, but he didn't have a human mouth here anyway.

Room after room.

Sweetmetal after sweetmetal.

As he screamed, less potent sweetmetals immediately gave up the ghost, plunging nearby vulnerable dreams into sleep.

Stronger sweetmetals seemed to channel him, as onlookers shuddered and exchanged glances to see if they were the only one to feel the change in the atmosphere.

He couldn't find Matthew. He couldn't find Declan. He couldn't find Adam.

He was trapped here.

All this time, he had judged Declan for being so staid as he took extreme measures to keep his brothers safe. But all this time, that was what Ronan should have been doing. He had so much power before the ley line was shut down. He should have been guarding his family, not the other way around. Instead he acted like a petulant kid. He made up the task of guarding the world, which meant nothing to him, instead of guarding his family, which meant everything to him.

But how could he have protected them, when everything about him had to be secret?

He was an old Irish hero with a *geis* placed upon him to dream so hugely that eventually he would not be able to hide it, and another *geis* placed upon him to never reveal that true self to anyone else.

He shouldn't have existed. He was impossible. He was made for neither being awake nor being asleep. He'd killed Matthew and Adam with his dreaming.

Ronan spun and spun through sweetmetals, flinging himself through the dark sea, screaming, coming apart. This couldn't be real. Maybe none of this had happened, maybe he was still a high school student sleeping fitfully in an old warehouse, maybe he was still a child sleeping fitfully in a room a few yards away from his still-living parents, maybe he was a god dreaming of being a baby dreaming of being a god—

What was reality? He made reality.

Was he awake or was he dreaming?

Was he awake or was he dreaming?

Was he awake or was he dreaming?

Was he awake or was he dreaming?

Was he awake or was he dreaming?

Was he awake or was he dreaming?

Was he awake or was he dreaming?

Was he awake or was he dreaming?

Was he awake or was he dreaming?

Was he awake or was he dreaming?

Was he awake or was he dreaming?

Was he awake or was he dreaming?

Was he awake or was he dreaming?

Was he awake or was he dreaming?

Was he awake or was he dreaming?

Was he awake or was he dreaming?
Was he awake or was he dreaming?
Was he awake or was he dreaming?
Was he awake or was he dreaming?
Was he awake or was he dreaming?
Was he awake or was he dreaming?
Was he awake or was he dreaming?
Was he awake or was he dreaming?
Was he awake or was he dreaming?
Was he awake or was he dreaming?
Was he awake or was he dreaming?
Was he awake or was he dreaming?
Was he awake or was he dreaming?
Was he awake or was he dreaming?
Was he awake or was he dreaming?
Was he awake or was he dreaming?
Was he awake or was he dreaming?
Was he awake or was he dreaming?
Was he awake or was he dreaming?
Was he awake or was he dreaming?
Was he awake or was he dreaming?
Was he awake or was he dreaming?
Was he awake or was he dreaming?
Was he awake or was he dreaming?
Was he awake or was he dreaming?
Was he awake or was he dreaming?
Was he awake or was he dreaming?

27

This year, the New York Fairy Market took place in the General, an old hotel near Fifth Avenue. It was exactly the kind of place that usually hosted the Markets; after the Market was complete, the host building always burned to the ground. Presumably it was to burn the evidence of some transactions—Declan darkly suspected this involved bodies— and it was possible insurance fraud was involved, as all the buildings were always moving toward obsolescence in some way.

Declan didn't really want to know why the buildings burned, or who burned them. The black market was a book where the pages got smaller and darker the farther you got into it, and Declan preferred to simply reread the first few chapters again and again. At the second-to-last Fairy Market, the one before he'd brought Ronan (was that a mistake?)(something had been a mistake)(the cards of the house had all come down for *some* reason), one of the antiques merchants Declan had known his entire life told him, "Diaspora always prefers an idealistic view of the homeland." Declan didn't know what he'd said to provoke such a statement. The Fairy Market wasn't his homeland. Declan was not Niall Lynch. Declan was nothing like his family. He was family-less.

(Matthew was dead.

Dead for good.

There would be no planning for school, no reason to make

coffee in the morning, nothing stopping Declan from doing everything, nothing stopping Declan from doing nothing.

Dead.)

At the General, Declan was waved directly inside by a doorman in an anonymous black suit. Inside, the small lobby was barely more updated than the nineteenth-century building that housed it, but the two security guards before the check-in desk were shockingly modern in Kevlar and face shields. They seemed pasted into the scene, which was otherwise paisley wallpaper and deeply scarred wooden floors and vintage light fixtures with dead insects heaped inside the glass.

"Invitation," said one.

Declan showed his hard-won invitation, which they scanned with an electronic device. That was new. It seemed crass and ugly to be scanned into the Fairy Market, no different than a gun show or concert. What was the Fairy Market when you took away the courtly ritual and the art? It was just crime. Jordan wouldn't have been able to forge her way into this one, Declan thought, which made him feel strange and nostalgic, even though he didn't want a world where Jordan *needed* to be here instead of in a gallery.

"Weapons?" asked the second guard, even though he'd already begun to pat Declan down.

"This isn't my first Market," Declan said. Weapons had always been forbidden inside the Market. It was supposed to be a place where everyone held equal power. Weapons broke that balance.

The first guard found the silver flask in Declan's suit pocket, the one he'd made special arrangements to stop and pick up on the way here. He lifted it. "What's this?"

Declan's stomach churned, but in his usual bland voice he replied, "You know what it is."

The guard shook the flask and listened as it sloshed. Alcohol wasn't prohibited inside the Market. Neither were sweetmetals, which the flask was. A very weak one, but a sweetmetal nonetheless.

Don't take it, he thought.

They didn't. The guard tucked it back into Declan's pocket and said, "Through that door. Preferred invite uses the elevator at the end of the hall, tenth floor."

Declan pushed open the heavy fire door and found himself in a low-ceilinged, narrow hall.

The first thing he noticed was the dated, cheaply framed black-and-white photographs of New York hung between each door that lined the hall. They were so aggressively ugly that they came right back around to nearly being art.

The second thing he noticed was the rat. He'd had a long debate with Matthew about rats, back at the DC town house they'd shared a lifetime ago, because Matthew had wanted one. As a pet. Declan had said Matthew wouldn't want one if he'd seen a city rat. Matthew had replied the only thing that was different about a city rat was that no one loved it. This rat, creeping fast along the edge of the hall before disappearing into a crevice, was different from a pet rat in many ways. It was enormous. It was manky. Its eyes glittered with a sort of empty enterprise. If only Matthew were here, he would have understood that a life on the streets did something to a rat.

(Except Matthew wasn't here, he wasn't anywhere)

The third thing Declan saw, as he put one foot after another, was a number of people lined up along the hotel hall between him and the elevator at the end, all sitting exactly the same, with neatly printed signs in front of each. All of them had a precise square of duct tape over their mouths. Most of them were women. He had no doubt that this was the work of Boudicca.

This was unpleasant. It represented another line crossed at this Market, and Declan didn't like it. Of course there was violence around the Markets; any unregulated industry eventually gave way to violence, which is just another kind of order. But because weapons and clannishness weren't allowed in the actual Markets, it was usually subtly off camera. It was not presented to everyone who arrived, whether they were there for stolen vases or for the services of hitmen. Before, one could go to the Market with, say, your ten-year-old son, if you were Niall Lynch, and pretend that it was simply a secret club for people who thought the legal world was a little stodgy.

This was an obvious show of force on Boudicca's part.

Power had shifted.

The first five prisoners (because they had to be prisoners; their wrists were zip-tied) had no ears. They clearly *used* to have ears, but at some recent point in time, their ears had been removed without much care. The signs before these prisoners read I HEARD WHAT WASN'T MINE TO HEAR.

Declan tried his best not to look at these people as he walked down the hall toward the elevator, even though they were clearly meant to be looked at; he didn't want to be involved, and looking at them felt like being complicit in the methods.

It was harder not to look at the next few people, who had no hands, a more dramatic deletion than the first group. These prisoners' signs read I TOOK WHAT WASN'T MINE TO TAKE.

One of these was Angie Oppie, looking nothing like the

voluptuous thief and broker he knew from previous Markets. Her red mouth was hidden behind the duct tape. Her clothing was torn and bloodstained. Her arms were zip-tied together multiple times above and below the elbow, ending at blunted, bandaged stumps. This was as hard to understand as Matthew being dead. He had been alive, and now he was dead. Angie had had hands, and now she did not.

Declan's steps flagged.

He wasn't friends with her, but they also weren't enemies. They had more in common with each other than most people. That felt like something.

He met her eyes.

Ever so subtly, Angie shook her head. Her eyes cut to the door he'd just come through, and he could tell without turning that someone else was in the hall behind him, maybe one of the guards.

Declan's stomach hurt.

He kept walking.

The hall felt like it went on forever.

It was not just these people who were ruined. It felt like Declan's childhood was ruined, too. He had not realized until he walked past all these people how much he had relied on the ritual of going to these Markets with his father, how they had felt like subversive conferences, not grimy battlefields. This felt like he himself had joined Boudicca, the mob, signed up for this viciousness in his daily life. He could not get away from it.

The final group of prisoners had been placed next to the elevator, so that one had to stand directly beside them while waiting.

They had no eyes.

Their signs read I SAW WHAT WASN'T MINE TO SEE.

Declan couldn't help it. He looked at them as he waited for the elevator car to come.

He realized he was scanning the group for his mother. Not Aurora Lynch, the woman who'd raised him. Mór Ó Corra, his real mother, his birth mother, the woman who'd been used as the prototype for Aurora, the dreamt copy. There was no reason why Declan should have expected Mór to be among these prisoners, apart from the fact that he knew she worked for Boudicca. He had gone to so much work to track her down, he thought, and in the end, she hadn't wanted to see him. Instead, a dreamt copy of his youthful father had warned him to stay away and keep Ronan safe.

Well, he hadn't done that, had he?

The elevator doors opened to reveal a final prisoner inside. This person, a gangly young woman, was collapsed against the paneled wall of the elevator car, neither gagged nor tied, because there was no need. She was sleeping.

The sign leaning against her knee said I FORGOT I WAS HELPLESS.

Declan made himself get into the elevator. He could hear his breathing when he stepped in, as if he had a bag over his head.

The doors slid shut.

He hit the button for the tenth floor.

He hated everything about this trip, he thought. Everything felt twisted.

The display at the top of the elevator blinked as the car rattled upward, as rickety as the rest of the hotel.

When it read 9, the girl's eyes opened. Not much. Just a flicker. But they stayed open when the elevator dinged at 10.

Sweetmetals, thought Declan. His preferred invite was taking him to the floor with sweetmetals, and something there was strong enough to wake the girl in the elevator. Not enough to fully animate her body, but enough to rouse her mind.

As the elevator doors opened and the girl sighed, Declan realized that her placement in the elevator was torture. Or punishment. Pick your noun. For the entire length of the Fairy Market, the girl would ride the elevator up to consciousness and then slide back into darkness, over and over.

And then burn with the rest?

Declan hesitated.

"Lot 531," the girl whispered. "That's me. Bid high."

Declan backed out of the elevator.

He found himself surrounded by sweetmetals. This floor had previously been a top-floor suite, and each room had been transformed into a showcase for pieces of art. There were glass cases filled with jewelry and silver and fragments of sculptures. Bronzes on pedestals. Drawings in protective sleeves. Paintings hung behind velvet rope. Dresses and jackets, shoes and gloves, intricate with beads, jewels, and embroidery. Even the bed was clearly a sweetmetal, marvelously carved, draped with spectacular quilts and tapestries.

Posted at each doorway was a bulky guard with an unsubtly displayed weapon.

Whatever the stakes of the Fairy Markets had been before, they were higher now.

Declan found himself facing a Magritte.

It was such a surprise to see the painting in this context that he could not even pretend it had not stopped him in his tracks. It was a famous image, officially named *The Son of Man*, but known by most non-art people as *Man in the Bowler Hat*, which was actually the name of another, lesser-known Magritte painting featuring a pigeon. In this one, an anonymous businessman in a dark jacket, red tie, and bowler hat faced the viewer from in front of a stone wall, his hands hung slack by his sides. One of his elbows was subtly bent the wrong way. His features were completely hidden behind a green apple floating in front of him.

For a period of time in high school, Declan had been moderately obsessed with this painting. Or perhaps he was obsessed with what Magritte had said about it, which was that the viewer desperately longed to see the man's face not because it was necessarily more interesting than the apple but because, unlike the apple, it was hidden. Declan had written Magritte's words about it at the top of his English notebook for that quarter and he still remembered them, word for word, like a Bible verse.

"It's a real looker, isn't it?" Barbara Shutt said, sidling up to him. As before, the Boudicca representative was deceptively disarming in appearance, in a dowdy blouse with an abusively artless rooster pin attached crookedly to it. She was holding a fizzy drink that cast tiny bubbles just above the rim of the glass. "The first look-see you get at it is just a *wow-ee, that's a painting!* And then you realize, whoopsee, you've *seen* that painting before, this is *that* painting."

She was shoulder to shoulder with Declan, close enough that he could hear the slight nasal wheeze to her breath and smell her perfume.

He said, "'Everything we see hides another thing, we always want to see what is hidden by what we see.'"

"What's that?"

"Magritte said that."

"Oh! You clever thing. I don't have a head for quotes. Jokes, though! Here's one: Why can't a nose be twelve inches?"

Declan didn't reply until the silence stretched out long enough that he realized he was supposed to. "Why not?"

"Because then it would be a foot!" She laughed hard enough that she had to take care not to spill her drink. "What a hoot. Where is your friend Jordan at? Is she looking at the necklaces? Maybe the rings, if you know what I mean, you dog?"

"She didn't come," Declan said, and then realized as soon as he'd said it that she already knew that.

He had to rethink his opinion of her in light of this.

"Oh, sweetie, we really did want her here," Barbara Shutt said. "It's not that we don't want to see you, handsome guy that you are! But—"

"When we ask for something, and you agree, we expect that to be followed through," said Jo Fisher, cutting in. The young woman had pulled her straight hair into a very tight bun so that there was nothing to hide the coolness in her expression. "And I think the deal was you arrive here with Jordan Hennessy and the information about your father's property."

"We haven't made a deal yet," Declan said. "This meeting is to discuss a deal. I was clear on that."

"Oh, I didn't get that at all from the phone call," Barbara Shutt said to Jo Fisher. "Did you get that? That's a big fat no from her, too, shoot. I'm really sorry you came all this way, but we can't help you."

Declan kept his voice as level as possible. "There's plenty to interest you at the Barns. Jordan's choices are her own, not mine, separate from all this."

To his astonishment, Barbara Shutt and Jo Fisher simply

turned away from him and began to leave, chatting as if in a completely unrelated conversation. He was meant to chase them, perhaps, and beg, so they could turn him down again.

He said, raising his voice, "Is that how you end a conversation with all your contacts?"

The two women paused and turned back to him.

Barbara Shutt said, "Sweetie, your father and brother are dead and gone, and all that's left is you. You're a nice bit of pudding for the eyes, if you get my whiff, but otherwise, what good are *you*?"

"Please escort this man out," Jo Fisher told the guards.

And escort him out they did, the two guards flanking him. Back to the elevator, where the girl woke up and said "Lot 531" until one of the guards kicked her in the mouth. She moaned a little until the car sank too far down for the suite of sweetmetals to affect her. Back down the hallway of the other Boudicca prisoners, including Angie without any hands. Back to the lobby, where the men in Kevlar stood, making sure that only those with the correct means could get access to this newly precious commodity.

Back out onto the dark sidewalk, where New York made its ordinary night noises of cars and sirens and shouting. The wind howled down the long block. It would whip the fire of the hotel into quite a frenzy later.

Declan stood there for a long moment in the middle of the sidewalk, shivering. He had just been surrounded by sweetmetals that would have made Matthew's life infinitely easier, that would have prevented the argument between them in the first place, that would have kept him—

(he's dead)

And *The Son of Man*—if he had that famous piece, he had

no doubt he'd be able to wake Ronan. And if he woke Ronan, then—then—

(he's dead, he's dead, he's dead)

Declan had a feeling like there was a version of himself that might never take another step off this sidewalk. That might just stand here forever until his heart stopped beating, however long that took.

But instead he squared his shoulders. He took a breath. He felt empty.

He texted Jordan: *you were the story I chose for myself*

Then he walked back into the hotel.

"What do you need?" asked one of the guards.

"I forgot something," Declan said. He took out his phone. "Could you tell me what this means?"

As the first guard leaned in to look at the screen, Declan took the gun from his holster and used it to shoot the second guard.

The first guard reeled back, reaching for his missing gun, and Declan shot him, too. He leaned down and took the first guard's combat knife from his belt, then he took the second guard's gun as well.

He shoved open the fire doors to the hall. The prisoners looked at him.

Without a word, he stalked down the hall, using the knife to slice the zip ties of each of the prisoners.

The elevator opened. A guard stood in it over lot 531.

Declan shot this guard, too. He took his gun, then dragged lot 531 into the hall.

He turned to the prisoners.

"Get out," he said. "Why are you still sitting there? They're dead. Take her. Get out."

More uniforms appeared from side doors. He heard gunfire but he was already rolling into the elevator and firing back.

Floor ten. He was headed to floor ten.

Up.

There was blood spattered on his hands and shoes. Not his. He could hear shouting from the floors he passed.

The elevator doors opened. Floor seven, not ten. More security. He let off covering fire while mashing the door-close button.

Up.

The door opened again on floor nine. More security. Already right on top of him, no time to shut the elevator.

He stabbed the closest, shot the next, burst out of the elevator and rolled against the wall as gunfire peppered where he'd just been.

More of them came as he went down the hall, striding straight for the stairwell to keep going up, up, up. The bodies piled behind him. The doors to the rooms he passed opened long enough to see the fighting before shutting again. Up the stairs, up the stairs.

Floor ten.

He was surrounded by sweetmetals and guards and he was out of bullets.

The Son of Man looked at him from behind the apple.

(dead, everyone's dead)

Declan removed the silver flask from his jacket pocket and unscrewed the lid. As bullets flew at him, creatures suddenly exploded from the newly opened mouth of the flask. The creatures were both hounds and smoke, dark and menacing as they billowed across the carpet. When they bayed, light as brilliant as the sun flared out of their mouths, powering them from within.

They were starving.

They devoured the flying bullets as they leapt upon the guards. They were not neat.

These were Ronan's sundogs. Dreamt to protect his brothers, but willing to tear them apart, too, once the work of destroying villains was all done. All they knew was killing.

Declan fumbled for an unlocked door and just had time to slip into the space behind it as the screaming began. It was a closet. He stood in the darkness, gasping for breath. Somehow the sound of his breathing and the pounding of his heart was louder than the hideous sounds happening on the other side of the door.

When it was finally quiet, Declan counted a full sixty seconds to be sure.

Then he unscrewed the flask again to reveal the liquid inside, and risked stepping back into the room.

Bodies littered the space; the sundogs still swirled among them, panting, hungry. A glowing inferno was visible in the open mouth of each dog; there was no sign of blood on their amorphous mouths, although the rugs suggested there should be.

"It is time," Declan said, "to be done."

At his voice, the pack surged toward him. Identical glowing mouths burning toward him, starving, thoughtless, never satisfied. For a moment he thought: *This is it.*

But then the sundogs swirled right back into the flask, neat as a video played in reverse.

He screwed the lid on tightly.

In the hushed silence of the deadened room, Declan strode

over the ruined bodies toward *The Son of Man*. He tried to picture it riding beside him in the car back to Massachusetts. He tried to imagine giving it to Ronan in that dark corridor where he was trapped forever. He tried to imagine seeing Jordan again.

But all of that was hidden by what he could see before him.

"Don't," Barbara Shutt said. "Young man, you've done enough."

She emerged from the elevator, blood spattering her face, too. Not hers.

"This is already done," Declan said.

Raising her eyebrows, Barbara Shutt looked past him. Maybe it was a bluff, but Declan looked, too, following her gaze.

He saw a figure holding a gun. He just had time to see that it was his mother, Mór Ó Corra.

Then she shot him.

28

"What do you think the Forest wants from us?" Niall asked. He said *Forest* because Mór also called the thing in their dreams a forest, but he knew that it wasn't really a forest they were dealing with. *Forest* was just shorthand for a place where the thing lived, a representation of how it was a vast entity, roots in one world and branches in another, although it was entirely uncertain if they lived in the branches or in the roots. Niall would have assumed they lived on the side with the sun, but perhaps they were underground.

These were the kinds of thoughts dreaming of the Forest provoked. Niall didn't like it. It was stretching his brain, and he could feel his brain wanting to break from the enormity of existence. He had not been built to understand this.

"I don't know if that's the right question," Mór replied. "Rather, it's, what does the Forest want?"

"How is that any different?"

"Why is it here? Why is it talking to you and me instead of doing whatever it wants back where it comes from?"

Niall said, "Do you reckon it's a demon?"

Mór gave him a heavy look. She thought he was foolish for being religious still when the two of them could pull things from their dreams, but he thought there were plenty of things in the world that weren't explicitly mentioned at Mass. He was fine being one of them. He needed to believe someone beyond him and Mór and the thing in the Forest had a plan, so that *he* didn't have to have one.

"More a god if you're going to use names like that," she replied. "Whatever it is, I think it's curious. Sometimes I think it wishes it could be us. Human. It wants to see more than it does; that's why it's always prodding us."

"See more what?"

"More of our world. I think it would like legs, is all I'm saying."

"Well, it can't have mine—I've got cows to feed!" Niall retorted. He kept his voice light, but both of them knew he felt uneasy about the conversation. They had entered a closeness with the thing in the Forest that made giving away one's legs feel more possible than it had at the beginning. Niall called out for Declan, put a pair of gloves in his hands, said, "You're helping me, boy, let your mum have some time to herself," and went out.

It felt important to let Mór have time to herself, because increasingly it felt like if he didn't give her a little freedom, she would take *a lot* of freedom instead. After making contact with Boudicca—that was the name of the group attached to the card Niall had gotten—she'd started taking trips away from the Barns. At first they were just for an hour or two, and then they were for an afternoon, and then a day, and then many days. She left without warning and came back the same way, with no explanation or apology, like a cat. She always came back from these trips with a ferocious and living look in her eye, so it wasn't as if Niall could oppose them. Whatever was out there, she needed, and who was he to stop her? Like the Forest, she wanted legs and space to use them, and he wasn't going to be her chain.

Declan took it hard, though. He was growing into a child

of rigid rules and diligent plans, and increasingly, plans that involved Mór could not be relied upon. She might be gone by the time they came to fruition.

"Marie," Niall said, one night when she came back late and crawled into bed with him, "do you think you might be after ever taking big D with you on your trips here and there?"

"Mór," she replied. Marie Curry was her real name, which made her married name Marie Lynch, just like Niall's mother, a truth she'd always hated.

"What's that?" He thought she'd said *more*. Not *Mór*, which meant *big* in Irish.

She said, "I'm changing my name. Mór Ó Corra has a ring, don't you think? I'll be Marie Mór and your mum can be Marie Beag. I've won."

"You don't want to be a Lynch anymore?"

"I don't want to be Marie Lynch anymore, no."

It felt a little as if Mór had managed to slip one of her painful dream objects into the conversation, but Niall said, "All right, then." He wasn't going to call her a name she didn't want to be called. It would be like an insult every time.

"You aren't upset with me?"

Those weren't mutually exclusive. In a low voice, he said, "I want you to be happy. It makes me happy for you to be happy."

The dark Virginia night made its dark Virginia night noises in their bedroom—the crickets whirring, the trees shushing, a fox barking warningly high out in the fields.

Mór rolled up onto one elbow and said, "You really mean that, don't you? You have so many feelings. Can I tell you something about me I've never told anyone else?"

He kissed her cheek. Her eyes were wide open on him.

"I don't think I have any," she said.

Niall shook his head, smiling a little, not understanding if she was trying to turn a phrase.

She went on, "No, truly, when you say that you're happy for me, happy that I'm happy, you feel it, I can tell. You aren't just saying that so I'll do something for you; it really does something inside you."

Niall pushed himself up now, too. "I don't understand, love—are you telling me you just say things because you think I want to hear you say them?"

"Right, yes!" She seemed glad that he'd figured it out, rather than ashamed. "But you see, that's what I thought you were doing, too, for a long time. I thought everyone was. I thought we were all in this grand play on a stage, where it's like when someone asks how you are and you say 'fine,' because that's what you're supposed to say. But it's not really like that, is it? Because when you say you love me, you *feel* it, don't you?"

Niall rubbed his fingers against hers to be sure they were real, that he was awake, that this wasn't a nightmare, that this was his real wife. He felt a little jittery, like the night they'd decided to flee from Ireland.

"You don't?" he asked.

"I don't think so, not like other people do," she said. "Other people, it seems to hurt them to love someone, or it seems to make them happy. I just watched how other people said 'I love you' and I tried it out, I tried out all the things other people did, to make sure I was doing it right. I've been pretending to be like others for a long time, but I don't think I *love* things—I think I am *interested* in them. It's hard to tell because I'm not in anyone else's head, but I think that's how you experience it."

Niall said slowly, "Are you like a psychopath, then?"

She laughed merrily. "Sociopath, I think, because I've got a conscience! I looked it up. But an agreeable sociopath, lucky for you."

"So you never meant it when you said you loved me?"

"I'd be sorry if you died," she said. "I've never cared about that before. I used to imagine my sisters dying. My mother. I tried to decide if I'd be upset about it. I tried to tell myself I would be, but I knew better. I think I can get upset, but it takes me more than most people. You are the only one I've ever talked about this with."

She kissed him then, but he didn't know what that meant anymore.

"Let's give the Forest what it wants," she said, suddenly girlishly excited, "so it can give us what we want."

But now he didn't even know if she was truly excited, or if she was being excited just for his benefit. He asked, "What do we want again?"

"Everything," she said.

The Barns and Marie Lynch and Declan had been enough for Niall. But he could feel he was in danger of losing one of those things.

He asked, "What does it want?"

"Greywaren."

Why did it have a name already? Had it done this before? What did it mean if it had? He didn't want to know any of the answers.

But he loved her and he was afraid of losing her, so he said, "All right."

29

The problem with being very old, Liliana thought, was that feelings got all soft and blunted. It was so hard to remember how sharp and important they used to be. What it felt like to lose sleep to anticipation. How much it used to hurt to lose someone.

Liliana well remembered the shape of feelings, but these days, it often felt as if she were acting out the ones she used to have. She had seen so much, survived so much, said goodbye so many times.

When she was with Carmen Farooq-Lane, it helped her remember how *big* they used to be. It also reminded her of how little hers had become.

And Farooq-Lane's feelings were very big in the days following Nathan's bomb blast. It was as if she and Hennessy had swapped roles. Hennessy had become silent, studied, ruthless in her attack on the art in the basement, trying, failing, trying, failing to make another sweetmetal. Farooq-Lane, on the other hand, had become a wall of ceaseless noise. Everywhere she went, she turned on opera, if it wasn't already spontaneously playing for her anyway. Tenors warbled in the kitchen as she stared out the back window toward the little garage. Countertenors rippled seductively over the grocery store speakers. Sopranos mourned in the car as she went to the police station to discuss any new findings about the explosion or the hunt for Nathan. Baritones rumbled punitively over the top of bewildered drive-through attendants. Mezzo-sopranos dueled louder than her earbuds could contain as she jogged around the block until she was slick with sweat and out of breath. Opera, opera, opera. Farooq-Lane and her ghost. They couldn't take it anymore, and the only other person who could understand it was the other.

Liliana had caught Farooq-Lane by the elbows after one of her runs and held her gently still. Farooq-Lane's skin had been both burning and frozen, a contradiction made possible by running for miles during the still-frigid morning. "Carmen."

Farooq-Lane had said, "I have so much blood on my hands."

She was impossible. She could not be talked down or reasoned with. She could not be made to put down her feelings for anything. She simmered during breakfast. She smoldered while showering. She charred and blistered right until the moment she managed to fall asleep in bed. All she could talk or think about was what she had done, what Nathan had done, and what she might be able to do to stop it from happening again.

One evening, Farooq-Lane confronted Hennessy as she came up from the basement. "Can you turn the ley line back on, Hennessy?"

"What?" asked Liliana and Hennessy at once.

"Does the orb work the other way?" Farooq-Lane said. "If the ley line was working again, *you* could dream something to find him and take him down. Or at least help bring him in. Find out if he has a bigger bomb, something even worse—"

"Whoa, whoa, whoa," said Hennessy. "Pump the brakes, as the Pope would say. First of all, no, the orb was a one-use toy, meant to be thrown out or recycled depending on your proximity to the closest waste facilities. It's just an off button, not a toggle switch. Secondly, I am not the dreamer you're thinking I am. I just played one on TV. All I got for you is that sword, I promise. Thirdly, you'd throw me to the Lace just to stop your brother? Fourthly, I have got to piss like a racehorse, can I go?"

In response, the television above the mantel burst into a panicked aria.

It all reminded Liliana of how long it had been since she'd felt that strongly about anything.

On a particularly mild day, Hennessy and Liliana stood on the little porch and watched Farooq-Lane vacuum out the car, opera blaring, her eyes scorched. Hennessy tapped the ash off her cigarette before blowing a smoke ring in Farooq-Lane's direction. "Thing of beauty, isn't it? Like watching a volcano take out innocent villagers one at a time while they sleep."

"She blames herself," Liliana said.

"Good! She fucking should. 'I was following orders' isn't many schools' mottoes for a reason." Hennessy flipped around to lean on her elbows and eye Liliana instead. With her enormous hair, vintage coat, and leather pants, Hennessy looked completely out of step with this cottage, as if she had been dropped here for an ironic album shoot. It occurred to Liliana that Hennessy was not quite the opposite of Liliana, but she was close. "What do you think, Visionary—do I have to worry about buying Christmas presents this year?"

Liliana said, "I am worried."

But what she meant was, *I remember what it is like to be worried.*

"I know it's rude to not ask a woman's age," Hennessy went on, "so how old are you? Oh, wait, maybe I got that wrong. But now that it's out there, how old are you?"

This was not the first time she had asked. It was not the fifth time. It was not the seventh. Liliana asked, "Hennessy, why is it you keep asking me that question?"

Hennessy lit another cigarette with the first and put both back into her mouth. She spoke around the two of them as if they were vampire fangs. "Because I have had a lot, l-o-t of time to think about the decision to shut down the ley line these past days, and to generally, you know, relive the experience of getting to that point of being willing to do so in the coffee shop, and it seems to me it was your idea to do it. Then good ol' Frookla there backed you up on the idea, because that's her big thing, isn't it, being vaguely suggestible to avoid having bad ideas herself."

"Now, that is not quite—"

"Please hold, Liliana, a representative *is* waiting to take your call and will be with you shortly, but until then, hear me out: Every way I cut it, shutting down the ley line was pretty damn cold." Hennessy glanced over to watch Farooq-Lane, Italian still blaring from the speakers. "I mean, who's to say if it was wrong or right. Maybe it will have worked, down the road. Apocalypse averted! Eight hundred billion people saved or however many people live on this place. No matter how you cut it, those are good numbers, even if you figure it killed more people than Nathan's bomb just did. However, I think you'll agree it takes a certain personality to make that call, yeah? Without a bit of hesitation. Yes, push the button, Hennessy, pillars of salt are a go. Feels like something either a real asshole would do, or someone who's just *so fucking crispy* their heart has become a chicken nugget. So on, so forth: How old are you, Liliana?"

Liliana felt caught between two storm fronts. Buffeted by opera on one side and Hennessy on the other.

"It was not easy," Liliana said.

Hennessy held her gaze.

"I knew it was not easy," Liliana corrected herself.

Hennessy stubbed out her cigarettes, satisfied. She did not seem to expect Liliana to offer regret, or further contextualize. She said, "Do you think regular cops will be able to take out this brother of hers while we sit here playing house? On a scale of *one* to *reprehensible*, just how bad is it to hope the situation will sort itself without us doing anything about it?"

Liliana tried first to think of what Hennessy might be trying to get her to say, and then about what she really thought the answer was. She shook her head.

Hennessy pushed off the railing as some old Handel aria trilled from behind her. She quirked an eyebrow and rocked her fingers in the air as if conducting the music. "How old were you when this one came out, Lil? When are you going to do the right thing?"

"What is it you want me to do?"

Hennessy stalked past her into the cottage. She shrugged. "But the rest of us gave everything up at the office already."

30

Matthew Lynch had never spent so much time *inside* furniture before.

When he was younger, he and his brothers used to play hide-and-seek at the Barns, which had involved a fair bit of time inside furniture. There was an armoire in their parents' room suitable for hiding a child of reasonable size. A chest in the living room that could fit a child of unreasonable size, if they were willing to remove some quilts first. Some dressers in the garage for the slightly more daring. A broken washing machine in one of the larger outbuildings, for the truly adventurous.

But that had been minutes inside furniture. Hours, at most, when the washing machine lid had fallen shut and latched on Matthew.

Not days.

Days was a very long time to be sitting quietly inside a table, especially if the only company one had, on the other side of the space, was Bryde.

I think the room is empty now! Matthew signed to Bryde. He had taken a course in American Sign Language the year before to make up for hideously failing French I. He was delighted to have someone to practice on, although Bryde had not been quick to pick it up.

In the dim space, Bryde's eyes glittered as he stared at Matthew. He was about three feet away, the farthest away he could get. The table was eight or nine feet long, with solid sides, all the way to the floor, made of MDF board or something similar. The only light came from the narrow gaps where the corners did not meet quite perfectly and the occasional gap in the place where the sides met the high-traffic carpet.

We can probably talk! Matthew signed.

Bryde, unmoving, signed back, spelling out the final word with surprising adeptness: *I'm busy.*

He was not busy. He was not doing anything. There was nothing to do.

Bryde wasn't at all what Matthew expected him to be.

For starters, he didn't seem interested in committing crimes. Based upon everything Matthew had heard, he'd expected the first thing Bryde would want to do when freed from the assistance center was destroy some stuff, or steal some things, or maybe try some culty behavior on Matthew or at least some bystanders. But he hadn't tried to do any of that. The closest he'd come to crime was shortly after they'd snuck him out of the Medford Assistance Center. He used the last of Matthew's change from the console to take a taxi into the city to search for Burrito, Ronan's invisible dreamt car. After spending hours trying to find it, Bryde had lost his temper and kicked someone's Mercedes. He left behind dents but no note. Criminal.

He also wasn't scary. The way Declan had talked about him, Matthew had expected him to be a terrifying bogeyman. At school they were often saying that dictators didn't seem scary in person, they seemed cool, like people you'd want to hang out with. Bryde *looked* cool enough, but he sure didn't act cool. He was silent for long stretches, looking windblown and put-upon with his hands in the pockets of his jacket, and then when he did talk, it was in long blocks of words that usually involved vocabulary Matthew had never memorized. He and Matthew would be talking about something entirely different and then suddenly Bryde would break off and be all *consciousness is a map to every place we have ever been and ever will be and yet no one here will consult it and thus is lost* and Matthew would ask, "Have you ever read anything about clinical depression?"

Bryde also didn't seem obsessed with Ronan. Matthew had worried that all he'd want to do was find Ronan to mess with his head, since Declan had seemed quite sure that was all he'd done before. Instead, Bryde looked pained whenever Ronan was mentioned. The only time he mentioned Ronan without prompting was when he went into a pub that first night and came out with an absolute wad of cash. He muttered, "Thank you, Ronan Lynch," and said nothing more.

"You know, I never really liked museums before," Matthew said in a stage whisper. He was *pretty* sure the gallery was empty, but not one hundred percent. "I didn't see the point of them. I used to make up songs in my head when I had to go on field trips. I had this one about a chiropractor once, because I liked the word *chiropractor*. Do you know if you have bones?"

The two of them were in a museum now.

They had to be.

The escape from the Medford Assistance Center had gone off without a hitch. Once Bryde was freed from the bed, he had hurriedly zipped his blue windbreaker all the way to his chin, making it look more like a company jacket, draped a sheet over the cot, stacked it with all the visitor chairs and fake potted plants from the room, and then threw a clipboard on top of it. Then he and Matthew wheeled it from the room like a dolly, as if they had been called upon to move the furniture for some mundane purpose. They met no one in the hall as they went directly to a side exit and wheeled the furniture to the garbage bins. Matthew had pulled out the car keys, but Bryde had said cops would find the car in a hot minute, and did he want to be caught in a hot minute?

They were not caught in a hot minute, but the swan pendant hadn't lasted too much longer than that.

They'd just stepped out of a convenience store after buying a disposable phone, but before Bryde could activate it, the skin around his eyes had gone tight and he'd said, "The whine in this place is unceasing—I wish I was dead. I wish I had never agreed to come."

Matthew didn't remember what happened after that.

He'd woken up here, under this display table, which turned out to be right outside the Klimt exhibit at the MFA. A girl named Hannah and a guy named Musa and another girl named Claire had brought them here. Two of them worked here and one of them was an art student, but Matthew couldn't remember which was which. Bryde had apparently come to them in their dreams, and in return for that, they brought him and Matthew sandwiches until Bryde could "figure something out."

Bryde had yet to "figure something out."

Matthew had started to keep a little journal; Bryde had given it to him. He asked Matthew if he would write down what he was thinking instead of saying it out loud if he bought a journal, and when Matthew said yes, Bryde had immediately doled out some of the cash from the pub for Musa to buy it from the gift shop.

Most of what Matthew wrote about was the voice.

The voice was a thing Matthew had heard for ages, especially after the ley line started to get a little funky and Ronan started to nightwash more. It always said the same sorts of things, like *Matthew, are you listening* and *Matthew, there's a better way* and *Matthew, come find me* and *Matthew, don't you want more?*

Here in the museum, the voice started up every night. Matthew listened to it. There wasn't much else to do. They could not wander the museum, even when it was closed, because of the security cameras and the guards. One could either curl up, as Bryde did, and sleep, or curl up, as Matthew did, and listen.

"What are you writing?" Bryde asked in a low voice.

"What the voice is saying," Matthew replied. *Don't be afraid, Matthew. It is simpler than you imagine.*

"The voice—is that what you call it?" Bryde said. "It doesn't matter anymore. This world isn't dead, but it might as well be, dragging its corpse from café to ballroom to alt-rock concerts, unable to do anything but keep itself awake, nothing more."

"Don't be bummed you can't do what you were doing before," Matthew said encouragingly. He ripped out a blank page of the journal. "Hannah brought an extra pen—would it make you feel better to draw a li'l somethin'?!"

"The world prepares to burn and we entertain ourselves with trinkets and crafts while pissing into bottles in the dark." But Bryde sat up stiffly and accepted the scratch paper.

"See, this is a perfectly cool time," Matthew said soothingly.

"I was not made for a *perfectly cool time*," Bryde said. He had drawn something that looked either like a tornado or like someone had been trying to take the pen while he wrote. "This place you call the world is only half of one. On the other side of a mirror is the rest of it. It is like loving the night without ever seeing the day. It is a sentence, cut off. A book, abbreviated. It is the first half of anything. Awake, asleep: they are two different things now. But there is a reality where there's simply one condition, perfectly braided, both things at once. That feeling you have when you hear the voice, don't you know something is missing?"

"Yeah, totally!" Matthew said. "For a while I thought it just meant I was hungry for a snack, though. Tell me something more about the voice."

"There is a voice from the other side calling your name. And on the other side, you're calling to something else, too. Who knows who is listening to you over there. Fools, on both sides, to listen, to draw close, to want . . ." Bryde closed his eyes. "I don't know if what I know is true."

"Let's pretend it is for now," Matthew suggested. "Just go with it, say what comes to mind. Spitballing—that's what Declan calls it."

Bryde seemed to misunderstand the concept of spitballing. He went on, "Am I old or am I young? I don't know if my memories are real, what real is anymore. Does it matter if I am not thousands of years old if I have been dreamt to be?"

Matthew had pondered this, too, when he'd first found out he was dreamt, not that long ago. People liked him, they always had. Was that the way he was made? Or was it something he'd earned? In the end, did it matter? He told Bryde all this as Bryde made the tornado larger and larger on the scratch paper and the voice continued talking, and then Matthew finished, "Anyhow, loads of people have things that are just the way they are, like red hair and stuff, does that make sense?"

"No," Bryde said morosely.

This was the problem with getting Bryde talking. He either got boring or sad. Matthew didn't mind being here under the table so much. It was hard to remember there was a real world out there when this one was so small and unchanging. Hard to really believe Declan was out there, mad that Matthew had stolen his car, that Ronan was out there, mysteriously sleeping.

Matthew, do you want to be free? Are you listening?

As Matthew continued to transcribe, humming a little, looping the words in different cursives to interrupt the monotony, Bryde asked, in a sharper tone, "You aren't afraid of the voice. Of what it's asking you to do?"

"*Is* it asking me to do something?"

"Yes."

"I didn't get that at all."

Bryde said, "It will change you, if you let it. It will change you for good."

Matthew asked, "Will it change *you*?"

"The voice doesn't ask me."

"Why not?"

"Probably because it knows I would say no. I am not interested in keeping myself awake. I am interested in keeping the world awake. Not me, but us. Dreams and dreamers. Imagine what this place would be if you did not have to beg at the feet of a painting for your life."

"Dudifer, you are the saddest dude I have ever met," Matthew told him. "It's like you're always wet. Seems to me that if *I* had to learn to be sad, *you* have to learn to be happy. Why don't you draw a, I dunno, chinchilla or something, instead of that, uh, thing. Not that's it not good."

"What's a chinchilla?"

"You're sort of a funny person," Matthew told him. "You know a lot of stuff but you're also pretty stupid."

For the first time, Bryde sort of smiled at this. He kind of had Ronan's smile, which meant that now Bryde was a little happier but Matthew was a little sadder.

You must know you cannot hide forever. Bryde, you know it comes to an end.

Bryde's expression turned intense.

"It's talking to you!" Matthew said. "Why is it talking to you now?"

Matthew, are you listening? Bryde, can you hear me? Matthew, there's a better way. Bryde, this is the only way. Matthew, come find me. Bryde, you know how to do this. Matthew, don't you want more? Bryde, don't you want to be free of him anyway?

Matthew couldn't keep up in the journal. "Why is it talking so *much*?"

Leaning forward, Bryde swiped his fingers under Matthew's ear. With a sigh, he studied the nightwash smeared across his skin. It matched the thin black liquid gathering in the corner of Bryde's eye.

He said, "Because now it knows that we're listening."

31

Farooq-Lane burned and haunted.

She needed an action item, but there was no action item. Last time, after Nathan had killed their parents, she could take up a gun and travel with the Moderators to make it right. Now there were no Moderators. The local law enforcement was not about to make a plan as dramatic as the Moderators, although they were equally intense about apprehending Nathan Farooq-Lane. Yes, Nathan was on their radar; yes, they had seen the memo on how the individual ID'd as him in Ireland was a mistake; yes, let us know if he contacts you and if you think of anything relevant that could help our search; no, you can't do anything else to help.

Of course she couldn't help.

Farooq-Lane had only her heart to follow, and that had already been established as an unreliable source.

She knew just two things for sure: Nathan was going to do it again. And all of this was about her.

The Medford bomb had gone off just minutes after she'd left the storage facility, just minutes after they'd heard Lock admit that someone else had been calling the shots. As if Nathan had been invoked by the admission. More likely was that he'd been watching her—for how long?

She couldn't shake the eerie idea that Nathan had somehow

been stored with the other Moderators and she simply hadn't noticed him lying silently in the dark, waiting for her.

She turned the sequence of events at the storage facility over and over, trying to come up with a clue that would give her a next step. It took her several days to realize—in the middle of the night—she'd completely ignored one other set of eyes there: Hennessy. Of course Hennessy had been there! She could be in on it. Anything was possible. Anything! Deep down, Farooq-Lane knew this was a spindly tree to bark up, but nonetheless, she could not stop moving, stop looking for an action item, stop searching for something to cross off a list or shoot in the face. If she didn't, something terrible would happen inside her. She could feel it.

So she leapt out of bed and went down to the basement for a confrontation.

To her surprise, Hennessy had picked up the mess her tantrum had left and replaced that disaster with a new one: a disaster of canvases, sketches, paint palettes with plastic wrap on them, sofa cushions brought down to make a nest to sleep the day away. But unlike the results of her tantrum, this clutter clearly had a system to it. It covered every available space, but it was also a place of work.

Hennessy herself currently stood under glowing lights, working away at a self-portrait. It was a wonky, mirthful piece of art, the lines were long and tangled together, everything elongated and wry, intentionally misshapen. It was not the ghoul Hennessy could be but rather the laugh-out-loud-funny Hennessy she sometimes was instead.

One the worktable next to her, in a hamster cage, the dreamt mouse ran on a wheel, its golden tail clinking rhythmically against the plastic. Something in the basement was humming with enough sweetmetal energy to keep it awake, for now.

Without introduction, Farooq-Lane demanded, "How did Nathan know that we were at the storage facility? No one was there but you and me."

Hennessy, her back to Farooq-Lane, didn't bother turning from her portrait as she added, "And all the Moderators."

"They were asleep. Lock was talking to us. That leaves you and me."

Scratch, scratch, scratch. Hennessy scumbled shadow under her eyes. "It certainly does."

"We would have heard someone else come in, surely."

"So you've come round to the idea that it's got to be me, then?" Hennessy said. She sounded unworried. She continued painting. "Do what you gotta do, I guess."

Farooq-Lane knew she was being unreasonable, and she knew that Hennessy knew, and that made her feel *more* unreasonable. This was usually when opera began to play.

Just then, she noticed a familiar paint-stained rag tossed over the edge of one of the tables. "Is that my blouse?"

Scratch, scratch, scratch. Hennessy carved tattoos into her portrait's neck. "It was on the floor."

"It must have fallen out of the dryer!"

"Stuff that falls on the floor is only good for ten seconds, that's what I heard. Still smelled like you, though."

The blouse looked beyond repair, but Farooq-Lane strode over to snatch it up anyway, on principle. On her way back, her steps flagged. The massive portrait of Farooq-Lane looked back at her from the shadows of the opposite wall. Hennessy had finished it.

Farooq-Lane couldn't resist looking at it closer. It was better since the last time she'd seen it, which she wouldn't have imagined possible. The eyes were stunning, liquid-real perfect, watering, glistening, watching from inside the canvas. The hair was touchable and shiny.

And the expression. It was Farooq-Lane, but better. Now the portrait version of her didn't just burn callously. Now she burned with purpose, with confidence, with loyalty, with justice, relentless, powerful. Powerful. Farooq-Lane had not been powerful, ever.

Conversationally, still scratching away at her paper, Hennessy said, "That Zed you guys shot in Pennsylvania, Rhiannon Martin? She dreamt mirrors. That was all she dreamt. Never anything else. Never anything that was gonna end the world, not that that mattered to the Mods, as you know now. She didn't dream a lot of them; they took her a long time. The thing about these mirrors, they were just nice. Can you imagine? They liked you. You know how they say that mirrors never lie, well, these didn't, either, but they were just fucking nice. Only way to say it. They showed you all the things you liked about yourself bigger than all the things you don't."

Farooq-Lane knew Hennessy was actually talking about the portrait, and it was true that she wanted to be the woman in the portrait. This was how she longed to be seen. She wasn't there yet, but this beautiful portrait of this beautiful woman seemed aspirational.

It was more than that, though. This painting wasn't just nice. It wasn't *fond*. It was full of dynamic desire. The redone brushstrokes on the face quivered. The skin seemed like it should be warm to the touch.

Farooq-Lane hovered her fingers over the surface, just millimeters away. She badly wanted to actually touch it. The temple, the cheek, the chin, the throat.

Hennessy grabbed her wrist.

Farooq-Lane hadn't even heard her cross the room.

"I wasn't going to touch—" she started, but then Hennessy used her wrist to pull her close. Hennessy kissed her.

It was not Liliana's sweet kisses.

This was a whole-body situation, a whole-day situation. Hennessy gripped her close and, the moment Farooq-Lane's lips opened, she bit one of them. There was not a single part of the kiss that did not firmly underline that Hennessy the person felt exactly the same way about Farooq-Lane as Hennessy the artist.

Opera burst through every speaker in the house. Strings coursing. Harpsichord galloping. Voice clean and high as a cloudless day.

There wasn't a part of Farooq-Lane that wasn't on fire, as living and vivid as the brushstrokes of the portrait.

Farooq-Lane, Burning.

She staggered back. "Don't you— There's such a thing as— Why are you *like* this?"

"You dropped your blouse," Hennessy said.

Farooq-Lane couldn't think of a reply. She finally managed, *"Liliana."*

Hennessy shrugged.

With a strangled noise, Farooq-Lane backed away, her lips still hot. All of her still hot. Turning, she headed up the stairs, taking them two at a time, pursued by a blushing aria. This was awful. She burned with fury—but not at Hennessy, at herself.

Hennessy was just being Hennessy. But Farooq-Lane was supposed to be someone of principle, of character, of poise.

Who was she becoming?

Farooq-Lane, Burning.

The problem was, she thought she might like that person. But what did that mean for the rest of her world?

At the top of the steps, she ran right into Liliana.

Liliana gently took her by the same wrist Hennessy had just held. She gazed at Farooq-Lane's disheveled appearance.

"Liliana," Farooq-Lane said. "I—"

Liliana interrupted, "We have to talk."

They drove just a few minutes away to Red Rock Park, a small preserve that jutted out into the ocean. During the day, it was pleasant to look at, even in cold weather, the grass green even when the leaves on the small decorative trees were bare. At night, however, the park felt barren and exposed, with the winds coming in straight and pure off the waves. It was not a place most people would choose to stroll at this time, in this weather.

But Liliana led them all the way down the sidewalk to the point and then stood there with her hands in the pockets of the big ugly coat a trucker had given her earlier that year, looking over the water. It was not quite black; Boston was too bright to ever let the ocean near it truly sleep.

Farooq-Lane fidgeted and shivered, her arms wrapped around herself. She tested her words. She anticipated Liliana's. *Hennessy did it!*

But Farooq-Lane knew that. She didn't feel guilty about Hennessy kissing her. She felt guilty about how it had made her feel.

"It started with a voice," Liliana said eventually. "I could tell it was different. It was not a human voice. It was something different. Something that spoke to me directly, in a language I did not otherwise hear. I do not know if anyone else could have heard while I was there, because it always spoke to me when I was alone, but I am sure that if they could, they would not have been able to understand it. It was a language for dreams."

Farooq-Lane frowned at her, taken off guard.

But Liliana continued, still gazing out into that endless ocean. "I was afraid when the voice came to me. He—the dreamer I told you about— was getting sick and I thought probably he would soon die. Everyone else was getting sick in the same way, and they were all dying, so I knew how it would go. I had wished for him to die for a long time, but not in a genuine way. I knew I would fall asleep without him. But the voice told me something different. It told me there was another way. It would keep me awake, it said, in exchange for just one thing."

"Liliana—"

Liliana shook her head and went on. "If I would hold its nightmares, it said, I could stay awake forever."

The visions. She was talking about the visions. Nightmares? But—

"I know what you are thinking. You are thinking that nightmares are imaginary, and it is true, that they are usually not real, but they are not *entirely* unreal. They show you people you know. Places you've been. Situations you've lived through. Perhaps the details around them are untrue, but there is always at least one true part, or they would not be frightening." She took a heavy sigh. "That is why the visions are true more often than not.

The visions are imaginings, uncolored by human nature, and informed by inhuman senses, of the worst-case scenario, which, more often than not, is the real scenario."

"Why are you telling me this?" Farooq-Lane asked. "Why now, when . . ."

It was a lot to take in; to realize that Liliana hadn't been intending to talk about Hennessy at all, to think of young Liliana being lured into becoming a Visionary. Parsifal must have been, too, when he was just a child.

"How old were the other Visionaries?" Liliana asked. "Have you ever seen one as old as me?"

In the dark, Farooq-Lane shook her head. She didn't know if Liliana had seen, but it didn't matter; the question had been rhetorical.

"That is because eventually, they all make the decision you saw: They turn their dangerous visions inward instead of outward, because they are tired of hurting people every time the voice has a nightmare. I never did that. I took the option, every time, that kept me alive. For a very long time."

"I don't judge you for that," Farooq-Lane said.

"I know," Liliana replied. "I know why I did it, and it does not make it wrong or right. But it is time to stop now."

"What!"

"If the world is destroyed, my selfishness will have been for nothing anyway." Liliana shrugged off the trucker coat to stand there on the edge of the point, an impossibly old, graceful woman with determination in her eyes. She fetched out a piece of paper from the pocket and showed it to Farooq-Lane. It was one of Hennessy's strange, stylized self-portraits, done in smudge charcoal. "I stole this from Hennessy, but I think she will forgive me; I can imagine she might be flattered, in fact. It is just enough of a sweetmetal to let me have a vision, if I turn it inward to make the energy more potent."

Farooq-Lane's pulse accelerated. "Liliana, you don't have to do this."

"You know as well as I do that this is your brother's apocalypse," Liliana said. "And you know that you are the one who will have to stop him."

Tears spilled down Farooq-Lane's cheeks. There had been no pause between Liliana's words and their appearance; her body hadn't even offered her an opportunity to fight them back. "We can find a more powerful sweetmetal. You don't have to—"

"I need you to see the vision," Liliana said, "and you can only do that if I turn it inward, so that I can be touching you when I have it. This is how it has to be."

"It certainly isn't!" Farooq-Lane felt as if Liliana was unfairly punishing her for letting Hennessy kiss her, and just as quick realized she only thought that because her anger made the truth easier to bear. "It doesn't matter if there are other ways, does it? This is the way you want it."

Liliana smiled her graceful smile at Farooq-Lane, pleased to be understood. "You have made me as happy as I can be. You reminded me what it was like to be young. More full of feelings. More human. I have no regrets."

Farooq-Lane didn't protest, just continued crying quietly as Liliana put her arms around her.

She whispered in Farooq-Lane's ear: *"Watch closely."*

Then she had a vision.

The images washed over both of them, searing and immediate and precise.

And then there was just Farooq-Lane, holding the limp body of a very, very old dream in her arms, shaking with what had just happened and what was still yet to come.

32

Hennessy dreamt of the Lace.

This was the real Lace.

She had painted a sweetmetal, and she was sleeping just feet away from it, so now the Lace could come to her again. The door, cracked open.

As before, the dream slowly lightened to reveal the jagged edge of the entity. Once again, the dread rose inside her, completely primal, unattached to any conscious thought. This was a side effect of seeing the Lace itself, something so different from herself, and of being seen by the Lace, feeling its hatred buffet her.

Once again, the Lace began to hiss its hateful refrain. She was so useless, so awful, so needy. She'd ruined things with everyone. Driven Farooq-Lane away, up the stairs, just like she drove Jordan away. Wasn't Hennessy just like her mother, hadn't she always known she was like her? Wasn't that why she had carved those memories free of Jordan, to see what she'd have been like without her?

But it didn't sound as compelling as before.

Her mind was shouting new refrains: Hennessy had painted the most powerful sweetmetal Boudicca had in Boston. Hennessy could paint them again. Hennessy could paint energy into art, magic into art. Hennessy could lure the *something more* that normally was reserved for dream magic into her pigments.

Hennessy was powerful even without her dreams.

These are lies you tell yourself to distract yourself from the coming disaster, the Lace said, but it was a weak parry, done on the fly. It couldn't pierce Hennessy's soaring realization: Awake, she was as powerful as Ronan had been asleep. In control. Wielder of magic. Knower of secrets. Creator of things that hadn't existed before.

And deep down, she knew that Carmen Farooq-Lane liked her.

"Let's stop dancing," Hennessy shouted to the Lace. Her voice was loud now, the loudest thing in her own dream.

The Lace moved slowly and intricately on the horizon, but it came no nearer.

"All you do is attack me—that's your only trick, isn't it? You do what you always do; I do what I always do. It's a deal, right? So let's do it!"

She began to walk toward the Lace. The ground was littered with broken-off bits of Lace that glinted like paper-thin razors. It cut her clothing and legs, but she kept going.

In fact, she started to run.

The Lace told her to come no closer. It loathed her. She was meaningless. Powerless.

"Then why do you care if I'm here? Why do you keep coming to me? Who needs who?"

I will make you do what I say, I will kill what you love, I have it in my possession now, I am ready to—

She ran right up to the edge of the Lace.

Fixed in place, it seethed and grew in its strange, dreamy way.

She knew from experience that if it reached toward her, it would pierce her one thousand times, and pain would explode through her.

But that was all it was. Pain. Right? If it could not make her mind feel any worse, it was just physical pain.

She threw herself at the Lace.

There was no pain.

The Lace howled and quivered, but it didn't stab her. It was like a needled hook that only hurt when you tugged against it, or shark skin, abrasive when you rubbed it against the grain, smooth with it.

Hennessy found she was inside the entity. The lacy shapes fell all over her, and now, from this perspective, she could see they were exactly the same shadows cast by the lights in her mother's old London studio. In here, as it muttered to itself, she could hear that the Lace's deep voice was actually just her own voice. It was using her thoughts against her. All its weapons were just her weapons.

They had been very effective weapons for a very long time.

It was then she noticed there was someone else here, backlit with the same bright light that pierced the Lace itself.

She shielded her eye against the bright glow.

He was curled up, his hands twisted behind him to pull his tattooed neck closer to his knees, as if he could make himself smaller still. His back was to her. But even without seeing his face, she would have recognized him anywhere.

33

Was he awake or was he dreaming?
Was he awake or was he dreaming?
Was he awake or was he dreaming?
Was he awake or was he dreaming?
Was he awake or was he dreaming?
Was he awake or was he dreaming?
Was he awake or was he dreaming?
Was he awake or was he dreaming?
Was he awake or was he dreaming?
Was he awake or was he dreaming?
Was he awake or was he dreaming?
Was he awake or was he dreaming?
Was he awake or was he dreaming?
Was he awake or was he dreaming?
Was he awake or was he dreaming?
Was he awake or was he dreaming?
Was he awake or was he dreaming?
Was he awake or was he dreaming?
Was he awake or was he dreaming?
Was he awake or was he dreaming?
Was he awake or was he dreaming?
Was he awake or was he dreaming?
Was he awake or was he dreaming?

Was he awake or was he dreaming?
Was he awake or was he dreaming?
Was he awake or was he dreaming?
Was he awake or was he dreaming?
Was he awake or was he dreaming?
Was he awake or was he dreaming?
Was he awake or was he dreaming?
Was he awake or was he dreaming?
Was he awake or was he dreaming?
Was he awake or was he dreaming?
Was he awake or was he dreaming?
Was he awake or was he dreaming?
Was he awake or was he dreaming?
Was he awake or was he dreaming?
Was he awake or was he dreaming?
Was he awake or was he dreaming?
Was he awake or was he dreaming?
Was he awake or was he dreaming?
Was he awake or was he dreaming?
Was he awake or was he dreaming?
Was he awake or was he dreaming?
Was he awake or was he dreaming?
Was he awake or was he dreaming?
Was he awake or was he dreaming?
Was he awake or was he dreaming?
Was he awake or was he dreaming?
Was he awake or was he dreaming?
Was he awake or was he dreaming?
Was he awake or was he dreaming?
Was he awake or was he dreaming?
Was he awake or was he dreaming?

Was he awake or was he dreaming?

Was he awake or was he dreaming?

Was he awake or was he dreaming?

Was he awake or was he dreaming?

Was he awake or was he dreaming?

Was he awake or was he dreaming?

"Ronan Lynch," Hennessy said. "We need to talk."

34

Hennessy was watching a memory.

A man who looked very much like Ronan was asleep in an idyllic bedroom. Almost everything in the room was either dark brown or pure white. White comforter on the bed. Dark curls on the pillow. White linen curtains fluttering in the bright morning. Dark floorboards patterned with morning sun. White knotted rug covering the scarred floor by the bed. Dark suitcase sitting upon it.

Only the bed was a riot of color. The sleeping man was smeared with blood and covered with tiny star-shaped blue flowers. Handfuls of petals, tinged with more blood, were scattered on the floor. It was a strange sight because it seemed like a scene that should be hidden, and yet it was bright morning.

Ronan himself stood in a square cast by the window, his face glowing in the sun, watching the man sleep. He was younger than Hennessy had ever seen him, and at first, she did not recognize him with his long hair, his fuller cheeks. But then his expression honed and Hennessy saw the man he would become.

Niall's eyes opened. The light from the window made his skin incandescent. The both of them looked like angels.

"I was just dreaming of the day you were born, Ronan," Niall said to his son.

He wiped the blood from his forehead to show his son there was no wound beneath it. He was not wearing a wedding ring.

Ronan seemed about to say something, but then he changed his mind and said something else instead: "I know where the money comes from."

Niall looked at his son with such tenderness that Hennessy felt anger automatically rise in her. It was still hard for her to watch love like that, especially from a parent. He said, "Don't tell anyone."

Outside the window, the Lace moved restlessly, and Hennessy realized there was a second Ronan, the Ronan she had come to know, curled on the floor at the end of the bed. Checkered shapes fell over the top of this Ronan, though, because this Ronan, the real Ronan, was in the shadow of the Lace.

She wasn't really in a memory. She was in a dream.

She'd done it.

She'd changed her dream from the one she always had. Before this, Bryde and Ronan had needed to force her dreams into something else. They'd tried so hard to teach her tricks and techniques to mold her subconscious.

In the end, it was so easy. Not so different from painting over a canvas.

Hennessy walked across the Lace-checkered floorboards to stand directly in front of adult Ronan.

"Hey, bruv," she said, to try to lighten the atmosphere. "Want to talk about it?"

He did not lift his head. He sat there, still and dark. He sat there for so long that he started to get terrifying. He appeared less and less human the more she looked at him, until she started to wonder why she had ever thought it looked like Ronan Lynch to her at all.

She psyched herself up to bravery, and she touched his shoulder.

He screamed.

She jumped back with the suddenness of it.

He kept screaming.

Lifting his head, he screamed and screamed and screamed. Tears were streaming down his face, and his voice was hoarse, but he didn't stop. The whole dreamspace was filled with the sound. It escalated until the light and the shadows pulsed with it. The misery and desperation flooded up through the jagged roots of the Lace and made it big and strong.

Ronan kept screaming. He didn't take a breath. In a dream, you could scream forever without needing one.

Hennessy didn't know what to do.

She could wake herself up, she thought. There was no ley line; there was no danger of her bringing anything back from here to the waking world. Ronan's physical body was asleep somewhere, presumably unable to wake without the ley line. He wasn't in danger of bringing anything back, either.

She could just leave him here. Screaming. It was obvious he could not take it, but there was no way for him to stop taking it. This was his existence now.

Seeing him reminded her of a day not very long ago when they'd driven to the server farm to destroy it. Bryde had been trapped. Caught by the sound that seemed made to horrify him, he'd silently screamed until the server farm was destroyed, unable to remove or protect himself. In a way, she thought, Ronan had been screaming since she'd met him. She just hadn't been able to hear it, since she'd been screaming, too.

Did it matter? What did they owe each other?

There was so much that had gone down between them. Ronan had lied to her and himself about Bryde. She'd tricked him and shut down the ley line. He was supposed to have all the answers; she was supposed to be less fucked up. She didn't have the language for this.

He was still screaming. It was incredible how it never grew less raw, the pain refreshing over and over, never decaying.

Ronan himself had begun to transform with a kind of lace, all wires and thorns and talons. It covered his skin. It was inside him, bursting out, not the other way around. She'd fed her Lace where she could see it. He had buried his inside.

Ronan Lynch was becoming a jagged, shaggy horror of a thing. She could feel the same wordless dread that the Lace invoked rising up in her.

Hennessy hugged him.

She didn't even know where the impulse came from. She was not a sentimental hugger. She had not been hugged as a child, unless the hug was being emotionally weaponized for later. And Ronan Lynch did not seem like the sort of person who would care about getting a hug. Giving someone care and receiving it were two unrelated actions.

At first it did not seem to do anything.

Ronan kept screaming. The hug had not made him appear more human. He seemed more like Bryde than ever—and not Bryde when he was his most man-shaped. He just seemed like a dream entity that hated everything.

"Ronan Lynch, you asshole," Hennessy said.

Once, he had hugged her. At the time, she had thought it didn't help, but she'd been wrong.

So she held on now, and kept holding on, though he became even less recognizable as Ronan Lynch for a little bit. Then, after a while, the scream gave way to quiet.

She could feel his body quivering. Like a pencil sketch, it conveyed misery with the smallest of gestures.

And then there was nothing at all, just stillness.

Finally, she realized he was hugging her, too, tightly.

There was a strange sort of magic to being a person holding another person after not being held by someone for a long time. There was another strange sort of magic to understanding you'd been using words and silence the wrong way for a long time.

Finally, Ronan said, "You aren't dreaming the Lace."

Hennessy said, "I got tired of it. Are you going to wake up?"

He looked as grim as she'd ever seen him. "I can't on my own."

"Why not? Are you a dream?"

"I don't know what I am anymore. I thought I did. I know fuck all." There was no bluster. No razor hidden in his words. It was just raw truth, nothing protecting him.

They didn't say sorry. They didn't have to.

After a pause, Ronan said, "They're all dead. Nathan's going to kill the rest. I can't wake up. I don't have anything left. This is all there is to me now."

Hennessy stepped back from him. He looked once more like the dreamer she'd met, the one she'd thought might have all the answers. Her first true friend who didn't share a face with her. She asked, "If I told you I was going to help you get out of this, Ronan Lynch, would you believe me?"

"You're one of the very few people I would."

35

The night after Mór had confessed her true nature to Niall, the two of them put Declan to bed and went outside to dream together in the fields, like they used to do back in Ireland.

They dreamt of the thing in the Forest.

The Forest explained that their dreaming was like a request to the other place, the place where the Forest had its roots. That was where the ability to take dreams into the waking world came from. The farther a dreamer had their hands stretched toward that other place, the easier it would be to bring dreams back when they woke. It was making the two places one place, like a tree connecting the earth and the sky. Roots stretching toward the air, branches turning into the dirt. A dreamer could be like that. Dug in deeper. But in order to do that—

"I know what you want," Mór told the Forest.

Niall could feel the thing in the Forest reply in the way it always did. In images, in feelings, in sensations beyond waking human ones. He could imagine a tree, branches and roots both visible. The branches longed to see what was buried beneath the dirt and the roots longed to investigate the sun. Mór was one of these seekers. The thing in the Forest was another one. They both longed for more from the other side. They were so hungry.

Niall just wanted to be human, he just wanted it all to be easy, to be happy—

"Why do you want to leave where you come from?" Niall asked.

More.

He saw this desire echoed in Mór's face.

And so they dreamt, the three of them all together—Mór, Niall, and the thing in the Forest. What did they dream? *Greywaren.* Like *forest*, it was just a name for something beyond understanding.

It looked like a child, just a little younger than Declan.

The dream's form was Mór's contribution. With her precise way of dreaming, she imagined it down to every detail. Its features looked just like Niall's toddler photos. A human toddler. The least threatening thing in the world, a young human with bright blue eyes like Niall's.

Except that they were too bright, too precise, these eyes. They reminded Niall of the night before, when Mór had said she didn't feel feelings the same way as anyone else. That seemed like a terrible idea, to give the thing in the Forest a shape that wouldn't feel bad if its family died.

So Niall's contribution was feelings.

Feelings, feelings, so many feelings, as many as he could think of, and all the ways one could possibly show them. He poured feelings into the kid in the dream, as big as he could think of, love and hate and fear and excitement.

And the thing in the Forest—the thing that had been dwelling in that Forest, all the farther it could get from that other place it was originally from—poured itself into the child. As it stretched into the child like roots, like talons, like vines, like veins, like twisting roads through a midnight forest, it shivered with newfound fear as it felt the peculiar sensation of its experience shrinking and growing to fit its new home. There were many things the entity in the Forest could imagine and remember that a human toddler's brain couldn't manage, and they mostly had to go. And there were many things a human toddler, especially one full of feelings, possessed that the Forest had never imagined.

This was a terrifying experience for all involved.

All three of them felt sure this was the only time this had ever been done before.

None of them thought for a moment they were part of a pattern, a cycle, of longing and manifesting and destruction, longing and manifesting and destruction. None of them wondered why the word *Greywaren* already existed before that night.

When Niall and Mór woke in the field, the grass around them was thick with ravens and blue petals, and the air stank of iron. When Niall finally got his sense of movement back and stood, his feet sank into the mud and blood squelched around his boots. The ground was soaked with it.

Mór stood up opposite him. Clinging to her slacks was a blue-eyed toddler, smeared with blood and petals. The last of the dream entity's wisdom was fading from its eyes as waking life set in. All that was left was the longing and the feelings.

She pulled its fingers free from her slacks to look at it.

It began to cry.

She just kept looking at it. Was it her dream? Was it his? Was it the Forest's?

Niall's heart was howling in terror, but he knelt and held out one hand, and then, when that did nothing, the other. The child hesitated before stumbling to him. The two of them were covered with the still-warm blood and the little bright flowers. The birds in the nearby trees were making a huge commotion, shouting or laughing. The moment felt substantial to Niall and Mór. Otherworldly. They had always done magic, but it hadn't felt like magic for a very long time. And certainly it had never felt like this. This had changed something. For them. For the world. For that other world.

"Greywaren," said Mór.

Niall looked into its blue eyes, at the anguished shape of its mouth. Inside this body was the thing that used to be the thing in the Forest. It seemed very, very important that it feel human.

"No," Niall corrected her, holding it tightly despite everything. Warmly, despite everything. It seemed very, very important that it feel loved, too. "Ronan."

36

Declan Lynch was alive.

He was alive, but resenting it.

He hurt in every way imaginable. His head was resonant with pain. His shoulders were seized and twisted. His stomach growled with hunger. And his side roared with a throbbing heat that radiated every time he breathed.

Light played off the ceiling overhead. The air had the mildew scent of an old building. Somewhere, a piano was playing. It had the imperfect sound of a real piano, not a recording.

He worked up the nerve to turn his head; even this sent a shiver of pain through him. His imagination was awash with the image of a bead of pigment dropped in a glass of water, billowing out as it expanded to color the entire glass: That was his pain.

Breathing unevenly, he got his bearings.

He was in a spacious, shabby apartment. Outside the large window, downtown shop facades were visible. He recognized the partially visible word on the old sign jutting from the building he was in: PIANOS. Someone had situated him on a striped sofa with a pillow and blanket, as if he had caught a cold, not a bullet. He would have doubted his memory of everything that had happened at the Fairy Market except that when he lifted the blanket and the T-shirt (which was not his), he saw a very neat, professional dressing on his side, and a bedpan next to the sofa. He had no memory of anything since being shot. Actually, he wasn't certain he could remember that properly, either. Adrenaline had erased everything but the moment of Ronan's sundogs flashing free.

He felt for his phone. It was gone. Wallet, too.

Declan closed his eyes again.

"Hey, boyo, how are you feeling?" a soft voice said. Declan knew it so well, this voice, the cadence of it, the accent, the nickname.

It provoked a different sort of pain.

Declan opened his eyes. The face that looked back at him was a face that looked a lot like Ronan's, except surrounded by long hair, and a lot like his dead father Niall's, except twenty years younger. It was the new Fenian, a dreamt copy of his father as a young man. Unchanged, unaging.

"You seem to be doing all right in the healing-up department," the new Fenian continued, "all things considered."

Declan licked his lips. They felt dry as a floor mat. He put a hand down and pushed, testing his ability to sit up.

No. His body wouldn't lift him, not a bit. His side howled and failed.

The new Fenian said, "You should appreciate your mother did a fine job of shooting you. All soft tissue, not a bit of guts or stomach or liver, the things you really don't want messed with. And the blood loss wasn't bad, considering the size of the hole. Look at you sweating bullets from the pain. You'll be wanting some painkillers."

Declan's stomach rumbled audibly.

"Or a sandwich."

"No meds," Declan said. "I want my mind."

The new Fenian laughed, a short, sharp bark that brought

back a wave of memories of Niall's surprised laugh. "You've been drugged off your head for days, boyo—why stop now?"

As the piano rambled into yet another sonata, Declan started to rub his hand over his face. Then he put his other hand on his face, too, blocking out the light. Normally, after a setback, he would have come up with another strategy, another coping mechanism, another life restructure that was just a little shittier than the one before. And it seemed as if getting at least one good thing—being happy with Jordan—should have made him more resilient. But instead, it was the opposite. Whether it was the taste of the good life or the muzziness of the drugs and injury or the grief of losing Matthew or the impossibility of saving Ronan from the nightwash, he found himself completely floored. He could not sit; he did not really want to. He wanted to go back into nothingness and never return.

"Come on now, Declan," the new Fenian said, "let me get you something. It hurts me to see you like this. Let's get a look at the sunshine, maybe."

He dragged Declan up to sitting and stuffed a pillow behind his back, a well-meaning move that sent pain winging, soaring, flapping through Declan's body. A sound of agony escaped him; he was mortified.

"Declan," the new Fenian said regretfully. He put his hand on Declan's temple, just as Niall would have in his youth. If Declan closed his eyes, he could imagine it was his father. But it *wasn't* his father. It was a man made with the Niall Lynch template, a man who'd lived another life. The last time Declan had seen the new Fenian was while tracking down Mór Ó Corra, trying to find out if she felt any more like family than his actual family had. Then, as now, the new Fenian had had a tidy bag with him, one that he'd never put down. Declan saw that it was still directly next to the chair the new Fenian had pulled up to the couch. He wondered what was in it. Weapons, perhaps. Money. What else could be precious? He could not think of any other options now.

"Do you have a name?" Declan asked. "Not the new Fenian. A real name."

The new Fenian smiled. "One for everyone I meet. Would you like to give me one, too?"

"I know his real name," said a voice from the doorway. "But it's not for you."

It was Mór Ó Corra. In the flesh.

Previous glimpses of her had in no way prepared him for this: a woman with Aurora Lynch's body stalking across the room toward him, wary and muscled, the product of a very different life than Aurora's. Her eyes were bright as a predator's, shocking in the face of Aurora, the gentle woman who'd raised him as her son. She had less of an Irish accent than Aurora, but that, at least, made sense—Mór had been living out and about in the world more than the cloned dream his father had made for himself.

She handed him a glass of water. "Do you know who I am?"

He drank the entire glass and wished for more. He did not think the new Fenian was practiced in tending to gunshot victims. He wasn't sure if that made him feel better or worse. "Mór Ó Corra. My birth mother."

"Good," she said, although it was unclear which part of it she thought was good. She studied him. "And you are Declan Lynch, Niall Lynch's son. It was quite something to watch you fire through the hotel. I did not think you were that sort of person."

"Is that why you saved me?"

"I don't know," she said. "I don't know why I did. I am very interested in all of you. You. Your brothers. You are like a show I can't stop watching."

"And you didn't want me to go off air." Declan hadn't meant for his voice to sound bitter, but it did. He was the only rerun still playing. It should have been Matthew she saved. Ronan. "Did it burn? The hotel. Did they burn it?"

She raised an eyebrow. "Of course. But the prisoners didn't burn, thanks to you."

Declan shook his head. He wasn't intending to be a hero. "Why didn't you just kill me? I could have been dead all this time and you wouldn't have known any better. And this must cost you something. You must be in trouble."

"Not yet," she said. "As far as Boudicca knows, you died. And you'll have to stay dead for a while, until he and I sort some things out. They are not pleased with me at the moment because I am useless to them, so they are already looking for reasons to take the new Fenian's sweetmetal from him."

Of course. The new Fenian would have to have one. Niall, his dreamer, was dead. A sweetmetal was a good leash to keep Mór obedient.

Well, mostly obedient.

"Can you call someone for me?" Declan asked. He was not stupid enough to ask for his phone. "She'll have heard."

Mór said, "If they find out I have disobeyed, then it will be very painful for me. They'll make me kill you again, for real, and take my time with it, if I want to keep the new Fenian. And of course you know who I'd choose between the two of you."

He looked at her to see if she'd meant for this statement to be hurtful. It did not seem so. It was just fact: *You are not important to me. He is. Of course you know who I'd choose between the two of you.*

Declan refused to let this sting; it wasn't new information. She'd *been* choosing a life without him for years. "She won't tell. She has all my secrets."

Mór frowned over at the new Fenian, who replied in a low voice, "The forger."

She nodded once, quickly, and he took out his phone and placed a call. After a moment, he lowered it. "Perhaps she won't pick up an unknown number."

She would. She would, especially if she knew Declan had been at the hotel when a gunfight broke out.

But she wouldn't if she was asleep.

Waves of nausea rose in him. He wasn't sure if it was the pain, or the stimulation of the visit, or just remembering everything that was waiting for him outside this apartment. Everything that *wasn't.*

Mór peered at him with that bright, intent look of hers. "Are you upset about it? About how things are between us? You and me?"

He hadn't expected her to simply ask. Of course he was upset about it. He would never stop being upset about it. Why? Why? Why? He had been just a child. Mothers were meant to love unconditionally. Fathers were meant to know best. He'd been denied both. But he said blandly, "I'm curious about it. I remember you leaving."

"You remember? You were very young."

"I have a good memory. Are you upset about it? Did it bother you to leave?"

Her voice was vague. "I don't remember."

This felt like quite a lie to deliver with a straight face. "You don't remember if it bothered you to leave your son?"

"I don't have a good memory," she said.

"Did you know my father replaced you with another woman who looked like you?"

She frowned. "Yes, I think so. I don't remember that, either."

"You don't remember if your husband dreamt a clone of you to play house with?"

"I don't have a good memory," she said again.

"Declan—" the new Fenian started.

But Declan went on, "And then I suppose he dreamt the new Fenian for *you* to play house with?"

Mór stared at him for a long time until he realized she was actually looking through him, thinking. "He must have. The new Fenian would know."

Just then it was too much: The roller coaster of losing Matthew; failing to acquire a sweetmetal for Ronan; getting shot, finding out he still had to live; being trapped here, in pain; spending all that time to track down his biological mother only to find out he didn't matter enough for her to remember the details.

He turned his face toward the back of the couch and closed his eyes so that she wouldn't see the single tear that ran out of his eye into his shoulder. He just stayed there like that until he heard her footsteps take her out of the room and then heard the new Fenian scoot his chair even closer to the couch.

The new Fenian said, "I told you before I didn't think meeting her was what you were after, didn't I? She's not easy. This world's not easy. You have to understand that she cares; it just doesn't look like what you would think."

Declan didn't answer.

Reaching down, the new Fenian pulled his bag into his lap. It was worn from years of handling. He patted it with those long hands that were identical to Niall's, to Ronan's. "Have you heard in all your prodding what it is I do for Boudicca?"

Declan shook his head.

The new Fenian pressed his fingers on the bag's clasp. "This bag's full of memories, Declan, that I've pulled from people's heads. Things that make them feel bad. That keep them looking back at the past instead of moving forward."

He watched Declan's face closely, searching for disbelief, but Declan did not have the luxury of disbelief in these matters.

"The first memories I put in this bag were Mór's. The next were your father's. She wasn't lying about not remembering. They both gave a lot away."

Declan pressed his fingers lightly into his side as it began to throb again. He felt very ordinary and human in this world of dreams and dreamers. "I don't even know if I care enough to ask why."

"Ah, Declan," the new Fenian said. "Telling yourself that won't make caring hurt less."

"Why doesn't she put them back in her head, then?"

The new Fenian opened the bag. It was full of strings as shiny as instrument strings but soft as hair. He picked one after another, thumb and forefinger, showing them to Declan before dropping them back inside. "Memories in the bag can only be experienced by someone new; those are the rules. I don't know why. People who give them to me usually leave them in their wills or use them for mediation, but that's not why Niall and Mór asked me to keep theirs."

Declan felt light-headed and insubstantial. The real world seemed far removed from this piano-murmuring apartment with his birth mother and a man with a bag of memories.

"They asked me to keep them because they thought, we thought . . ." The new Fenian trailed off. "Well, I guess I always hoped you might have them."

37

Ronan.
Ronan.
Ronan.

In the weeks and months after, both Niall and Mór did their best to keep calling the uncanny child by name, because the situation did not seem survivable if they could not begin to think of him as human.

Since that night, their dreams had changed.

Their dreams had become *bigger*.

They were more productive. Niall was more readily able to concentrate on what he wanted, which meant fewer peculiar dream appliances that did no job well. Mór was able to dream her precise dreams far more often.

Their dreams were also more porous.

Now when they slept, Niall and Mór felt connected to something even beyond the Forest, clear on to the other side, where its roots were. They kept seeing images of what it must be like there. Visions of things they couldn't fathom. Visions of a world that felt completely unlike theirs. It wasn't that it was like an alien planet, because even that was too concrete. This world was unfathomable, designed for senses they did not have.

Sometimes, even worse, Niall and Mór dreamt visions that seemed like they must be premonitions, because it seemed like they were looking at their own world, but after everything from the other side had broken through and transformed it. Everything was music and rain and tree roots and ocean, and it was so beautiful that neither Mór nor Niall could stop screaming.

The dreams were only like this if they dreamt near the Greywaren. The child. The conduit, one hand reaching into their world, one hand grasping back at where he had come from.

Ronan, they reminded themselves.

Ronan.

Ronan.

It felt like they should get more comfortable with him, but instead the terror grew.

One afternoon a few months after they manifested the child, he woke up from a nap surrounded by little star-shaped flowers that had not been there a few minutes before.

The thing in the Forest had been a dreamer, too, on the other side of all this.

And it was now a dreamer again.

It had not occurred to them that their talent might be mirrored on the other side, or that when the thing in the Forest got legs over here, it might bring this skill with it.

Their own subconsciouses were already odd enough. Imagine its dreams once it got older. Once it remembered. If it remembered.

If *he* remembered.

Ronan, they reminded themselves.

Ronan.

Ronan.

That night, Mór whispered to Niall, "We should kill it before it's too late."

"You'll lose the power you have now," he replied.

"The power's not worth it," she said. "What we had before was enough."

Niall was filled with such a rush of relief.

The relief was not that she'd suggested violence, but because Niall realized that she *did* love him. He didn't know why he hadn't realized it before, that it didn't matter if she felt love the same way. Love, for her, was her confession to him that she *didn't* feel it the same way, that she'd trusted him enough with this truth about herself. Love was that she wanted him to know her truly, rather than love a version of herself that she simply wore for him. That love might not ever look like the love he gave to her, but it didn't change what it was.

"Do we have to kill him, though?" he asked. "Can we just send him away somewhere? Give him up?"

"It's too much power," she replied. "Can you imagine if another dreamer found it and they were evil? What if someone wanted to dream a nuclear bomb? Can you imagine if *it* wants to dream a nuclear bomb?"

When she put it that way, the situation seemed obvious. Because Niall's dreams were so fanciful and undirected, the idea had never occurred to him how, in a different brain, such a power might be a danger to society. Ronan was not just a manifestation of an ancient thing that used to be a forest. Ronan could also be either a weapon or a weapon-wielder.

It seemed horrid but necessary to do something about it before it got bigger.

But when they went into the room where Ronan slept, they discovered the child wasn't alone.

Declan was there. He was curled just next to Ronan, an arm draped over his side. They thought he was sleeping, but when

Niall's foot set off a floorboard's squeal, his eyes came straight open. He looked at his parents so directly that they squirmed, consciences guilty. But of course Declan didn't know—that was simply his ordinary expression, even as a little kid.

"He was lonely," Declan explained.

"How do you know?" Niall asked.

Declan carefully moved away from the child to join his parents. "He was crying."

Niall put his hand in Declan's curls, trying to sound light, unfettered. "I didn't hear anything."

Declan's voice was somewhat haughty. "He was very quiet about it."

Niall and Mór fidgeted. Finally, they sent Declan back to his own room and stayed there for a long while, saying nothing. Debating.

Love had changed the situation. Niall didn't yet love the strange, dangerous child, but he loved Declan, and Declan loved Ronan.

So Ronan lived.

And the Barns became rich.

Money gets used differently on a farm, where it isn't seen by anyone else, where it's not for status, but still, you can tell when a farm has fat after a long time of lean. Three-board fences become four-board fences, and they get painted. Roofs have sharp, neat edges. Feed rooms have mice, because the mice have bags of grain to worry away at. The herds grow because calves don't have to get sold straightaway. Decorative ducks, potbelly pigs, dogs appear—animals that don't have to do jobs are allowed. Inside the farmhouse, the furniture gets more comfortable and more handsome. The appliances get newer. Tiles and fixtures get more exotic, shipped from farther away, chosen for aesthetics, not for price point.

Ordinarily, when a farm gets very rich, more people arrive, too, so that the owners of the farm can travel and leave the farm in qualified hands. But most farms were not secret, as the Barns was, filled as it was with discarded dream things, so it at first swelled to match the farms of Niall's youthful imaginings and then shrank again as they sold the animals that could not be left for a few days and replaced them with dreamt versions that could.

And traveling was a must, if the Lynch family was to stay together. Mór often traveled for her work with Boudicca. She said it was to research what they might want to sell, to expose herself to other exotic trinkets to get ideas for exotic trinkets she might dream. This was not true. Boudicca just wanted her to keep dreaming her dreams with secret pain for them, and she already knew everything she needed for that.

But—

Ronan.

Ronan.

Ronan.

That was the real reason Mór traveled. As Declan and Ronan grew, Niall fell for both boys. Completely, thoroughly, in a way that he couldn't imagine ever loving anyone else, not even Mór. They were his sons, he was their father, they were a family. He was making them in his image, and they loved him for it.

And Mór loved Declan. But she could never love Ronan.

She could never see Ronan as a boy.

He was always *it*: the Greywaren.

And she could not bear dreaming of the other side so

completely anymore. Sometimes she thought it was asking for yet another Greywaren. Another, another, another.

A world completely mingled to unrecognizable chaos.

One summer afternoon, Niall watched Mór pack the car for yet another trip, although she had only just come back.

"I have to go," she told him.

It was a thorough sort of statement. Niall knew at once what it meant.

"But Declan," he began.

"I can't stand it," she said. "It's driving me mad. I'll hang myself. What if we do it again?"

"We won't," Niall said.

"What if *it* makes us?"

Niall looked off over the yard to where Declan and Ronan were sitting in the grass. Declan pretended to not be anywhere near laughter as Ronan flapped dandelion heads at him while making an outrageous face. "He's just a boy now. He's just an ordinary little boy."

Mór said, "It woke up with a duckling last night. It dreams living dreams, too, now? I wrung its neck."

"I dreamt a duckling once," Niall said. "Are you after wringing my neck, too?"

She waved this away. "It could dream an army. It could dream more Greywarens."

"He's just a boy," Niall said. "He doesn't remember any of that. He only knows what we tell him."

"Even if it stays that way, if Boudicca found out it existed . . ." Mór shook her head. "They would use it. They'd use it until they couldn't think of any more ways to use it, and destroy the world to boot. They don't know how to handle that sort of power. It was a mistake. It was such a mistake, but it's too late now."

She knew that when it came to brass tacks, Niall would sooner watch her leave than cut Ronan's throat so they could go back to the way it was.

Which meant it was over, the grand experiment in paradise. Niall said, "You'll miss me."

Mór just looked at him. It was not a disagreement. "I could take Declan, if it was easier."

Niall shook his head. She didn't argue with this, either. He said, "I'll miss you."

Mór glanced at Ronan, her expression full of disgust and dread. "The Forest will help us make this parting easier. If you're going to keep *that* alive, the Forest, the other side, they can make it worth it. We don't have to miss each other, you know. We don't really even have to know."

Because Niall knew both her and the dreaming, he could already imagine what she was thinking. A Niall to go off with Mór. A Mór to stay here with Niall. Perhaps a bag to keep their old memories in, so that they never did it (manifest a god, fall in love) ever again.

"It won't be real," Niall said, but his heart was breaking so hard that he knew he would do whatever she wanted.

"Haven't you seen? We dream reality," Mór said. "We make reality."

At some point during this, Ronan had joined them, and now he clung to Niall's leg. When Mór looked at him, he hid his face in Niall's jeans. She'd smacked him over the duckling, and he hadn't yet forgiven her.

Niall softly laid his hand on Ronan's head.

He looked over at Declan to see if he was close enough to hear, but he was picking up strewn-about dandelion stems in order to lay them in a neat row.

So it was decided.

Later, the Forest did what they asked. Not what they asked with words, but rather with thoughts. Niall had to be the dreamer, in the end, because he was better at living dreams, but Mór came along to the dream to make her intentions clear. Mór asked the Forest to help Niall make a copy of her, but softer, so that Niall could finally feel loved. And Niall asked the Forest to make a copy of him, but younger, so that it looked more like he had when Mór had run away with him.

And the Forest gave them a bag to discard their memories in, anything they chose.

Niall's first memory in the bag was the day Declan was born, because it had been such a happy time he thought he would die if he had to remember it.

That was not the first memory Mór put in the bag, but she got there eventually.

Here was where she started:

Ronan.

Ronan.

Ronan.

38

I thought he preferred Ronan," Declan said.

It was the most ridiculous thing to say.

It was the most meaningless of takeaways.

But out it came.

Declan and the new Fenian were situated just as they had been when they'd begun this: the new Fenian on the wooden chair he'd pulled up, Declan on the couch, memories tied up and down his fingers. The new Fenian had sorted through the bright strings with supernatural skill, finding just the ones he'd wanted. Then he'd carefully tied them onto Declan in chronological order, from the day his mother had arrived at the Barns with Declan until the day she'd left the Barns without him.

Niall had stayed, always choosing Declan, a life with Declan beside him as much as possible. A life with Ronan, because Declan had cared for him when no one else yet did.

It had only taken minutes to experience the memories, but it had felt like years. Dream logic. Dream time.

Declan wasn't the same person he'd been on the other side of it.

His father had loved him, adored him, favored him. Given up everything for him.

"You had to know you were the favorite," the new Fenian said. "Didn't I—he take you everywhere with him that he could?"

"He fussed over Ronan all the time." Ronan was just like him,

Niall was always saying, the spitting image. But now Declan's eyebrows pinched together in confusion, trying to reroute his own memories. Because Ronan *was* the spitting image of Niall. He had been made so. "Everything Ronan did was impressive and wonderful; he remembered everything Ronan said and wanted."

"It was important for Ronan to know he was just as loved as you," the new Fenian said. "The consequences of something like that feeling wronged . . . It was important he be raised a son, not a monster or a pet."

But the problem was that Ronan *had* ended up feeling like a monster or a pet, Declan thought. And he *had* turned out to be dangerous to the world, and to himself. A lifetime of being raised as a human and then told, upon adulthood, that no, being human was not going to work out for him. Back to the Barns to wait for the others to come and throw a bone.

"I don't blame him," Declan said, but he didn't mean Niall.

"You can't blame Mór, either," the new Fenian said anxiously. "She did love you. It wasn't easy. If you'd been there, you would have—"

"I don't blame her, either," Declan interrupted. "I don't judge her. Easy to stand back from the end of the tragedy and say how it could have been done differently. She did her best." He kept going, less because he thought the new Fenian needed to hear it and more because he needed to hear himself saying it. "I've seen the sorts of things she's seen. I know what it's like, being afraid all the time. Holding back a tide no one else knows exists. No one can judge her. She's who I . . . she's the kind of person I wanted to find when I went looking for her."

The new Fenian's face was slightly turned away. Mór was standing in the doorway.

"Did you know I was here when you said that?" she asked, but she already knew the answer.

It was difficult to tell what she was thinking. She wasn't like Aurora. Soft Aurora, easy to read, easy to understand.

"I couldn't get rid of all my memories of you," Mór said. "It would have taken too many years out of my head and been too confusing when I tried to piece my life together. So I remember you, a little. You were always practical. Even when you were little. Fair." She paused, dredging through her checkered, lacy memories. "Dauntless."

Declan realized she'd been expecting him to be angry. Betrayed. To hate her and to judge her. And he had been and done all those things, before he saw her story. But that had dissipated now. He'd loved dreams and dreamers, too. Mór hadn't been wrong about how dangerous dreamers could be. She hadn't necessarily been right about how to handle it, either, but that was because there wasn't a right or wrong. Long before any of them were born, the planet had already been made up of both dreams and non-dreams, and what was good for one wasn't necessarily good for the other.

"Where is the Greywaren now?" Mór asked.

"Dying," Declan said. "Ronan needs a sweetmetal, and I was trying to get him one."

Mór Ó Corra turned to look out the window, and when she did, she looked just like the portrait that Niall had dreamt of her, *The Dark Lady*. The jutted chin. The hands on the hips. The defiant stance.

She was the sort of woman Declan would have wanted his father to fall in love with.

She *was* the woman his father had fallen in love with.

All this time, the biggest lie Declan had told himself was that he hated his father.

What he'd really meant, every time he thought it, every single day, was: *I miss him.*

Mór Ó Corra jerked her chin at Declan. "Get him packaged up best you can. Pack everything you can, but no more than three bags. Be ready to move fast."

"What are you up to?" the new Fenian asked.

"I stole the ink from Boudicca during the shoot-out," Mór said. "I was getting it for you, love, but you're going to have to wait."

39

Test the untested blade.. Will it cut.. That is the only question.. Can it be made to cut.. If it cuts me then I will be remade in a better form.. Truer form.. Less noise.. Better able to think.. Less unwinding.. I corrupt as I age or the world corrupts.. Need to start over.. Hate it.. Will she learn to cut.. Or will she have to leave the drawer.. Either way this blade will get remade remade remade.. The drawer tipped over.. Only sharp blades from now on.. I think she can do it.. I don't want [illegible]

—NATHAN FAROOQ-LANE,
The Open Edge of the Blade, final page

40

Hennessy woke up.

The basement was dark. This made sense. It was night.

Her head ached, as if the sheer distance her thoughts had gone to find Ronan Lynch had exhausted it. And before that, the Lace. And before *that*, the kiss.

She heard the scuffling of the dreamt mouse in its cage, paws against shavings. It was nocturnal, like her.

It wasn't supposed to be dark.

Slowly, this thought occurred to her. She'd gone to sleep after dark, which meant all her work lights had been on, the ones that had to be turned on by hand, not operated by the cord at the top of the stairs or the switch at the bottom. Whose hand? She could imagine neither Farooq-Lane nor Liliana coming downstairs to pull all those cords, click all those switches, turn all those knobs.

Moreover, it was silent. The power must have gone off. There was no hum. No buzz. No click. Only the organic sounds of the mouse's tail clinking against the sides of the cage. Bryde would have approved, she thought, because it sounded like humanity had died.

For a few minutes, she remained motionless, thinking about him. Thinking about sitting on a floating hoverboard with him and Ronan Lynch, looking down at the world hundreds of feet below. Thinking about him being dead. Blown to bits.

Poor bastard, she thought. *The world did get him in the end.*

She heard a door close somewhere overhead. Although it was an ordinary-enough sound, something about it immediately raised the hairs on her arms. There was something cautious about the sound, perhaps. Furtive.

Perhaps it was nothing. Perhaps the power had gone out, the rental company hadn't paid the bill. Perhaps that was Farooq-Lane or Liliana going outside to quietly conduct a phone call to resolve it.

Perhaps the Moderators had come back to gibbering awareness to kill the Hennessys they hadn't gotten the first time.

Hennessy was very awake.

She eased off the sofa cushions she'd made into a bed, careful not to make a sound on the concrete floor. She took her sword from the worktable. Then she crept up the stairs, turning her feet sideways and jamming them closest to the riser to prevent creaking.

At the top, she paused. Listened. Tightened and loosened her grip on the sword's hilt.

There was nothing to hear. Nothing to see.

The house was dark. Not just dark, but incorrectly dark, the time on the microwave extinguished, the night-light on the wall dark.

There was no sign of either Farooq-Lane or Liliana. Their coats were gone, but their luggage was here. Hennessy was beginning to feel . . . not *afraid*, because that wasn't a feeling that came easily to her. Wary. She couldn't see the whole picture here, but what she could see suggested danger. She considered calling Farooq-Lane, but the idea of lowering her guard enough to get her phone out or raising her voice enough to ask a question felt ill-advised. She'd see if the car was in the drive instead.

One, two, three strides down the back hall. When Hennessy reached for the knob, she discovered the door was already ajar. Not good. Neither Farooq-Lane nor Liliana were the sort to overlook something like that. Gripping the sword hilt tightly, keeping herself tucked behind the door as much as possible, she eased it open and took a look around.

On the threshold was a pair of open scissors, pointed directly at her.

Oh, Hennessy thought, *shit.*

A moment later, two bombs exploded.

41

They were unusual explosions.

The first was an explosion of noise.

It took place right in the heart of Boston, cater-wauling out of the Museum of Fine Arts. Years and years of sound, compressed into just a few seconds, rolled out from the visiting Klimt exhibition.

The thunderous noise flipped a display table. Reverberated paintings from the walls. Roared down temporary barriers. Keened through every living creature within earshot.

Turn that music down! You're making my ears bleed.

Sound kills from the inside out. All around the museum, things died. Scuttling mice, sleeping squirrels, and roosting pigeons dropped dead, their insides liquefied.

At the heart of this explosion was a portentous vision, but only one person was alive to experience it.

The second explosion tore through a small rental house in Lynn, not far from the water.

The bomb had been placed inside the oven. It blew off the door with enough force to propel the entire piece of metal through the kitchen table, and then convey both door and table straight through the outside wall. The other walls had already blistered into the yard and street. The kitchen tiles and light fixtures were already skybound. The ceiling shivered, the floorboards fragmented, the ductwork vaporized, the roof disintegrated.

So much energy, so little room. Out, out, out. It took less than a second for the bomb to finish the business of making space for itself and nothing else.

As the sound of the second explosion echoed away, a nightmarish premonition overtook every person in the surrounding area.

This vision followed the same progression as the others. First, they saw the explosion itself as it tore apart the Lynn house. They had a front row seat to ground zero, where a determined young woman wielded a flaming blue sword. As the bomb blew, just feet away from her, she began to swing the blade around her body like a rodeo clown doing roping tricks.

She should have died instantly.

But she did not.

The front of the sword's edge cut through the hectic debris and fire. The back trailed brilliant blue and silver and gray nightshine, which absorbed the blast.

The young woman was maintained in a circle of swirling nighttime. Darkness and midnight within. Bomb-menace and firelight without. A supernatural force field.

The house came down around her.

She kept spinning that sword.

There was something hypnotic about the steady swing of the blade, the grim smile on her face.

Then the vision moved on, as it had before, from present to future. Everyone caught in the bomb's premonition saw a burning city, a frightened population. Rippling, smoky air. The starving, never-satisfied fire whispering, *devour, devour.*

Then the vision was over, and the street in front of the MFA was quiet, and the Lynn house was completely destroyed.

Hennessy picked through the rubble until she found a flattened hamster cage. She put the sword down long enough to tug the bent wires into something less 2D and examined the contents. Miraculously, the dreamt mouse was unharmed; it had wrapped its metal-plated tail around itself like armor. It was, however, asleep, as all of Hennessy's artwork had been turned to ash.

Taking the mangled cage, she made her way to her car, which had a doorknob embedded in its side.

"Fuck me," she observed. She tossed the sword in the backseat and placed the hamster cage on the passenger seat. Then she called Farooq-Lane.

42

The fear of discovery had always been present during Declan's childhood. They were not to speak of any of the dreaming that took place at the Barns—not Ronan's, not Niall's. They were not to speak of where the money came from. They were not to speak of where Matthew had been born. They were not to have friends over to the Barns; Ronan was not to ask to sleep elsewhere.

Aurora and Niall talked plenty about magic, yes, but only in bedtime stories about gods and monsters and kings and holy men. The magic in these stories came in the form of bottomless cauldrons. Sentient sighthounds. Bloodthirsty spears. Horses with special powers. Boars with secret knowledge. Sunbeams strong enough to hang coats on.

Never boys who brought dreams to life.

Even in the most obvious circumstances, the dreaming was never spoken of out loud.

Declan could remember a day he'd been home sick, a disgusting amalgam of snot and fever, unable to sleep, unable to be awake. He was alone on the couch. Niall had been gone for weeks—where, why, no questions asked, the usual. Ronan was at the county day school; Aurora was upstairs whistling and tending to Matthew, who was still too young for school.

In the midst of the listless afternoon, the door opened to present Niall, his eyes pouched, his skin hanging with exhaustion.

He lifted Declan right off the couch into a hug. His clothing had an acrid, unpleasant odor, like he'd walked through hell to get home, but Declan endured it while Niall stroked his curls and put his knuckles against Declan's forehead to test his temperature. *Poor boyo*, he said.

Declan ragdolled on Niall's shoulder as he kicked his shoes off by the cold fireplace and tossed his car keys on the end table, only coming to when his father sagged onto the couch and put his head down. Together they lay in the sick-day nest of blankets and pillows.

Niall let out a long, shaky sigh.

Declan had not rested easy all day, but in the arms of his beloved and capricious father, he finally fell asleep.

Later, Declan had woken to find everything covered with bits of metal.

It was jewelry. Hundreds of claddagh rings, each of them featuring two hands cradling a heart, so many that they banked against the walls. Aurora had waded through them to kiss Niall's mouth and whisper, "Look at this mess, you hooligan. It will take forever to get them all up."

Upstairs, toddler Matthew had begun to gleefully shout "po-weece!"

Police. Police?

Sure enough, a squad car was inching down the Barns's winding driveway. Stopping every few feet. What did they want? No one knew, only that it was coming to the house, and the house was full of inexplicable metal. The claddagh rings posed a question, but Declan understood that the answer—*dreaming*—was secret.

Without a word, Niall vanished into the kitchen.

Aurora made a game of hiding the evidence, singing rapidly to keep the boys scooping in time to her song as she propelled clinking claddagh rings toward the hallway. Declan's illness was forgotten as he employed a saucepan to shovel rings into a garbage can. Matthew plowed rings into the ashes of the fireplace.

Outside, softly squealing brakes announced the squad car's arrival.

Aurora froze.

The downstairs was still a dragon's hoard.

Niall burst back into the room with an unfamiliar velvet bag. He said, "Out of the way, boys, out of the way. I don't know where the bottom of this thing goes."

He opened the bag so that its top formed a monster's yawning mouth, and then pointed it at the closest pile of claddagh rings.

Magic, magic.

The bag began to eat. It sucked up the pile of rings closest to him, then it sucked up the rings and ashes in the fireplace. It sucked up the rings shoved beneath the end table. It sucked up everything he pointed it at, growing no larger despite all that it ate.

Aurora warned, "Don't let it take the lamp, Niall!"

Declan understood that his father had vanished just a moment before in order to dream the bag on the spot; a secret solution to a secret problem, an ouroboros of silence eating its own tail.

When the knock came at the door, it was only animal control looking for a lost dog, and there was nothing unusual for them to see. The heroic dreamt bag had taken all the claddagh rings, and also the lamp. Later, Niall disappeared on another business trip and took the bag with him. Doubtless he sold it to the highest bidder; probably crime bosses who used it to vanish bodies. In any case, it had served its purpose.

Declan had been practicing secrecy his entire life.

He had never practiced trust.

"Declan tells us we can trust you," the new Fenian said. "Is he right?"

"What happened to him?" Carmen Farooq-Lane asked.

She peered in the passenger-side window of the little car Mór, Declan, and the new Fenian had taken out of New Jersey. They had arranged to meet her in a remote, boggy state park about fifteen miles north of Lynn. Everything was pitch-black; both vehicles had extinguished their headlights, and there wasn't a house within sight. A good place for secrecy.

"I shot him," Mór said, from behind the wheel. "And I'll do the same to you unless you answer the question."

Farooq-Lane's voice was aghast. "Is he *hurt*?"

"Of course he's hurt," the new Fenian replied. "Have you ever been shot?"

Declan sat in the backseat, his head off-kilter against the headrest, his hand resting lightly on his throbbing side. It was hard not to think about being shot. Every thought began and ended with it. The pain didn't even feel like it was coming from the wound anymore; it was radiating through every part of him, a sun of agony, shining out through his fingertips, his eyes, out his parted lips like a sundog. The new Fenian had told him he had something that would knock him out for a good long while, but Declan couldn't sleep until he knew this was taken care of.

You can trust us to do this, the new Fenian had said.

Declan was not good at trusting anyone.

"This changes things," Farooq-Lane muttered.

Mór said, "How?"

"I thought he'd be . . . stronger. I thought he might come with me."

"How would he be after doing that?" Mór asked, as if she thought Farooq-Lane was a little slow. "Didn't he tell you? Boudicca thinks he's dead. They know they're missing a sweetmetal. They're about to find out I've disappeared. Those edge pieces'll solve the whole puzzle once Boudicca connects them. If any of their contacts sees any one of us—am I making the situation clear?"

Farooq-Lane's mouth flattened. Yes, the situation was clear. No, she didn't like it.

Declan wondered why she might have wanted him to come with her. Possibly she was afraid of Ronan. Possibly she knew how valuable the sweetmetal was and wanted him there as a sort of chaperone, proof that she delivered it where it was meant to go. Possibly— *God*, he thought, *the pain, the pain*. Everything else was beginning to feel a little imaginary.

"So you don't think I'll be followed," Farooq-Lane said.

"Once we get a little farther west, we'll make certain they see us, so we can lead them on a merry chase," the new Fenian said, patting the side of the little car. "And give them the slip after we're sure you've done the deed."

What a life, that Declan was in a car driven by the woman who'd shot him, handing over a precious sweetmetal to one of the people who had driven his brother into hiding in the first place.

He would have rather brought the ink to Ronan himself. Or

had Jordan do it, if he couldn't. But she hadn't taken the new Fenian's calls and there was no way he would have risked driving to her place with it. He'd seen the line of victims at the hotel. He knew the consequences of being caught with Boudicca's sweet-metal. He would not risk her being connected to it, which meant he needed to think of someone else he trusted.

But everyone else he trusted was sleeping or dead.

"So again," Mór said, "is Declan right about you, Ms. Farooq-Lane?"

Farooq-Lane's voice was clipped as she jerked her chin toward the other car, hidden in the darkness. "I assume Declan trusts me for the same reason the dreamer I came here with does: When I found out I was playing for the wrong side, I stopped. We . . . need the dreamers to stop all this. I need Ronan awake just as much as you do."

"You make the final call, Declan," the new Fenian said.

Farooq-Lane switched to Declan's window, leaning in to study him. This close, he was shocked by how different she looked from when they'd last met. Gone was the polished, pro-fessional woman who seemed untouched by the chaos of the world. Now her hair was a mess and she'd clearly been crying. Her eyelids looked puffy and tired of holding themselves up. He was sad for her, because he knew she wouldn't have let her exte-rior betray her inner turmoil without a hell of a fight.

He could see her looking at him and arriving at a similar conclusion about him.

"I don't feel comfortable with this situation," Farooq-Lane told him. "Do you know these people? Are you a prisoner? They shot you. They *shot* you! Are they going to drive you someplace to dump your body?"

"Christ," said the new Fenian, sounding an awful lot like Niall.

"Call a fecking social worker," added Mór, sounding nothing like Aurora.

"Shut *up*," snapped Farooq-Lane, making no effort to polish her tone. This was not really *Farooq-Lane*. It was just *Carmen*. "There aren't any jokes in this for *us*."

It was a bold way to draw the line across the board. *Us*: Declan and Farooq-Lane. *Them*: Mór and the new Fenian. But she wasn't wrong, was she? He had more in common with her than he did with the dream and dreamer who wore his parents' faces. They both had so much skin in this game.

Trust pressed in on him.

Pain pressed out of him.

"Look." Declan wished he had better words, but he didn't. He felt like he was digging each one out of his own flesh as it was. "You're talking about what's left of my family. You know how it is. What would you give to not be the only one left? I can't . . ."

Her eyes glistened and then cleared. "I know."

Declan nodded.

On cue, the new Fenian handed her the ink through the window. Then he swiveled to Declan with a single pill pinched between thumb and forefinger and said sharply, "Not a minute longer, boyo. I can't stand you like this."

This pill was marked with Mór's name.

"Dreamt?" Declan said faintly.

"It'll put you down for longer," the new Fenian said. "You need it."

How badly Declan wanted it. How badly he wanted to trust

that someone else would make sure the world didn't burn down without him. How badly he wanted to be a son again, a kid again, to let someone else carry this. Carry *him*.

"Declan," Mór said sharply, "there's nothing else you can do. Your moves in this game are over. Let go."

It was the closest she had come to being his mother.

Declan imagined his father's velvet bag swallowing up secrets as he tipped the pill into his mouth.

It did not immediately take away his pain. Instead, it did the opposite. New pain ground into the back of his head, nothing like the bullet wound. For a brief moment, he felt he was on the windy shore of a cold ocean. Bird wings scissored overhead. A rock dug into the back of his head. He was shredding from the inside out. His mouth was full of sand. The air was screaming.

Then he was back in the car, and drowsiness was fast replacing the pain of his wound.

Mór's intense gaze pinned him against the seat. Sleepiness was dragging him under the surface.

"Will he be okay?" Farooq-Lane asked.

"You have your job," Mór replied coolly. "We have ours."

From the darkness, the other car revved impatiently.

"She's right," the new Fenian said. "We both need to get miles under us."

Farooq-Lane stepped back, holding the ink in both hands, like she was praying. "I will get it done."

"One more thing," Declan said as the car began to pull away. "Tell Jordan I'm coming back."

In the red glow of the taillights, he just had time to see her frown fleetingly, and then sleep took him from the pain.

43

Ronan Lynch was in pain.

It wasn't an unbearable pain. It was a heat, a scratching, like his topmost layer was being stripped away by a gentle but insistent razor.

He was half awake. Half aware.

The moment of truth had come, and he was aware he had a choice.

Ronan Lynch.

Greywaren.

He could feel that heat flaying him, but he could also feel a chill on his chest, his stomach, the palms of his hands. There was something familiar about all of it. He smelled something like hickory, like boxwood, a comfortable sadness, an out-of-reach happiness.

That was the world he lived in with Ronan Lynch. The world he had *built* with Ronan Lynch. A world of limitless emotions and limited power. A world of tilting green hillsides, purple mountains, agonizing crushes, euphoric grudges, gasoline nights, adventuring days, gravestones and ditches, kisses and orange juice, rain on skin, sun in eyes, easy pain, hard-won wonder.

On the other side was the world he lived in with Greywaren. The world he'd left, stretching farther than any of the other entities that dwelled there, stopping not at the sweetmetal sea, stopping not as just a forest with his memories still rooted, but begging to explore even more, unrooted, beyond where his memories could follow him. In that world, the air was music. The water was flowers. There were new colors born every moment. It could not be described with human words; the systems were too different.

The pain was getting hotter on Ronan's skin. He was remembering he *had* skin.

He belonged in both those worlds.

He belonged in neither.

Here in the sweetmetal sea, in the in-between, he could choose either.

Why isn't he waking up? I thought he was supposed to wake up right away?

He could give up on the experiment called Ronan Lynch. He could return to the other side, and he knew what he would find. He would expand beyond the form he'd had in the dark sweetmetal sea. He would become arcing and searing, able to bound across universes and time without pause. *Greywaren*, the others would say, although it would not really sound like *Greywaren*— that was simply a human translation of what the name for him *felt* like. Concepts had to get so much smaller to fit inside humans. *Greywaren*, they would say. *Greywaren, it is good to see you again.*

He was and was not like the others there. A few, when they glimpsed the human world, felt homesick for a place they'd never been. A very few stretched through dreams to become something more, their roots still dug back into their memories in this place. And only one had cared about both worlds equally for as long there were worlds. Greywaren.

He did not know why he had to care about both. A flaw in his creation.

He was pretty . . . far away when I saw him last. Ronan Lynch, you are *coming back, aren't you?*

He could give up on Greywaren. He could return to the human world, retreat to a place that would sustain him for as long as possible, and ignore that there was anyone else who also relied on the ley line. A tourist to humanity, he would seize joy and victory where he could manage it, until the world beat him. Humans only lived for decades, but it turned out, when you were human, that felt like a long time.

He was beginning to hear voices more clearly.

Come on, Ronan Lynch. I went through the Lace for you, asshole. I need you now.

Greywaren, said the voices from the other side. *Please come back. We don't want to see you suffer.*

Neither was enough. He would always want more.

It's time to put on your big-boy pants and fix this shit. We don't have time for this! Wake up!

Greywaren, the voices said, *come back before that world ends.*

Quite suddenly Ronan was cross with both voices. He was cross with himself. Both sides telling him what he was, and him believing it. How long had he been asking: *Tell me what I am?*

Never once had he simply decided for himself.

It wasn't a choice at all.

He woke up.

44

The hum of a space heater sounded in the background. The smell of gasoline and oil and old meatball subs filled his nostrils. His cheek was numb; he was lying on a worn work surface lit by the cold but friendly light of morning. His shoulder was stinging and warm.

Ronan had forgotten what it was like to be in this body.

He rolled himself to sit, inhaling sharply as he did, from the newness and intensity of all the sensations, and twisted to see what had been done to him.

"Hold on, pillock, keep your mitts off. I've got to wrap it," Hennessy said. She came into view, bearing down with a roll of plastic wrap in one hand and a towel in the other. On the shop bench behind her sat her sword, a tattoo gun, and a small glass bottle shaped like a woman. "Say hello to your arm full of sweetmetal."

Of course. Now he recognized the familiar, warm pain that had punctuated his sleep—it was the same as when he'd had his back tattoo done.

But this tattoo was brand-new. Blood and ink still smeared his skin from shoulder to wrist.

He started to touch it but stopped just short. His fingertips were filthy, caked with the sort of thick, colorless grime of a car left unwashed for years. His bare arm was clean, and so was his chest, but his jeans and boots were similarly filthy. When he touched his scalp, he felt that his hair was still shorn short, but it, too, was dusty.

"Show me," he said instead. His voice was a growl, unpracticed, unfamiliar.

Hennessy carefully patted the blood away to reveal the tattoo. It was difficult to not be overwhelmed by the realness of it, the permanence of it. Part of him had expected her to just wipe the blood and ink away to reveal bare skin, but instead, his entire left arm was patterned darkly from shoulder to wrist with something like chain mail.

No, like snakeskin.

Each inked scale was a pure dark green, and the only place his skin showed through was in a narrow line to indicate the edge of each interlocking scale.

It felt like a lifetime ago he and Hennessy had held a snake in the abandoned museum. Bryde had ordered them to look at the reptile, to study it, take in its details in case they wanted to dream it later. They had. But Hennessy had been wide awake, not dreaming, when she'd painted these scales up and down his skin.

"Fuck you," he told her. "This is so good."

She gave him a ghost of a smile. "Welcome back, Ronan Lynch."

It was still jarring to *be* Ronan Lynch. Time behaved so differently here; it was *important* here. One did not have endless dark moments to fill; human lives were so short, so urgent—

"Where's Adam?"

Hennessy asked, "What?"

"Adam. My Adam. Adam!" He was across the garage bay and to the narrow, grimy corridor where his body had been kept before he even was consciously aware he'd jumped from the worktable.

He found it pitch-black and dusty—a place to store a corpse, not a brother. All he saw was a used-up mural, now just paint on the wall. A tipped-over scrying bowl, scattered rocks.

"He was here," Ronan insisted. "His body should be here still."

Hennessy said, "Ronan—"

"Where's Declan? Maybe he moved him."

But Declan had been shot. Ronan remembered that; he'd seen it. Seen it when Matthew died— He pressed his hands against the cold wall of the corridor. All of this was so impossible that Ronan wanted to kick the scrying bowl right off the opposite wall, hard as he could. He could imagine the sound it would make hitting the cinder block. The shatter of glass. But he closed his eyes, and in that darkness, he could still see the bright threads of the sweetmetals. The bright orbs of Adam's consciousness. Kicking was something this body had done back when he was younger, when he was a kid. He wasn't a kid anymore. He was barely even Ronan Lynch anymore. He didn't have to take up any of that body's habits that he didn't need anymore.

"Adam's not here," Hennessy said. "He was already gone when we got here. I was trying to go easy on you 'cause you just woke up from the great beyond. But there's no way around it: Things are fucked and we need you."

Ronan echoed, "We?"

When he opened his eyes, he discovered that they'd been joined by a third person in the corridor. She looked considerably more tattered than when he'd last seen her with the Moderators, but he recognized her at once: Carmen Farooq-Lane. He felt the sting of Rhiannon Martin's death anew.

Ronan snarled, "What are *you* doing here?"

She didn't flinch away from his tone. Instead, she just looked at him gravely.

"Listen to her, Ronan Lynch," Hennessy said.

He could not imagine what she could possibly say to change the dynamic between them.

"Right before your brother gave me the sweetmetal to wake you up," Farooq-Lane began, "I was with Lili—with a Visionary when she had her last vision. I saw the end of the world. I saw *my* brother there, making it happen. And I saw . . ."

She paused.

"Nathan has Adam and Jordan."

45

Jordan had a memory of going to the Metropolitan Museum of Art, but it wasn't hers.

It *felt* faultless as a memory. She could see herself climbing the stairs of the museum on a crisp autumn day. The sky above was brilliant ultramarine, wisped with the smallest brushstrokes of clouds in the highest layer of sky. She couldn't remember if the sidewalk was busy, or if they'd walked or driven there, or what had happened before or after. But she did remember that her eyes were on the shadows that made sharp, clean shapes on the museum's facade and beneath each of the long stairs. She was thinking about the colors she'd use to paint them, about the way the edges of the dark interacted with the bright to tell the eye that these two wildly different colored pieces were the same object, just in different levels of light.

Then the memory fragmented in the way memories and dreams do, just bits and pieces of the Egypt rooms and suits of armor, and then it came back into clear focus in front of a very familiar painting: John Singer Sargent's *Madame X*.

The portrait, which Jordan had now copied many times over in all different sizes, was large in real life, a little more than life-sized. Madame X's emotional presence was even larger. Her skin was sculpturally pale except for her pinked ears. One hand gathered her low black dress; the other braced fingers elegantly against a desk. Although her face was turned away, her open shoulders nonetheless invited the onlooker to explore the beauty of her body, her white throat. See her, but don't know her: Madame X.

Jordan remembered tilting her head back to see all of her. Then she remembered J. H. Hennessy, her mother, taking her hand, so they could absorb *Madame X* together.

That was how she knew it wasn't one of her memories. Jordan had never known J. H. Hennessy; she'd been dreamt after Jay had killed herself.

It was one of Hennessy's memories.

What would Hennessy have been without Jay?

Jordan.

Jordan thought her time at the Charlotte Club would have been a perfectly nice time, except for the dust, and the bombs, and the body.

The building was gorgeous. How could it not be? It had marked the best of the best of nineteenth-century architecture when it had been constructed, and over the decades, it had received the best of orthodontia, cosmetic surgery, and cute clothes to maintain its perfection.

The dark wood accents carried the weight and whimsy of the art deco period. The walls were surprising, subtle colors: leaf green, periwinkle blue, dull mauve. The ceilings, towering twenty, thirty feet overhead, were pressed copper or painted with restored murals. The furniture was shabby in the way only possible in antiques owned by those rich enough to cavalierly use them. The art on the walls was spectacular, the sort of stuff people didn't imagine could live in private collections. It was one of the finest old buildings on Beacon Street.

Jordan knew where she was, because she'd been in the Charlotte Club once before, and had never forgotten it. Her previous visit to the exclusive social club had been under false pretenses, sneaking into an event just long enough to see that it was true: One of their forged Edmund C. Tarbells was hanging on a wall inside.

The forgery still hung there now, although the building had not hosted a party for several months. In fact, its facade was gridded with scaffolding and covered with plastic sheets, hiding the interior from view.

Hiding the dust, the bombs, and the body.

"I probably won't use these," Nathan Farooq-Lane had said to her conversationally, the night he'd brought Jordan here, indicating the bombs. They were all different shapes and sizes, piled up against every wall, stacked on every one of the winding staircases. Some were squat like funeral urns. Others were flat and rectangular with printing on the side, like matchboxes. Some were needle-nosed cylinders, like rockets. Others were studded with spikes like maces. They were all the exact same color, a dull battleship gray, and they all had the number 23 on them as if it had been stenciled.

Jordan didn't need to be told they were bombs. The bombs told her as she walked past them.

"You just like the look of them?" she'd asked. *Bomb*, whispered the square object next to her.

"They remind me what's real. Sit down. I had dinner delivered tonight to calm you down." He said this all placidly, matter-of-factly, as if she had been anxious about a road trip rather than about being kidnapped.

He'd led her through one of the enormous doorways to reveal a long dining table, suitable for forty, with two plates at it, four seats away from each other. He seemed to have anticipated she wouldn't trust the food, because he waited to unpack the

Styrofoam cartons until she was there. It didn't matter; she still didn't touch it. She just watched him eat his portion.

He didn't try to convince her to eat hers. He simply shrugged, stacked the cartons, and said, "We can talk more tomorrow. All the bedrooms are upstairs. Pick whichever you like."

She hadn't done anything of the sort, of course. As soon as he'd gone, she'd stepped immediately and silently down the hallways to one of the exit doors.

When she'd reached for the door handle, a small voice had said, *Bomb.*

Jordan glanced up, in the direction of the voice. What she'd thought was a fire alarm was a steel-gray circle fixed to the wall above the door. The number twenty-three glowed white at her. She retreated slowly.

Bomb, warned another object behind her.

She eased back into the middle of the hall, reversing her path in exactly the way she'd come. A chorus of voices rang out from a collection of three steel-gray objects shaped like grandfather clocks: *bomb, bomb, bomb.*

At first, she'd thought Nathan was going to kill her straightaway. When she brought that up, though, he'd said, "I understand why you'd think that. But I'm only getting rid of your copies."

That was when she'd realized he thought she was Hennessy. Of course he did. She was awake, with no obvious sweetmetal, after all.

"Are you all right with that?" he'd asked her. "It's okay if you're not. I'll do it anyway. But I thought you might be glad they were gone. Clear out the space, you know. Less drain on resources."

This was nighttime Nathan. He was a narrow, tall figure in his thirties, with elegant mannerisms and heavy-lidded eyes with beautiful long lashes as dark as his hair. When the sun was gone, he was pleasant, dry, solicitous, eager for conversation even if she was not eager to give it.

"How many have you gotten?" Jordan replied. *Bomb,* said the door closest to her.

He was glad she'd asked a question. "Only one since coming here. How many were there, do you know?"

Only one. Hennessy. He had to mean Hennessy. Could that be possible? Jordan would no longer fall asleep if Hennessy died, but it seemed like she should have felt it anyway. Hennessy was part of Jordan, or the other way around.

It didn't matter how they'd parted ways before. Jordan was ill imagining Hennessy dying alone, slowly, like the murdered girls. She said, "I lose track."

Nathan gestured to all the steel-gray bombs in the building as if to say, *I know what you mean.*

Jordan asked casually, "How did you kill the copy?"

Again, Nathan spread a hand toward the bombs around them. Then he opened and closed his fingers at her, as if operating a puppet, and, with a rueful smile, admitted, "I don't like to get these . . . messy."

Jordan said faintly, "Right."

Nighttime Nathan ordered food, played music, watched television in the bar on the first floor.

Daytime Nathan was different.

He became reclusive, hidden somewhere in the building. Sometimes she heard his feet pacing overhead. When she did glimpse him, he was muttering to himself, scribbling furiously in a journal.

Daytime Nathan was the one who'd brought the body downstairs.

At first Jordan had thought they were dead. They seemed dead. The hand she saw dragging along the Persian runner was not a healthy color. The spine was limp in the way most people couldn't manage while alive. But when Nathan slumped Adam Parrish onto the bottom stair, Jordan saw that Adam's chest was still rising and falling, very lightly. He was skinny as a rail and his eye sockets were cavernous.

For the first time, Jordan felt something like true despair. It felt like they were circling a broken future, one beyond repair.

Nathan examined his palms, which were smeared with something dark. Blood? No. It was black nightwash, dried deep in the lines of his hands. He rubbed them on his pants legs and then took his small journal from his back pocket. Muttering, he began to read what he had written there in the past, mouthing the words even when he didn't quite say them out loud.

"Not to plan. Couldn't bring him back here. Ronan Lynch. Had to leave him. He started dying in the car. Had to take him back to the corridor so it would stop. Harvard student is not right, either. Doesn't matter. Not long now. Things falling into place."

Then Nathan began to jot furiously into the notebook, still reading aloud as he did. "Harvard student might not survive long enough. Brought him downstairs just in case. Nearly time. Everything starting to seem familiar."

He snapped the journal shut.

Without another glance at Adam, daytime Nathan strode from the room.

As soon as he'd gone, Jordan hurried over to assess Adam. There was no obvious injury, but he did not stir even a bit when she whispered his name or when she pinched him. When was the last time Declan had mentioned reaching him by phone? Had they heard from him since Ronan was put in the corridor? She didn't remember. Briefly, she wondered if this was a dreamt copy of Adam, but she dismissed the idea as quickly. When a dream fell asleep, their body was paused; they didn't age, and they didn't need to eat or drink. This body, on the other hand, was failing. Sickness? Scrying?

"Crumbs," she told Adam's body. "I don't know, mate. This isn't good. Whole situation is seriously not good."

Keeping an eye out for Nathan, Jordan slunk to the bar and emptied sugar packets into a glass of water. She returned to Adam's body and sat it up. He was worrisomely light, his skin dry and hot. She dribbled sugar water into his mouth, painfully slow, rubbing his stubbly throat to try to encourage it to go down. She got perhaps a quarter cup into him before she started feeling like she was drowning him instead. Better than nothing, she thought.

She was starting to get a little tired. For all the art in this place, none of it seemed to be a sweetmetal, and she hadn't painted in days. She probably ought to try to make something. If she was inventive, she could make pigments out of condiments and use her fingers for brushes.

But she didn't feel inventive. She felt like Hennessy might be dead. She felt like the end of the world was coming.

That night, Nathan got them cupcakes from a local bakery and ate his with evident enjoyment, four chairs down from her. She'd struggled to keep from falling asleep into hers.

She felt like she was drowning in sugar water, too.

After that, Jordan tried to kill Nathan. She used a knife from the bar and rushed him while he was working on his journal. He seemed to have anticipated this, because when she was two feet away from him, something under his shirt remarked, *bomb*.

She skidded to a stop, her shoes squeaking on the parquet floor.

He turned around and said, with some irritation, "It's not going to be much longer. It's only until the ley line comes back."

Jordan hadn't risked speaking much to him before now, unsure of what might push him over the edge, but it felt now like she had little to lose. So instead of backing away as she would have before, she asked, "What happens then?"

"You do what you do, and I do what I do," Nathan said. Pure relief broke out on his face then, an enormous, boyish grin, a weight off him. Just imagining the end was enough to completely transform his expression. "Finally."

She didn't like the sound of this. "And what is it *I* do?"

"Dream the Lace," Nathan said. "It says you will not be able to stop yourself."

Even now, Jordan had a very poor understanding of what the Lace was, besides something that struck absolute terror into Hennessy, a person who was not otherwise afraid of much, including death. She hid this ignorance best she could. "Hmm. And what is it *you* do?"

Nathan reached his hand out to nearly touch the fireplace mantel beside his chair. A steel gray cat resting there said, *bomb*. "The big one."

Again she was struck by his expression. Relief.

This was it, she thought. *The apocalypse. I'm looking right at it. All this time, all this wondering, all those dead dreamers. And here it is. The big one.*

She asked, "Why?"

"Don't look at me like that. It doesn't affect you," he said. "The bomb only gets rid of things that aren't useful. And you, as I just told you, are very useful."

The problem was that Jordan could not pretend to be useful much longer. She could not pretend to be *Hennessy* much longer.

She was falling asleep.

She had to talk herself through every sequence of events now, in order to stay alert. Sugar water for Adam meant ten steps to the back stair that led to the bar. Left hand on rail. Right hand pushed open the door. Glass was upside down on a bar towel to the right, where she put it after washing the last time. Fill the glass. Fill the—sugar packets. There were supposed to be sugar packets in this process somewhere. Wait—had she already done them? More wouldn't hurt. Was the water running still, had she not remembered to turn it off?

There were black rugs covered with stiff bristles on them behind the bar. Jordan didn't want to lie on them, not particularly, but they were there, and she was there.

Get up, she told herself. She had settled on the rug anyway. That was not ideal, but she didn't have time to be hard on herself. It would be all right if she simply got back up instead of sleeping.

Get up. She knew if she didn't, she wouldn't get up ever again.

Jordan became aware that a pair of shoes was just inches away from her nose. She hadn't noticed them approaching; she must have been drowsing off.

"Clever thing," said Nathan.

46

We are called Moderators because that is both what we do and who we are. It is important to remember that we are not law-makers, law enforcement officers, judges, or executioners. We do not enforce order; we enforce balance. Our goal is to make certain that power is not concentrated in the hands of the few, particularly those who may wish to harm the world. We moderate. We act only on those who force our hand by obviously stacking the deck. It is a lonely and necessary calling that hopefully will go extinct long before we do. Until then, Moderators should remember that we have each other.

The process for moderating a Zed is straightforward.

Step one. The Visionary has a vision. The structure of a vision is usually standardized in reverse chronological order. The first part comprises the apocalypse: city, fire, etc. The second part conveys the immediate future of a Zed. Usually this Zed is within close physical distance to the Visionary, but this is not always predictable. Bodies of water and electrical interference can prompt a Vision of a Zed much farther away.

Liliana's final vision had depicted the end of the world.

Farooq-Lane had seen it all. Because Liliana had been touching her, she experienced the vision as if it had been her own, her mind whisked from the ice-cold present-day shore to a bright, fiery day in the future. The last future there would ever be. The end.

It was as the visions always were: The flames devoured the city. The people fled. The world ended.

Then the vision shifted back slightly, showing not the end, but just before.

She saw a handsome, old section of a city. Big trees. Small crime. Big money. Small population. A building under renovation, its face hidden by plastic. She saw paintings on walls. Racks of steel-gray boxes. She saw Adam Parrish sprawled on stairs. Jordan or Hennessy splayed behind a piece of long furniture. She saw Nathan.

She saw Ronan Lynch.

An explosion. *The* explosion.

Fire. *The* fire.

In the future, everyone was dead.

In the present, it was just Liliana.

Step two. After debriefing the Visionary, a local team of Moderators works together to identify the physical location described in the Vision. Either local or remote teams of Moderators work on determining the possible ID of the Zed and then establishing, as best as possible, the Zed's schedule. Safety is a priority! Do not proceed to the next step without checking in with your team to be sure the plan has been made as secure as possible! We work together. Remember, we're called Moderators, not Heroes.

Farooq-Lane had thrown herself into researching the details of the vision, just as she used to do with the Moderators. It was easier than many of the other visions, both because Liliana's final vision was exceptionally clear and also because Farooq-Lane had gotten to experience it directly, rather than having to work with a stilted translation.

It made her feel a little better to know that Liliana's sacrifice hadn't been in vain.

In short order, Farooq-Lane narrowed down the neighborhood in the vision to Back Bay, one of the poshest areas of Boston. After that, it had taken only one drive through the area to see that just one building's renovation coverings matched the vision.

Nathan was in there.

The end of the world was in there.

Step three. With the other Moderators, devise a plan to moderate the Zed. The plan should be as subtle and low-key as possible; the general public should not be subjected to scenes that appear violent or dangerous. We are called Moderators, not Terrorists. Ideally, the Zed should be moderated after hours, in a quiet area, and then removed by at least two Moderators after the site is thoroughly documented (format for site documentation included in attached addendum).

Farooq-Lane did not have a team of Moderators. She did not have an arsenal of weapons. She had Hennessy and Ronan. Two dreamers without the ability to dream. Hennessy had her dreamt sword, and Ronan had a little pocketknife thing that exploded talons and wings when opened, but otherwise, they were no more powerful than any other human. They rummaged in their pockets for anything they might have forgotten—Hennessy said, "I wish I had one of those nasty little orbs of Bryde's still, the ones that confused time"—which was when they both discovered the dreamt masks they used to use to fall asleep immediately. The masks had been integral to their havoc before. Now they were merely curiosities, a cure for insomnia.

Farooq-Lane remembered just how terrifyingly powerful the

two of them had been with Bryde when the ley line was powering them. They had been limited only by their imaginations.

Now they were just two ex-dreamers made fearless by life.

It was a sunny day when Farooq-Lane, Ronan, and Hennessy approached the house. A workday. It was quiet. All around, people were puttering about on their ordinary city business, business that relied on the principle that *today* would become *tomorrow*. Even if they had been one of the many who'd seen the bomb's apocalyptic vision, none of them could have guessed that the sunny day they'd seen then was very likely the sunny day they were living now. Farooq-Lane was mired in the paradox of premonition: The vision had said she and the Zeds would be there at the end of the world, and so they were here now, kicking off the end of the world. Would the apocalypse still go on if they simply never showed up at this building? Or would the vision have reflected that, too? Cause and effect felt as murky as the day was bright.

Outside the Charlotte Club, Ronan hesitated.

"Wish you had your sword?" Hennessy asked.

"I wish I hadn't wasted so much time," he replied.

"Time's never wasted with youuuuuuuuuu," Hennessy sang tunelessly, some song Farooq-Lane didn't recognize.

"Bow *bow* bow *bow* baaaa," Ronan replied melodically, sarcastically, finishing the riff so Hennessy knew he got the reference. "If the world ends, that guy will stop making records."

"Simple blessings."

Farooq-Lane sensed the familiarity of this dark banter. It was strange to think they must have perfected it while sparring with the Moderators, when she was still their enemy. Ronan wasn't the only one who was sorry he'd wasted time, she thought. She put her hand on the butt of her gun at her belt. She stood on the front step of the house, thinking, *This is it. This is the last one.*

"Behold," said Hennessy. "The front door is unlocked."

Important notes: Zeds are unpredictable. Some will give themselves up immediately. Others will resist in ordinary human ways. Still others, however, will employ their dreams to intervene, creating instantly dangerous situations. Moderators must stay alert. Research of the kinds of dreams a Zed is prone to create before making a plan can help prevent mass tragedy. Remember that we are called Moderators, not Martyrs.

It turned out the front door was unlocked because Nathan Farooq-Lane was waiting for them. All the lights were aglow in the grand foyer. On the great stairs were two bodies: Jordan, curled up small, and Adam, leaned against the railing, head lolled over.

The walls were lined with steel-gray objects that all began to say, *bomb.*

Nathan sat a few stairs up from the bodies, a gun resting over his knees.

He watched Ronan, Hennessy, and Farooq-Lane come in, and waved the gun to encourage them to shut the door behind them.

Farooq-Lane did.

Bomb, bomb, bomb.

He said, "Carmen always does what she's told."

Ronan's eyes simmered and burned.

"I was getting tired of waiting," Nathan added. "I have something you want. You have something I want. I want *you* to dream the Lace, and then you can have this thing back, if you want it." This was to Hennessy; he meant Jordan. *The thing.* He turned to

Ronan. "And I want *you* to wake up the ley line again, and then you can have *this* body, if you want it."

He meant Adam.

Nathan looked at his sister. "And you—I just wanted to see if you would ever do a thing for yourself."

Farooq-Lane felt the sting of the words even before she parsed them for truth. This had been their relationship for years; her constantly trying to win his respect, him never giving it. It hadn't changed, despite everything.

"Wake up the ley line?" Hennessy sneered. "I'm afraid we're fresh out of your order. We can't wake up the ley line. Can we give you a substitution? Fries, a baked potato, side salad, eternity in hell?"

Stepping over the bodies, Nathan descended toward them. "Don't lie to me."

"She's not lying." Farooq-Lane projected her most professional voice. Poise was the only armor she had. She'd seen him shot. She'd *had* him shot. He knew all this. He was coming straight toward them. "We shut it down. We can't wake it back up."

Nathan stopped four feet away from them. Something under his shirt said, *bomb*. Lifting his gun, he pointed it directly at Farooq-Lane's forehead. "Wake it up, so this all is over."

The siblings stared at each other.

"It can't be done," Farooq-Lane insisted.

Nathan pulled the trigger.

Finally: Because of the nature of our task, some of the encounters may feel personal. They are not personal. A relationship is between the Zed and you; a moderation is between the Zed and the world.

Everyone in the room except for Nathan flinched.

The gun had let out only a mute click; he hadn't released the safety.

Farooq-Lane's heart rammed bullets through her body instead.

"Remember when you shot me, Carmen? Oh, that's right, you had someone else do it. Now, do you two want those things on the stairs or not?" he asked. "Wake up the line. The Lace told me it was possible."

"The Lace *lies*," said Hennessy. "It tells you what you want to hear, mate."

"I can do it," said Ronan.

This entire time, even as Nathan had descended the stairs, Ronan had not taken his eyes off Adam Parrish's body. He was still fixated on it now, his entire posture almost leaning toward him. Even if Farooq-Lane had not known anything about the relationship between the two of them, she would have guessed it by the shape of the space between Adam's motionless body and Ronan's coiled one.

All attention was on Ronan.

"He's right, I can do it," Ronan said gruffly. "When I was younger, we did a ritual to wake a ley line. We had to make a bargain with the . . . thing . . . the entity that could wake the ley line."

He lifted his chin, and the anger bubbling in his eyes would have made anyone other than Nathan step back.

"And you can speak to one of those things now?" Farooq-Lane asked faintly. "That can wake ley lines?"

He said, "I *am* one of those things."

47

Hennessy watched Ronan in the middle of that grand foyer, standing in a circle of light diffused by the plastic outside the scaffolding. She was reminded of when she and Bryde had nearly lost him to nightwash. His mind had wandered far from his body—not as far as she knew it could go, but far enough—and Bryde had insisted on Hennessy coming into the dream to help bring him back.

He'll be drawn to you more than to me, Bryde had said, a sentence Hennessy had puzzled over after.

But now she understood.

Ronan Lynch chose to be human. He had been drawn to it at the start, and he was still drawn to it now. What was Bryde? More dreamstuff. What was Hennessy? Human. What was Ronan? Torn between.

In that dream, Hennessy and Bryde had climbed and climbed until they'd found a version of Ronan curled inside a hollow tree trunk. He'd been older. Silvered. Powerful and sad. A Ronan who had seen the world. When he'd opened his eyes, though, Hennessy had realized he was still that young, human Ronan that she knew, too. Torn between.

Now, here was that Ronan in the waking world, looking both young and old. On one hand, a young man with a tattoo still new enough to be angry, a pugnacious set to his shoulders, a defiant way of planting his boots on the wood floor.

On the other hand, there was something ancient in his eyes. He no longer looked torn between. He was both at once; there was no dissonance.

I am one of those things, he had said.

She believed him.

"Give us Adam and Jordan first," Ronan said. It was not a request. "You have us surrounded with bombs, anyway. What are we going to do?"

Nathan shrugged. "Get them, then."

Together, they moved quickly to retrieve Jordan, and then Adam.

Hennessy checked Jordan's pulse—she was all right, just sleeping, unable to wake, even with the nearby sweetmetal tattooed in Ronan's skin, because he was such an expensive thing to keep awake. It was terrible to see Jordan this way. Jordan was meant to be larger than life, taking up space, making electric portraits, dominating the art world. Not curled on the floor of the Charlotte Club beneath bombs and their old Tarbell forgery.

"I'm sorry, Jordan," Hennessy whispered.

Standing, she saw Ronan kneel next to Adam's limp body to whisper something in his ear, too. Adam did not wake, but Ronan didn't seem to expect him to.

When Ronan lifted his head, she thought his face would be miserable, but it just looked furious. It was all the fire she'd poured into the portrait of *Farooq-Lane, Burning*, and then some.

"Enough of this," Nathan said. He lifted his hands slightly to indicate the steel-gray bombs lining the walls. *Bomb, bomb, bomb.* "Wake the line, Greywaren."

Ronan rose.

He twitched his fingers to make Nathan, Farooq-Lane, and Hennessy stand back.

He bowed his head. Hennessy saw his lips move. It seemed like he might be praying. Who, she wondered, did Ronan Lynch pray to now?

Then he held his hands before him as if he were holding one of Bryde's orbs in his cupped palms.

Nathan watched him, transfixed.

"Don't do it," Farooq-Lane said abruptly. "If he blows up the world, you won't get what you want anyway! I didn't bring you here to make the vision true. I brought you here to change it. Ronan! It's not—"

A gunshot rang out; she fell silent.

Ronan did not pause. It was taking all his concentration to do whatever he was doing. He opened his hands like a book, straining, as if the space between them was heavy.

The air in the room became visible.

Hennessy had never given much thought before to the movement of water, of clouds, of lightning, how the structure of all of these visible things were clues to the invisible. Now she saw a world where energy darted and arced and bright orbs glowed between them and threads of particles drifted and stretched in the sea they all strode through every day. The darkness, visible. The unseen, seen.

Power was building.

"Hennessy," Ronan growled, and Nathan suddenly smiled, knowingly, anticipating the challenge. "Be ready."

She knew the Lace would be waiting.

You've been through it once before. You made it all the way through to Ronan Lynch. Don't forget. You beat it once already.

Everything had changed.

She had changed.

She would not be afraid.

Ronan hurled his hands away from his body as if they held something hot.

In a single instant, the room was brilliant with colors Hennessy had never seen. An image she knew she would never forget. An image she knew part of her would be pursuing for the rest of her life, if they survived this.

The ley line sang to life.

"You better be very good," Ronan snarled at Nathan.

Nathan said, "I am."

All three dreamers threw themselves into a dream.

48

The dream was hectic with dreamers.

At first, it looked exactly like where they had just been, in the foyer of the Charlotte Club. But then Nathan tried to dart up the stairs and into his own corner of dreamspace.

Ronan and Hennessy pursued.

It was easy to see the three different styles of the dreamers at work.

Nathan's was precise, lifelike. Nothing was changed from reality unless it absolutely had to be. His subconscious held the stairs as close to the stairs they'd just left as he could, down to the scuffs on the banister, the pattern on the runner, the shadow of the chandelier across the wood.

Hennessy's was *more* than real. Her colors exploded bigger than the original, her shadows rolled deeper. The chandelier and the stair railing stretched and exaggerated into elegant, painterly forms of themselves. Nathan put his foot on a stair only to realize she'd painted him into a different room entirely; now his stair led him into a Vermeer painting. A woman stood by the window, bathed in light, turning her head to watch him go.

Ronan's dreams were full of emotions. Nathan reached beneath the table in the Vermeer painting; in his hands was a steel-gray stool. The stool said, *bomb*, as Nathan willed it to become one. Suddenly, music sang through the room, carrying dread. It battered Nathan like a storm; he leaned against the overwhelming feeling, his face horrified. He was losing his grip on the stool; Ronan's subconscious whipped the bomb away.

"I need a home-team advantage here, Hennessy," Ronan said, hoping she could hear him, hoping he didn't have to elucidate. It was taking all his attention to continuously snatch the bombs out of Nathan's hands as he reached for them again and again. It was clever how Nathan had decided his bombs could come in any shape. He didn't have to waste any time at all trying to hold a specific bomb shape in his head. Instead any object could be an explosive; Nathan only had to think the nature of the destruction into it.

"On it," Hennessy said.

The dream spread like watercolor into a different scene: It was now a landscape, but without land. The dreamers were falling through an endless stormy sky, nothing but lightning and clouds around them.

Clever, Ronan thought. *Nothing to grab.* But it was more than clever, it was personal. She'd seen what Ronan looked like in the dream before she held him, when he must have still looked a lot like the Lace-like entity he was in the sweetmetal sea. She knew what atmospheres he could thrive in. She couldn't be happy here, not in these clouds so checkered like Lace, but she knew Ronan's nonhuman side could succeed in this dream. And she knew Nathan was likely to be blindsided.

She was right.

Nathan was shouting through the sky, falling forever.

He began to shout for the Lace.

It was as if the Lace had been waiting. It grew and stretched, the dread rolling before it. Reaching out to surround Hennessy as it always did.

The entire sky was turning to Lace.

Ronan switched his attention to holding the sky in place, but he could not manage to focus on both that and trying to spare Hennessy from the worst of the Lace. Moreover, the Lace knew that Ronan's attention was divided, so it drove Hennessy farther and farther away, separating the two of them.

Nathan was beginning to make a new bomb. This was not like one of the bombs stockpiled in the Charlotte Club. This was *the* bomb. The Big One. Ronan could feel him pouring his intention into it, the intention to destroy everything in the world but dreamers.

Ronan tried to focus. He washed conflicting intentions over Nathan, giving him a bomb full of quacking ducks, a bomb full of deflated balloons, a bomb full of laughter, a bomb full of hope.

"You want this, too, Greywaren," Nathan argued. "Stop interfering."

"I don't know what the Lace told you about me," Ronan replied, "but not all of it was true."

He heard a shattered scream from the direction of the Lace.

It was the sound Adam had made when he was torn away.

The nature of it was so precise, so exact, such a perfect rendition of how Adam had sounded that he knew it was just a copy of that moment, not a new one. It was not Hennessy screaming now, it was Adam, screaming then. Not something he could prevent now. Something he had not prevented before.

Ronan knew it was just to distract him.

But it worked.

His feints toward Nathan were now less creative, repeated, and Nathan more easily batted them away as he pushed ever more complicated and deadly consequences into his bomb.

Now the Lace was whispering to Ronan. *I took Adam from you so easily. It was like part of you was always trying to give him away. You say it does not matter, it is in the past? We will do the same thing to Hennessy we are doing to him.*

It whispered how it had seen how well Adam knew how to strengthen the ley line, how hateful it seemed to the Lace that a human might have the ability to do that, to have knowledge it didn't. It was going to dismantle his thoughts, it said, every one, to get all that knowledge out of him, and then blow the rest of him away into the ether. It had already begun to tear Adam apart, starting the moment the Lace had stolen him away from Ronan. Did Ronan enjoy whispering in the ear of a dead person back in the Charlotte Club? Because he was never getting Adam back. There were not enough of Adam's thoughts left to animate his body again.

The dream changed.

There was a voice in Ronan's dream.

You know this isn't how the world is supposed to be.

It was everywhere and nowhere.

At night, we used to see stars. You could see by starlight back then, after the sun went down. Hundreds of headlights chained together in the sky, good enough to eat, good enough to write legends about, good enough to launch men at.

You don't remember because you were born too late.

Maybe I underestimate you. Your head's full of dreams. They must remember.

Does any part of you still look at the sky and hurt?

Ronan was having a dream he'd had before. He was in the dark. He turned on a light and saw a mirror. He was in the mirror. The Ronan in the mirror said to him: *Ronan!*

He woke with a start in his old bedroom at the Barns. Spine, sweaty. Hands, tingling. Heart, kick-kick-kicking at his ribs.

Usual nightmare postgame. The moon wasn't visible but he felt her looking in, casting shadows behind rigid desk legs and above the stretching wings of the ceiling fan. The house was silent, the rest of the family asleep. He got up and filled a glass with water from the tap in the bathroom. He drank it, filled another one.

Ronan turned on the bathroom light and saw the mirror. He was in the mirror. The Ronan in the mirror said to him: *Ronan!*

And he twitched awake again, this time for real.

Magic. It's a cheap word now. Put a quarter in the slot and get a magic trick for you and your friends. Most people don't remember what it is. It is not cutting a person in half and pulling a rabbit out. It is not sliding a card from your sleeve. It's not are you watching closely?

If you've ever looked into a fire and been unable to look away, it's that. If you've ever looked at the mountains and found you're not breathing, it's that. If you've ever looked at the moon and felt tears in your eyes, it's that.

It's the stuff between stars, the space between roots, the thing that makes electricity get up in the morning.

It fucking hates us.

Ordinarily, when one woke, it was obvious the dream was a pretender. But this time, dreaming about dreaming . . . it had felt so real. The floorboards; the cold, chipped tiles of the bathroom; the sputter of the tap.

This time, when he got up for that glass of water, the real glass, the waking glass, he was sure to marvel his fingertips over everything he passed, reminding himself of how specific waking reality was. The bumpy plaster walls. The rubbed-smooth curve of the chair-rail molding. The puff of air from behind Matthew's door as he pushed it open to see his younger brother sleeping.

You're awake. You're awake.

This time, in the bathroom, he paid attention to the moon

slatted through the blinds, the faded copper stain around the base of the old faucet. These were details, he thought, the sleeping brain couldn't invent.

Ronan turned on the bathroom light and saw the mirror. He was in the mirror. The Ronan in the mirror said to him: *Ronan!*

He woke up in his bed again.

There are two sides to the battle in front of us, and on one side is Black Friday discount, Wi-Fi hotspot, this year's model, subscription only, now with more stretch, noise-canceling-noise-creating headphones, one car to every green, this lane ends.

The other side is magic.

Ronan stumbled out of bed again. Now he had no idea if he was awake or asleep or if he'd ever been awake or asleep. He raked his fingers down the walls. What was reality?

You are made of dreams and this world is not for you.

"Ronan," Bryde said, and snagged his arm as he started into the bathroom. "Ronan, enough."

In the hallway of his childhood home, in a dream in his head, Bryde stood before him, taking both of his arms, holding him firmly.

"You're dead," Ronan said. "You're not real."

Bryde said, "Don't make me say it."

You make reality.

"You cannot beat him to the bomb," Bryde said. He shifted the dream enough that Ronan hovered outside the farmhouse, looking inside, as if it were a dollhouse, and saw Nathan in Matthew's bedroom, furiously finishing up the bomb that would kill every human and dream in the world. "I am going to dream an orb to slow the blast down as much as I can, to buy you time to come up with something to stop it. That's all I can think to do."

Overhead, the Lace tormented and twisted through the darkening sky. It was beginning to look a lot like the sweetmetal sea. Hennessy was entirely hidden behind it. It was possible she was already being torn apart as the Lace had promised.

In the farmhouse below, Nathan stood with the bomb in his hands. It could look like anything, but it looked like a journal. It was open to a page that said, *We live in a disgusting world.. The drawer is full of ugly blades made for nothing..*

"I'm sorry I lied," Ronan told Bryde.

Bryde opened his left hand. In it was one of his orbs at the ready. He put his other hand on the side of Ronan's face. "Greywaren, it's time to grow up."

Nathan vanished. The bomb did too. He'd woken up, which meant he'd just brought that bomb back to the real world.

A breath later, Bryde vanished, too.

Hennessy's voice came from the other side of the Lace, desperate and clear. "Ronan Lynch, do you remember what we saw at the end of the world?"

He had no idea what she was talking about, and then, because they were in each other's thoughts, he did. the fire.

The devouring fire, the starving fire, the never-ending fire.

But that wasn't what Nathan had created, was it? Nathan had created one of his nasty, cruel bombs. So when the visions had promised a world ending with fire, did they really mean a world ended *by* fire?

Or was a devouring, dreamt fire the only thing that could eat the blast before it managed to tear through Boston?

Ronan wasn't even sure he could control something like that. All the dreams he'd failed to control. The murder crabs. The sundogs. Matthew. Bryde. When something was really important to him, he always fucked it up. And this was important. The vision had been of the city on fire, people fleeing, the fire eating everything.

Farooq-Lane said it was a nightmare, not a promise, Hennessy thought, her thoughts loud as a shout in Ronan's head. *Don't be only human just now, Ronan Lynch.*

Ronan thought of how he had just woken the ley line, a thing he would have never believed possible only a few years before. He thought of how he would never again feel powerless, because he wasn't going to lie to himself anymore, hiding from the truth just because he was afraid of taking on the decisions himself, afraid of being wrong.

He was Greywaren, and he belonged in both worlds.

As he began to dig deep into the image of scouring fire— that was never far from his mind anyway—he glimpsed the Lace rotating as fast as it was able.

Turning just enough to let him see that while Ronan was making the fire, the Lace had gathered together the orbs that made up Adam Parrish's mind. And brought them just close enough for him to see. To reach. To save. To make back into Adam Parrish. One last chance to save Adam and bring him back to his body in the waking world.

All he had to do was put down the fire he had begun to build.

You have a choice, the Lace said.

49

For that first summer, the Barns was paradise to Ronan Lynch and Adam Parrish.

Having dropped out of school, Ronan had spent the winter working on renewing the faded outbuildings and broken fence posts. In spring, his friends graduated, and Gansey and Blue left on a gap-year road trip. Adam, however, came to the Barns. He wasn't there always—he still lived in his apartment above the church in Henrietta, and he took all the hours at the garage he could manage—but he was there often enough. When Ronan wasn't dreaming, when Adam wasn't working, they were together.

The Barns wasn't new to either of them, but the freedom to choose their comings and goings: That was a new kingdom.

"This is a terrible idea," Adam said, when Ronan proposed digging a swimming hole in one of the sloping fields. "It'll drain too fast; it'll breed mosquitoes; it'll smell like cow shit; we'll never be able to dig through the rock."

"Not with that attitude," Ronan said, full of his newly minted optimism. He was a charming young buck, handsome, persuasive, fast-talking. If the swimming hole could be dug, he was the dreamer to do it.

Adam looked at the future swimming hole site with his cool-eyed gaze. Ronan believed it could be done, and that was all that mattered. Ronan made reality, either through dreaming or stubbornness, both good and bad. Adam had recently realized Ronan was a weakness to his ambition, since it was harder to work with two moving pieces rather than one, but he couldn't talk himself out of it. He tried each night he was alone in the apartment over St. Agnes, and he failed every time he saw Ronan again. He was in love with Ronan, and he was in love with this lonesome green valley, and although he could not work out how either dovetailed with his addiction to the future, for the summer, he put his reservations away.

He just lived in the moment with Ronan instead.

It was a hot and inviting Virginia summer. They took road trips into the mountains. They made out in every room in the farmhouse. They tried to fix Adam's car. They sorted through the old dreams in the outbuildings. They burned food in the kitchen. They dug the swimming hole and it was a disaster so they dug it again, and then they taught Ronan's little hooved dream Opal to swim, and they took turns using a ragged pair of dreamt wings to hover over the swimming hole and drop themselves in again and again.

For a long time, it was paradise, and the dreaming was good.

Ronan had been practicing his dreaming in a long barn he kept locked when he wasn't there. He worked on ever more sophisticated dreams, dreams that had weather and emotions and magic hard-baked into them. He dreamt a security system for the Barns.

He meant to dream a new forest. His old one on the ley line had been destroyed, cataclysmically, when his mother had died, when he'd first experienced nightwash, and although he could not dream himself a new mother, he could dream himself another forest to ground him to that other place. That dreaming place. He meant to do it before Adam went to college.

College and *forest* were the same sort of concept, because both of them were full of both hope and dread. What would happen at the end of the summer?

Adam could not stay at the Barns forever.

Ronan could not leave the Barns forever.

They barreled toward a potential nightmare. As the days got shorter, they began to quarrel. Rarely about college. Often about dreaming. It was not truly about the dreaming. It was certainly about college. Ronan would not tell Adam not to go, or to go to a college near to him. Adam would not tell him he did not want to do a long-distance relationship, because he had lost the knack for being unhappy and tired and strung out with balancing acts. So instead they quarreled about the forest Ronan was going to dream, and they quarreled about Adam's car, and they quarreled about whether or not they both should have gone with Gansey and Blue on the gap-year road trip because didn't it feel like they were already becoming a different sort of friend group than they had been before?

But really they were quarreling about the impossible future. They could not go into it the same as they were, and they both knew it.

The nightwash began to come for Ronan.

The world was changing at the same time they were.

At the end of the summer, Ronan dreamt his new forest. He let Adam scry at the same time, so that he could be there, even though he warned that it might be dangerous; he intended to dream this forest with the ability to protect itself.

This new forest was a lot like the forests that already grew on the ridges of the blue mountains to the west of the Barns, but it was vaster. Deeper. It was a whole world. Lindenmere. Dreaming is about intention, and Ronan intended for this forest to last. He intended for this forest to tell him how to exist in the future as a dreamer. He intended for this forest to be able to survive without him. He intended for this forest to want him.

(It was about Adam, of course.)

And then it was fall. It was fall, and the leaves were turning, and colleges were starting up. The year was dying.

This paradise, this summer, it had been a dream. One didn't integrate dreams into waking life. One went away, woke up, and then returned to the dream only at night. They were separate.

"I know I'm going," Adam said, repeating the thing he'd said over and over, "but I'll always come back, as long as you're here."

"I'll be here," Ronan said. "I'll always be here."

They kept saying it. The less true it felt, the more they said it.

Magic is about intention. So are conversations.

Neither Ronan nor Adam had been trained in the difficult and nuanced art of having a future. They had only ever learned the art of surviving the past.

In the end Adam went away to Harvard as he had planned and Ronan was left alone with Chainsaw, as even his little hooved dream Opal had gone to live in Lindenmere where she belonged. Ronan stood on the porch of the farmhouse where he'd grown up, watching the fall mist move slowly across the property. He told himself he was not really alone; in just a few days he would drive to DC to go to church with his brothers, although he could not stay, because the nightwash was too bad there now.

You are made of dreams, he thought, *and this world is not for you.*

The Barns's stark fields already looked like winter.

Paradise, paradise, why would he ever leave?

50

It was an unusual bomb.

Everything about it was unusual.

The way it began to explode from its central core at the Charlotte Club had more in common with a Visionary's blast than any natural explosive. The deadly shock began to ripple out from the bomb itself, which was right next to where Nathan lay on the stairs. The weapon contained bits and bombs and pointy nasty bits meant to pierce flesh, but it also contained the Lace's overwhelming hatred.

How it hated this world.
How it hated the wasteful..
useless..
hungry..
self-defeating..
self-harming..
greedy..
sad..
mean..
narrow-minded..
destructive..
abusive..
passive..
excessive..

noisy..

pointless..

unreal..

occupants of this world, seething and destroying, taking and dying, leaving everything just a little shittier in their wake.

That was going to go away with this bomb. This bomb was going to scissor them to pieces, the dread and hatred cutting the humans into lacy corpses. The world would be blessedly empty once more, leaving room for the *real* to return. No more duplicate scissors in the drawer. No more sad lives choking out the resources for the productive ones.

But the bomb was moving very slowly. The time just around it had been tricked by Bryde's silver orb lying on the floor beside the staircase, still wobbling a little from rolling into place.

Moving much faster, by the door, was Jordan Hennessy, the dream not the dreamer, who'd woken at once when the ley line returned. As the strange steel-gray objects against the wall said, *bomb, bomb, bomb,* getting ready to explode themselves when the dreadful bomb's debris began to hit them, she had begun to drag people from the building and as far from all the bombs as possible.

First Adam, who was still limp in sleep. She hooked her hands under his armpits and dragged him down the stairs, underneath the plastic sheeting around the scaffolding, as far down the sidewalk as she could manage it.

Then Hennessy, who was awake, but paralyzed after waking with an unseen dream.

Finally, she hesitated over Ronan Lynch, trying to decide if she should wake him, or if she should leave him in the dream to do his work. *Was* he going to wake? Was he making a solution for this slowly rising bomb right now; would she ruin it by disturbing him? Jordan didn't know the rules of the unseen battle playing out for their lives.

In slow, dazed motion, Nathan was sitting up; he was finally unparalyzed after dreaming the bomb. But he couldn't really move yet. He was as trapped in the confusing, time-slowing magic of Bryde's tricky orb as the bomb itself was for now. His eyes on Ronan's sleeping form, he reached for his gun.

But before he could close his fingers around the weapon, a little popping noise burst from the ground beside Jordan.

Farooq-Lane, lying on her side in an oozing pool of her own blood, had shot Nathan. Then she fell back.

Jordan hadn't realized she was there, that she was alive.

As she began to drag her free of the building, Bryde's orb finally gave way.

The bomb burst free.

Bomb

Bomb

Bomb

Bomb

The building writhed with destruction. The end of the world was no longer on its way. The end of the world had arrived.

Suddenly, there was fire.

51

Ronan was paralyzed, as he always was after a dream.

As he had for the past several weeks, he floated above his body, looking down at it. It was lying on its back in the fancy foyer of the Charlotte Club; the dreamt mask that sent him instantly to sleep had slithered off onto the parquet floor beside him. He looked different than he had lying in the corridor. There, he'd looked abandoned, dusty, waiting.

This Ronan Lynch looked powerful even now. His unblinking eyes were full of furious purpose. He was not moving an inch, but no one would mistake him for a corpse. The Ronan Lynch floating above the Ronan Lynch down below looked at him and thought, *This is right.*

Everything around him was on fire.

It was the most powerful dream he had ever dreamt. Just as when he had reached past the sweetmetal sea to wake the ley line while awake, he felt he had reached farther than ever before to accomplish the fire. He felt as if even Greywaren had never arced as deeply into the ether as he had to pull out the power necessary to get something that could possibly have such a complicated purpose as the fire.

The effort of both traveling for the power and holding the intention of the fire in his head was impossible for one dreamer to pull off. The fire had to be all-powerful, but not burn down Boston. The fire had to eat the bombs, but not the walls. The fire had to devour every bit of exploding violence from Nathan's newest bomb, but not the feelings of every person it touched. It could not eat skin, it could not eat trees, it could not eat sharp things that were not part of the bomb. It had to only eat the bomb as if it would never, ever be satisfied.

But then it had to be.

The fire had to go out. It could not devour the rest of the world, it could not churn over the surface, ending everything, no matter how miserable Ronan was over Adam's ruined, empty body; no matter how miserable he was over the memory of Matthew's golden smile; no matter how remembering Declan saying *Be dangerous* made him feel.

As he struggled to hold the fire's purpose and draw the power required from deep in the ether, he realized that other entities had gathered around him to watch. The ones who had never reached through the sweetmetal sea to manifest on the other side, the ones who had only wistfully looked out through the sweet-metals and felt homesick for a place they'd never been.

Greywaren snarled to them, "Don't you want them to live?"

A handful of onlookers rushed forward to help him carry the fire.

Together, they kept reminding him as he struggled forward, power arcing all around him, of what the fire was meant to do, what it was supposed to spare, and they pressed it all into the dream that Ronan Lynch manifested in the foyer of the Charlotte Club. They added to it their curiosity, their longing, and their fondness for the world they'd glimpsed. The fire was too much for one dreamer to hold. But it was not held by only one dreamer.

That was the fire that devoured Nathan Farooq-Lane's bomb. *Devour, devour.*

It ate the dread. It was so hungry.

Devour, devour.

It ate the bombs lining the walls. It was still starving.

Devour, devour.

It ate the sharp, nasty bits at the heart of the bomb. It would never be satisfied.

Devour, devour.

It ate the hatred.

Devour, devour.

The fire went out.

52

There was quite a bit of commotion when Hennessy could move again. The finer details of what had happened inside the Charlotte Club were still hidden from the greater world, disguised behind the plastic sheeting, but there was no disguising that there was a woman bleeding on the sidewalk.

Jordan, who had been working ceaselessly since waking, had flagged down a car as it passed. Well, really, she nearly leapt in front of it—it had not been intending to stop. The moment it squealed to a complete halt, she made a telephone gesture beside her ear. When the window rolled down, just a suspicious crack, she had shouted, "Call 9-I-I! A woman's shot!"

The police came; the ambulance came. Phones and cameras came.

But by then, all there was for them to see was Carmen Farooq-Lane, collapsed on the sidewalk in front of the Charlotte Club, her hands covered with her own blood.

The dreamers and the people who loved them had not gone far, though, just a few blocks away to the Esplanade, a public green space surrounded by the Charles River. The trees were still bare but the sun overhead was surprisingly warm as they laid Ronan down in the dry grass.

It was taking him a very long time to become unparalyzed, but that seemed fair. He had to come back from a very long way away.

As soon as they put him down, Hennessy turned to Jordan

and, without a word, they threw their arms around each other. Hennessy couldn't remember a time they'd ever done this out of happiness. Over the years, Jordan had embraced her often, but it was always for comfort, when yet another thing had gone to shit.

"I thought—" Jordan began.

"Shh," Hennessy interrupted, pulling back. "Shit's about to get real touching and I worked too hard to not get the satisfaction of seeing it go down."

Jordan *Hennessy* and *Jordan* Hennessy turned to observe the scene before them.

Slowly, Ronan Lynch sputtered to movement, trying to sit up even before his body was fully willing, scrambling, his voice disbelieving: *"Adam?"*

Adam, who had been sitting quietly all this time beside Ronan, grinned weakly as Ronan seized him around the neck in a crushing, desperate hug. Hennessy and Jordan watched the two of them kneeling in the grass, just clinging to each other. It was an enormous, extraordinary moment, surrounded by mundane, ordinary things. The slapping of joggers' feet against the park's sidewalk. The sound of cars on the bridge. Distant voices shouting from the city behind them.

There was a time when it would have made Hennessy feel bad to see how gratefully Ronan's face was pressed into Adam's neck. To see how Adam's face just wore a raw relief, a peace, as he held on to Ronan, his eyes open and gazing up into the blue sky. To see Ronan finally say something into his ear and Adam close his eyes and sigh.

But not now.

Now she said, "When I look at moments like this, two men

in love, reunited against all odds, their feelings so pure, their commitment so deep that they'll literally cross space-time for each other, all I can really think is: I can't believe how these two blokes will owe Jordan Hennessy for the *rest of their fucking lives*."

Ronan lifted his eyes to her. She didn't say anything else, just let him autofill what had happened when he left Adam behind in the Lace to dart after the fire. *He* might have left Adam in order to save the world instead, but Adam wasn't the only one in the Lace, was he? Hennessy was still there with it stuck into her at ten different points in her mind, whispering poison. Too bad for the Lace that Hennessy didn't need it anymore. While Ronan had been plunging deep into the ether to build the fire to stop the bomb, Hennessy had been busily gathering all the orbs of Adam's mind and squishing them back together into his consciousness, then dragging all of it closer to the waking world. The moment of truth had come when they'd shaken Adam awake. For a moment, Hennessy hadn't known if she'd managed to recover enough of Adam for him to be . . . right. But then he'd woozily come to and immediately looked for Ronan, so she'd known she'd pulled it off. Who would have thought? That Hennessy could one day not only ignore the Lace, but take someone else back from it. Two someones, really, if you counted the time she'd found Ronan Lynch hidden amongst it, too.

"You really are a shithead," he told her.

"Check it," she said, digging into her jacket pocket. "I dreamt myself a better dreaming mask."

The mask dangling in her fingers had an intricate pattern like the threads through marble, or like lace.

Ronan shook his head, and for several long minutes, they sat there in the grass, listening to the sounds of the city around them. The sun was very good. Winter was not yet over, but one could tell that it *would* be over, which is nearly as good.

Eventually, Ronan said, "The orb that slowed the bomb—"

Hennessy asked, "Did you see him?"

Ronan frowned. "I don't know what to believe."

Hennessy mentally replayed the events. "I saw the orb myself. It appeared before you woke up."

"Maybe it was you."

"I wasn't thinking about an orb. I had my hands full with the Lace, thanks very much. I'd love to take credit for it, but my mind was being *fucking extruded* as I saved your boyfriend from madness and death."

Adam asked, "Jordan, did you see anything? Did you see Bryde?"

She shook her head. "Things were kind of crazy, mate."

Ronan knew why he wanted it to be true; he wasn't going to do that to himself. He stood, reaching a hand out to help Adam up. "I got more than I thought I would. It's going to have to be enough."

Hennessy couldn't disagree with that. She said, "What do we do now?"

Jordan flung her hand out in the direction of the sky, the wordless gesture for *anything*.

53

On the first day Declan was back at the Barns, he slept. Gunshot wounds were hard work, and running from Boudicca was hard work, and the business of trying not to worry and grieve was hard work, so for the first day, or possibly more, he slept and slept. In his childhood bed he dreamt that no time had passed since he had lived here with the rest of his family, and he relived the mundane days of waking and quarreling with his brothers and marching over the fields and going to school and being shaken awake by his father because, *boyo, I know it's early, but it's time for our trip if you're coming.*

When he finally woke up for good, he realized he had been happy here, before everything went wrong. His childhood had been a contented one, despite everything. It was a shocking, sun-washed realization to have; he had so thoroughly convinced himself otherwise. He'd told himself his father was hateful, his mother invisible, the Barns dreadful, the dreaming frightful. It had been the only way to bear losing it all.

Declan Lynch had become such a liar.

On the second day Declan was at the Barns—or, at least, on the second day he was *awake* at the Barns; he knew from the changing weather it had been far longer than one day—he took a very long time to limp down the driveway. Spring swooped and hummed on either side of him. The fields were coming alive with small bright flowers. Everything was beginning to smell warm and alive.

At the end of the driveway, Declan faced Ronan's invisible security system, the one that had made intruders and visitors alike revisit their worst memories. He had only been through it once before. After that, he'd just picked his way through the woods every time he wanted to leave or enter. But now memories didn't seem like they might have the same sting, so he stood there, willing himself to go through.

The new Fenian pulled the car up alongside him. "Mór says you're undoing your healing."

With a glance at the end of the drive where the security system was, Declan accepted the ride, and the new Fenian made a game of reversing the car the entire way back to the farmhouse.

On the third day Declan was at the Barns, it rained and rained, both sky and trees hidden by the drenching gray curtain. As the new Fenian and Mór played scratchy ceili band records in the living room, Declan went through postcards in his room. They were from all over the globe. *Wish you were here*, his father wrote. *Take care of your brothers.*

That afternoon, Ronan came home.

The rain had stopped and the sky was bluer than it had ever been. Masses of daffodils suddenly opened on either side of the driveway, trailing gold into the secretive spring woods.

Ronan walked into the farmhouse without any particular fanfare, scraping off his boots and hanging up his jacket. He looked older, but something else about him had changed, too. Now, when he held Declan's gaze, it felt less like a challenge and more like Declan was being examined thoroughly. It was still not comfortable, but it felt like progress.

Declan and Ronan embraced without words, an uncomplicated hug, no apologies, no words at all until Ronan said, "I brought you something."

The door opened again to reveal first Adam, and then Jordan.

"Pozzi," she said, and Declan smiled at her with all his teeth, with all his body, hiding his grin from no one.

On the fourth day Declan was at the Barns, Mór and the new Fenian left to confront Boudicca. Ronan had dreamt them something to take with them. He'd shown this dream to Declan first, but even having seen it, Declan wasn't sure what it was. It was a book. Or perhaps a bird. Or a planet. A mirror. A word. A shout. A screaming threat. A door. A spiraling day, a singing letter— whatever it was, it didn't make sense. Declan could feel it driving him mad as he tried to understand it. The only thing that was clear was the *power* behind it. Whoever could make such a thing had power beyond measure.

"Tell them to leave my family alone," Ronan told Mór. "Or I'll deliver the next one in person."

On the fifth day, Declan limped down the driveway once more. No one else was awake yet. Cool mist crept lowly over the grass, pierced here and there with the light of Ronan's dreamt fireflies, who glowed year-round. Birds, hidden from his sight, called sweetly to each other, sounding as if they came from everywhere and nowhere. He stopped at the end of the drive, facing the security system.

He did not know why he was so tempted to step into it now.

He supposed he wanted to know what it thought his worst memory would be. Every violent, miserable memory seemed toothless now.

Declan played his fingers over his side, testing it for tenderness, steeling his courage.

Then he stepped into the midst of Ronan's dream.

At once, the security system rewarded him with his worst memory. It was none of the memories he'd been expecting, but rather the one when he discovered that his father, in his will, had left him not the Barns, which Niall had loved, but rather a previously unknown town house in DC, because Declan had told him he wanted to be a politician, a desire Niall had not understood in the slightest. *Boyo*, he asked, *do you know what politicians* do?

Declan emerged from the security system to find Jordan standing there waiting for him.

He sat down directly in the middle of the drive with his hand tenderly over his wounded side and, for the first time since Niall had died, he cried. Jordan sat next to him and said nothing so he did not have to cry alone. After a space, a host of strange animals came out of the woods and sobbed with him, to keep him company. When he was finally done crying, Ronan drove to the end of the driveway to collect Declan's spent body and take him and Jordan back to the farmhouse.

"I miss them, too," Ronan said.

On the sixth day, Matthew came home.

(Matthew came home. Matthew came home. Matthew came home.)

It was late at night, and when the back door opened, everyone was at once on the alert. In walked the youngest Lynch, nearly unrecognizable. His hair was cut short and uneven, and his cheeks were gaunt. His clothing and shoes were very dirty.

"I walked," he said simply.

His brothers fell upon him.

"You couldn't call?" Declan demanded, after Matthew had finished wiping away his tears.

"I thought you'd be mad."

"What happened to Bryde?" Ronan asked.

"He listened to the voice," Matthew replied. "He became one of those Visionary things. And changed ages and stuff."

"You didn't?" Ronan asked.

Matthew shrugged. "Bryde told me it was better for me to ask you guys for help than the voice. He said you cared more."

Declan understood that Bryde had given both his brothers back to him; he understood that Bryde had always been like shallow water, only dangerous to those who couldn't stand on their own or who already wanted to drown.

On the seventh day, the Lynch brothers discovered they were friends once more.

EPILOGUE

FOUR YEARS LATER

This is a story about the brothers Lynch.

There were three of them, and if you didn't like one, try another, because the Lynch brother others found too sour or too sweet might be just to your taste. The Lynch brothers, the orphans Lynch. All of them had been made by dreams, one way or another. They were handsome devils, down to the last one.

Four years after the worst fight they ever had in their lives, they were back at the Barns for a summer wedding. It was a very small wedding. Later, there would be a big, showy one, but this one was for family and friends who might as well be family. Those were the only people allowed at the Barns, on the inside of the security system Ronan had perfected.

Who was there? Mór Ó Corra and the new Fenian, of course, because they were the only permanent residents of the Barns, after all, staying year-round to tend to the creatures that lived there, including the occasional appearance of a small, hooved girl.

Richard Campbell Gansey III, Ronan's oldest friend, was in the country for the wedding, and so was Blue Sargent. They had just graduated from the same sociology program with two very different concentrations. Both of them were very excited to talk about what they had studied to anyone who would listen, but no one except for each other was very excited to hear about it. Something something *trenches* something something *artifacts* something something *secret doors* something something *trees* something something *primary sources*.

Henry Cheng and his mother, Seondeok, were there. Henry was a sometimes friend of the family and Seondeok was a sometimes associate of Declan's. When they were not being fierce friends, they were engaged in fierce feuds, and it was fortunate for all involved they were in a friendly place when the wedding was scheduled. The last feud had involved two continents, seven countries, and a crate with contents too valuable for insurance, and had required international courts, a tense game of polo, and a divorce to bring it to a close.

Calla, Maura, and Gwenllian, the psychics of 300 Fox Way, who had helped guide Ronan through high school, were there. They had been made to swear left and right not to bring business to the proceedings and to keep any premonitions to themselves, but this demand had only made them insufferable. They kept pointing at people, whispering to each other, and getting fits of the giggles. Calla had been asked to officiate the wedding, as she was the only one responsible enough to have gotten the paperwork filed in time, but even she gave in with a mighty snort-laugh during the ceremony in the pasture behind the house.

Matthew was there, of course, although he'd had to postpone leaving for his summer internship for it. He had an unpaid internship on a sweet potato farm in North Carolina. It was unclear what he was supposed to be learning there, but his advisor had told him he'd get credit for it, so off he went.

The couple was there, of course: Declan and Jordan, the least surprising wedding of the decade. Jordan had refused to get married until she sold a painting for five figures, and she said it didn't count if it was Declan's name on the check. The honeymoon was a very Declan honeymoon: They were going back to Boston for it, but both had agreed to not work for two days.

Hennessy was there, but not for long. She was usually traveling this way and that to destinations she worked out with Ronan, finding places that needed to be taught how to create art that made people feel awake. She had a ticket booked to California for the next morning. So did Carmen Farooq-Lane.

And of course Ronan and Adam were there. Ronan had just returned from a ley line in Tennessee, and Adam had just returned from DC. He was enjoying his new employment, although no one knew what it was. After Harvard, he'd transferred twice before getting hired directly out of college by an organization with a dot gov email. It was unclear what they did or what they wanted Adam to do, but it was also clear that they both felt Adam was already well prepared. He traveled so much for it that neither he nor Ronan kept a permanent address, but rather continuously rejoined here and there. Ronan had a way of having doors opened to him (usually with dreamers on the other side of them), and Adam had a way of getting those doors paid for on the corporate credit card. And they always had the Barns, of course; it would always be there in the end.

The Barns was a paradise in the summer. Every field was lush with grass and wildflowers. The sweetmetals Jordan and Hennessy had brought kept Niall Lynch's old herd lowing softly as they grazed. Plums hung heavy on the tree by the freshly painted farmhouse. The leaves of the trees that surrounded the hidden farm flipped up to show their light undersides, promising a thunderstorm later, but for now, everything was blue skies and towering clouds.

Ronan and his friend Gansey stood on the back porch, leaning on the railing, watching the psychics giggling as they placed the flowers for the ceremony. Every so often, Ronan threw a cheese cube stolen from a snack tray at Chainsaw, whose claw marks scarred the railing.

"You want one of these?" Gansey asked. He gestured with his chin to indicate it. The all of it. The wedding.

"Yeah," said Ronan. "I think so."

"Well, that's a relief," Gansey said.

"How do you figure?"

"I asked Adam and he said the same thing."

They watched Matthew and Henry struggle with a table holding refreshments. Why they were carrying it was hard to say, but they seemed intent.

"It's good to be back," Gansey said.

Ronan studied his friend, understanding his life and deaths better than before. At some point, he thought, he'd ask Gansey to talk about it, what it felt like to be him now, but now wasn't the place. They had time. Years. Instead, he said, "Yeah. I missed you and Sargent droning on about shit."

"I missed your witty repartee."

"Aglionby taught me well. I'm glad you didn't get killed during that whole Pando thing last year."

"I'm glad you didn't get killed during that whole apocalypse thing," Gansey said. He paused, watching hummingbirds circle the flowers growing up over the garage roof. "It occurred to Blue and me the other day that being a teenager really sucked."

Ronan just drew his breath in through his nostrils and blew it out through his mouth. "Yeah."

After a moment, Gansey nodded to himself, and then he reached over to fist-bump Ronan. It felt like a language of a faraway country. "Let's go celebrate your brother not marrying an Ashley. Oh!"

He pointed; a hawk swooped down low from the sky, talons spread. It was a gorgeous creature, shaggy and fierce. Something about it gave the impression of age.

Ronan stretched out his hand as if to call it down to him as he would Chainsaw, but the hawk tilted upward sharply. In only a moment, it was just a speck in the clouds, and then it was gone.

After the ceremony, when nearly everyone had gone home, the group sat in the lawn among the fireflies, watching Jordan and Declan look at their wedding gifts. Neither Jordan nor Declan were amused by Ronan's and Hennessy's gifts to them: two matching swords, one with the words VEXED TO NIGHTMARE on the hilt and the other with the words FROM CHAOS.

"What are we supposed to do with these?" Declan asked.

"Something old, something new, something borrowed, something that can cut through walls," Hennessy said.

Jordan waited until all the gifts were open to give Declan hers. Ronan watched his brother hold Jordan's gaze before opening the tiny box. Inside, there was a postage-stamp-sized painting of a soft-eyed woman with golden hair. Jordan said, "It's a sweetmetal."

"For what?"

With a glance at Jordan, Matthew handed him one last box.

This one wasn't wrapped. It was a handmade glass-fronted display case. Inside was an enormous moth.

As fireflies and orbs hung around them, Declan swallowed and opened the box. Carefully, he dropped the sweetmetal onto the moth's furry back. It was already starting to flap, and two tears were already making their way down Declan's face. He didn't bother to hide them or wipe them away. He just lifted the box up toward the dazzling evening sky and whispered, "Goodbye, Dad."

And finally, after nearly everyone had gone to bed, Ronan and Adam lay on their backs on one of the roofs and watched the stars get brighter. Without taking his eyes off the sky, Ronan reached out his hand to Adam to offer him something. It was a ring. Without taking his eyes off the sky, Adam took it and put it on.

They sighed. The stars moved overhead. The world felt enormous, both past and future, with their slender present hovering in the middle.

It was all very good.

THE END

ACKNOWLEDGMENTS

This series has been in my life, in various forms, for over twenty years. How does one write the acknowledgments page in its conclusion? It seems as if it must be either very long or very short. I think if I make it very long, I'll make it very, very long, so instead, I'll be as brief as I can:

Thank you to:
- the readers who grew up with these characters
- David Levithan & the Scholastic team for letting me tell this story to the end
- Laura Rennert, for shepherding the series for a decade
- Will Patton, for bringing the audiobooks to vibrant life
- Adam Doyle & Matt Griffin, for their art
- Brenna, Sarah, Bridget, Victoria, Anna, who read and read again
- Richard Pine, for making room for future dreams
- My family, particularly when the nightwash seemed unsolvable
- Ed, who knows what I am

ABOUT THE AUTHOR

Maggie Stiefvater is the #1 *New York Times* bestselling author of the novels *Shiver, Linger, Forever,* and *Sinner.* Her novel *The Scorpio Races* was named a Michael L. Printz Honor Book by the American Library Association. The first book in The Raven Cycle, *The Raven Boys,* was a Publishers Weekly Best Book of the Year and the second book, *The Dream Thieves,* was an ALA Best Book for Young Adults. The third book, *Blue Lily, Lily Blue,* received five starred reviews. The final book, *The Raven King,* received four. She is also the author of *All the Crooked Saints* and the previous two books in The Dreamer Trilogy, *Call Down the Hawk* and *Mister Impossible.* An artist and a musician, she lives in Virginia with her husband and their two children. You can visit her online at maggiestiefvater.com.

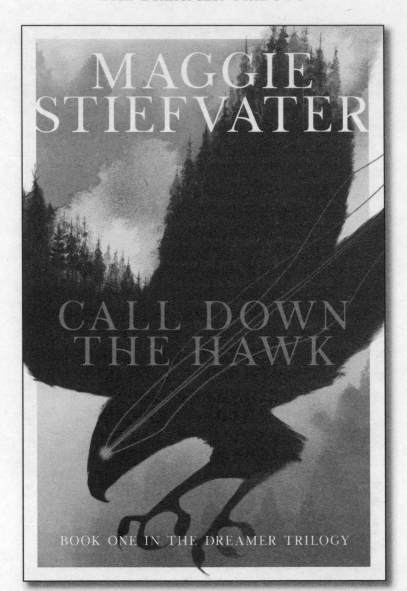

MAGGIE
STIEFVATER

CALL DOWN
THE HAWK

BOOK ONE IN THE DREAMER TRILOGY

MAGGIE STIEFVATER

MISTER IMPOSSIBLE

BOOK TWO IN THE DREAMER TRILOGY